A Lodge Affair

A Lodge Affair

RACHEL LABERGE

Copyright © 2024 by Rachel LaBerge

All rights reserved.

Paperback ISBN: 9798989130801

No portion of this book may be reproduced, distributed, or transmitted in any form without written permission from the author, except by a reviewer who may quote brief passages in a book review.

Developmental and line editing by Kimberly Hunt with HEA Author Services.
Copy editing and proofreading by Caroline Palmier.
Cover design by Love Lee Creative.

To every anxious millennial who would rather do everything on their own instead of asking for help (and being a burden). I see you.

PLAYLIST

1. **Motion Sickness**, Phoebe Bridgers
2. **Serotonin**, girl in red
3. **We Are Never Ever Getting Back Together (Taylor's Version)**, Taylor Swift
4. **...Baby One More Time**, Britney Spears
5. **Out Of The Woods (Taylor's Version)**, Taylor Swift
6. **The Weather (feat. Molly Parden)**, Ron Pope, Molly Parden
7. **Don't Wait**, Dashboard Confessional
8. **Vigilante Shit**, Taylor Swift
9. **Slingshot**, Zach Seabaugh, Chance Peña
10. **No Diggity**, Blackstreet, Dr. Dre, Queen Pen
11. **Autumn Leaves - Deluxe Edition**, Ed Sheeran
12. **Fallingforyou**, The 1975
13. **When You Look at Me**, Sara Kays
14. **Falling Into Place**, Leah Nobel
15. **Ghost On The Dance Floor**, blink-182
16. **Because Of You**, 98°
17. **I GUESS I'M IN LOVE**, Clinton Kane
18. **When I See You, I See Home**, Tyler Hilton

Scan the QR code with your phone to access the playlist on Spotify.

Letter from the Author

I know we all feel some type of way about a trigger list or letter from the author. If you're someone who isn't concerned about triggers, you can skip this next part.

Seriously. Skip it. This is your last chance.

In *A Lodge Affair*, there are a few scenes some readers may find distressing. I always aim to provide transparency to those who may benefit from trigger warnings or just a heads-up. While these scenes are integral to Ivy and Holland's narrative, they are not graphic in nature. *A Lodge Affair* includes themes involving the death of a sibling and on-page instances of assault and unwelcome sexual advances.

Take care of yourselves.

XOXO - Rach

CHAPTER ONE

I WOULD RATHER shave my eyebrows—and not be allowed to fill them in—than sit across from this halfwit for an entire ninety minutes. Working with your ex is as unfortunate as everyone claims—take it from me. Just when you think you've had a productive day, full of ass-kicking and sticking it to the "man," you see that stupid, smug face staring back at you. It brings down the hype girl energy really quick.

Our conference room has tall windows and modern vibes. Not only can everyone in the meeting see how you interact with said ex, but so can everyone who walks by during said meeting.

"Let's go ahead and get started." Stella, my boss, kicks off the meeting. Her voice is barely above a speaking volume and yet, she commands the entire room.

"I'd like to go over the finishing touches for the Bliss4ul event and the follow-up strategy." Stella speaks like the yoga instructors I pretend not to hate when I'm attempting a group class. Tell me yoga isn't one of the hardest things you've done and I won't believe you.

While the Bliss4ul—pronounced blissful—event is only two days, we've been planning it for months. One of our top-tier clients who brings in a quarter of our revenue, has made sure our team has been meticulous with the details. If this client wasn't so important, I'd definitely make fun of the random number in their company name.

Our marketing team discusses the tasks following the event, as well as social media content that will align over the next few weeks. Since this phase means everything is out of my hands, I zone out for a minute, once again mulling over that night a few months ago.

Jack was never all that creative; it's fitting he'd sleep with his assistant, without checking to see if his long-term girlfriend was still at work. Inconsiderate. Idiot. Hell, he didn't even check to see if anyone was still at the office; spoiler alert: I wasn't the only one still here.

Jack was a dickbag for many reasons, but especially because the thing keeping me late at work was a last-minute urgent task *he couldn't take on*. What he meant was he couldn't take it on because Misty was *taking it* on his desk—in an office which also has floor-to-ceiling windows. Classy.

I try not to laugh when I notice Jack's wearing two different Gucci patterns. For someone who "doesn't care about name brands and recognition," he's put himself in quite the outfit. I like how it screams "do you see me" with the worst kind of desperation.

"Jack. Ivy. What time's the flight?" Stella glances between the two of us.

Why is she asking Jack about flight details? I've made it clear that while I can work with him in an eight to five capacity, traveling is off-limits.

"Early. We board at 6 a.m.," Jack responds while running his hands through his hair. This habit comes off as staged like he's trying to be charming. In all reality, it makes his hair greasy.

We aren't boarding anything.

"*My* flight boards at 6 a.m., yes, but Jack isn't planning on taking this trip." I try not to sound confused but my brain is scrambled. I shoot Jack a professional look which could only be interpreted as a courteous, "What the fuck?!"

It feels like everyone in the meeting is holding their breath. People casually walking by the conference room have slowed to try to sneak a listen. No one dares to move and eyes dart from me to the front of the room, avoiding eye contact. Probably because at any minute, lasers could blaze out from my pupils.

Since it's a conference call, the video of the meeting room shows on a flat-screen TV. I'm sitting razor straight, not a hunch to be found, and I'm truly having a spectacular hair day. My long dark hair curls at the ends and stands out against my white top. When things are going south, it's the little details that matter.

After the longest pause, in the history of pauses, someone finally speaks.

"It was my understanding Jack would accompany you. Since the two of you couldn't find someone to get up to speed in such a short amount of time," Stella explains. She catches my eye and immediately knows something isn't quite right.

Before I can find a way to professionally ask, "What the fuck is going on?" Jack interrupts as we make eye contact.

"I've been working on a plethora of high-profile clients and urgent tasks. I didn't have a chance to get to it," he says like he's been working on a cure for cancer. "No worries, I'm happy to attend and make up for my client time elsewhere." He nods and smirks. "I love being a team player."

The nerve to turn something he didn't do into the greatest of deeds. Also, who says *plethora*? Dick. Bag.

Jack and I *were* supposed to attend this event together. Our relationship wasn't a secret but we kept the traveling to a minimum. We did our best to keep our work and romantic relationship separate. Turns out the separation was easy for Jack because he managed different relationships—and girlfriends—depending on the setting.

After the very-public-cheating-fiasco, Jack agreed to find another colleague and bring them "completely up to speed" for this event, which were his exact words. I asked if I needed to check in on the progress and he responded with, "Come on, Ivy. I know this stuff backwards. I'll get it done." No matter how questionable his morals were, it was rare for Jack to miss a deadline or forget a task.

Until now. How convenient.

It's official, I'll no longer be giving him any credit. My brain struggles to grasp what's happening all while trying to keep my cool. Don't want to feed into the emotional-woman-in-the-office stereotype. I relax my jaw and make sure my lips aren't pressed into a thin line.

Even though it was the least he could do, he flat-out didn't do it. Instead, he chose a monthly team meeting to share his "plethora" excuse, but not to worry because he'd be *happy to go*. I doubt Jack ever planned to follow through and this was his best shot at still attending the event.

No chance.

"No, no, Jack. I'd hate to put you out. Seems like a bit of miscommunication but I can handle it on my own. No problem." I look down at my notepad and act as if I'm nonchalantly adding something to my to-do list when I'm actually writing "what a loser" in my prettiest cursive. "It's a quick trip. I'll be back before you know it." My smile is forced and my voice sounds like a Stepford wife.

Stella nods in approval. Jack's mouth turns down just enough for me to notice. He's seething.

Good.

When the meeting is over, I make it a point not to be the first one to leave the room. I'm not running. I take my time to review notes and action items. When I reach the end of my list, I can feel Jack's eyes on me. I give him a saccharine grin, my painted red lips dramatic, as I stand up.

I know he watches me as I leave.

Flying across the country, solo, for a two-day client event was not my plan, but this is the universe's way of saying "I told you so." *I told you not to date someone at work, especially someone in leadership. I also told you not to avoid the countless red flags before you walked in on him engaging in late-night extracurricular activities with his* other *work girlfriend.*

I also told you to get to bed earlier because a 6 a.m. flight is brutal.

Told. You. So.

I don't love that Jack still works here after the sex in the office. Stella reiterated that while she wholeheartedly believed he engaged in an inappropriate act, and put him on HR's radar, there'd be no repercussions unless I filed a formal complaint.

We know what happens with those and the people who file them.

No matter how upset I was, I knew I'd never file. It'd follow me around as much—or more—as it'd follow Jack. Meanwhile, Misty—Jack's second girlfriend—never came back to work. Guess she couldn't handle being part of the catalyst of workplace turmoil and playing a part in breaking up a two-year relationship.

When I was dealing with the stinging realization that I'd have to see Jack every day, I put in a request to work remotely. I wanted to get up and move anywhere and work from a shared space or a new apartment. My body had this itch to get myself far away from Jack—proximity-wise—and maybe try something new.

I'd even considered moving somewhere much smaller. There'd still be a Target within driving distance, obviously, but change the scenery.

Yes, I'd miss the sound of endless traffic. Car horns. People yelling out windows. Sometimes the screeching brakes. I'm not sure how I'd function without the chance to get dumplings from my favorite Thai spot, paired with the spiciest Indian food, where they put extra garlic on my naan. It'd be difficult to leave the string of Indie bookstores which I pass on the short walk from the office to the bus stop.

But it doesn't matter. My request was denied. Well, sort of. The message was to re-evaluate in twelve months. Stella never mentioned it and neither did I. I planned on getting through the year and seeing how I felt before bringing it up again.

I love a plan. And at thirty-three years old, mine was ripped from me. Believe me, it's not Jack, specifically, but the idea of knowing what's coming next.

I worked hard to move up in the company and become a senior consultant in the five years I've worked at Sparks Wellness. Stella's been fair and transparent about my trajectory. She's given me quite a bit of opportunity and responsibility in my role.

No way am I letting a walking misogynistic disaster like Jack derail this part of my life. I can do the bare minimum and keep the peace at the office.

This whole fiasco is also my doing. I knew it was bad news, and a total cliché, to get involved with a colleague. Now, my outlook on men is shot and I've opened a whole jar of trust and self-worth issues. I made this bed and here I am lying in it.

Nonetheless, here I sit on a 6 a.m. flight, after three short hours of sleep. There wasn't enough time to bring any of my colleagues up to speed, courtesy of Jack and his last-minute lack of follow-through. I jumped in, head-first, after the meeting from hell and did everything I could to be 110 percent prepared.

It helps that I enjoy my job. Working for Sparks is exciting and rewarding. We build wellness strategies for employers to roll out for their employees, encouraging changes that'd make them happier people, both at work and home. Before starting here, I had no idea about the breadth of corporate wellness and how much fun I'd have in the field. I feel like a nerd saying it but it's true.

I get settled in my seat and my phone rings—Vivian.

"Up and at 'em early, I see. I just boarded." I yawn into the phone.

"I set an alarm to check-in. Wanted to make sure Jack didn't meet you at the airport or do anything his entitled and equally egotistical self would do," she retorts in her own yawn.

That might seem like a long-winded insult for pre-sunrise but it's very much how Vivian is. I adore her for it. She's the first friend who showed me what it's like to say what I want in a friendship without making me feel needy or childish. She means what she says. No bullshit.

"No sign of him. I don't think he'd want to risk a scene."

I know Jack skipping this trip is significant. The client is expecting him since he's one of their key points of contact. The compromise we silently made was that he wouldn't accompany me, and I won't tell said client any details about him getting caught having sex in the office on a Tuesday.

"He loves all attention—no matter how slimy it is. Dude isn't even smart enough to get his rocks off somewhere other than your place of employment," she shares with enough contempt appropriate for 6 a.m.

"Things we know and I don't want to get into while I'm sitting next to a stranger. I'll text you when I land," I say as my seatmate's tired eyes meet my gaze.

"You're right, you're right. Remind me. Where are you staying?"

"The Emerald Canopy Lodge." I try not to roll my eyes. "The room rates are ridiculous but it has good feedback on their website."

"Jack *would* get a client to crack their budget on a place that starts with "the." Ivy—this also sounds like your nightmare." She remembers my desire to spend most of my time indoors.

Vivian knows how Jack immediately blew through the client's budget on this "must-stay" lodge. There were many other options within their price range, but Jack couldn't let it go. I love how Vivian and I can confide in one another about work. We support each other, even though I work in corporate wellness and she works at a bakery, plus other odd jobs.

"I'll be at the lodge for just a few days and then I'll head back for our trip!" I exclaim with as much quiet enthusiasm that's allowed this early.

"Yesssss. Spooky sisters unite!"

I quietly laugh as we say our goodbyes. Viv and I are going to Salem, Massachusetts to live out our spooky dreams. It's only a few days, shorter than we originally imagined, but we'll take it. This trip has been planned for months and I could jump out of my skin with excitement.

We've wanted to go for years and the split from Jack finally gave me room to make it happen. Viv and I were supposed to go last year, but a high-profile client request came up. Our leadership team, including Jack, encouraged me to cancel. Jack was pleased; he always treated me like a child for liking all things witchy. I think I put it off for so long because I didn't want to hear the argument he'd mask as a joke. Deep down, he meant every scathing word he said.

This trip is the start of a challenging few weeks. I'm headed out west, followed by Salem, followed by another event out west. It's not ideal putting vacation between two high-profile client events, but it was the only way to make it work.

Going to Salem will be the first honest vacation I've taken in three years. I'm a little sick about how much PTO I've lost by not using it.

My boss has never denied any of my vacation requests. When she approved this time-off, I could see her relax knowing I'd still be able to make both on-site client events; she's slightly calculating in the sense of knowing exactly how to get what she wants. It doesn't bother me. Maybe I'll learn some of her ways. When it comes to running a team, Stella is efficient, transparent, and cuts right to the chase *without* people calling her a manipulative shrew.

I pull up my email a final time and find the shipping confirmation for a few boxes we'd sent to the lodge. The boxes were marked "delivered" as of yesterday. They're full of about $10,000 in promised items for the client, aligning with their strategic launch of a sustainability-focused wellness challenge, as well as giveaway items for my table. It works best to have something people can come and take—it makes it easier for people to start a conversation.

Our flight is being held up by a few passengers who've decided their assigned seats weren't where they were going to sit. It's a whole thing and makes me anxious. And whenever I feel a bit overwhelmed, I make a pros and cons list.

Pro: The trip is quick—I'll be back in my cozy apartment in a few days.
Con: A mom, flying solo, has a baby who sounds like what I bet the flight attendants feel internally—screaming.
Pro: Packing was easy because of said quick trip.
Con: These people may get put on the no-fly list before they relinquish their seats.
Pro: I'm heading to the Pacific Northwest for the first time.
Con: The pilot is now joining the flight attendants in the seat debacle happening at the back of the plane.
Pro: My blazer and skirt combination is exactly what I'd hoped for.
Con: No coffee until after I land. See above.
Pro: I'll be free of dickbag Jack for the next few days.
Con: My seatmate is snoring.

Finally, the seats have been situated and we're about to take off. Gone is the slam of overhead compartments and clicks of seatbelts being fastened. I lean my head against the seat and smirk. It feels good to go somewhere new. And leave Jack behind.

CHAPTER TWO

I'M THANKFUL FOR the uneventful flight and the opportunity to get some broken sleep. I roll my eyes, thinking about the *lodge*. It's not a hotel. Jack loved to make that distinction. He pushed the client to host their annual meeting at this very woodsy location, tying it in to their intense sustainability and "all things planet" initiative. To be honest, it's not a bad idea; it would've been better if someone else came up with it.

The amount of luggage I have surprises the driver. Most of it—part of a tabletop display—is for the client event; while I want to scream about how small of a bag I brought for myself. Look at me, I didn't over pack! Where's the confetti?

The lodge is almost two hours away from the airport. My first reaction to the Pacific Northwest is there are a lot of trees. Many trees on many mountains. After that, it's pure surprise to see people hiking. Like trekking on the side of the road. I could never. Their packs are much bigger than what I've brought for a cross-country event. Again, I'm proud of myself.

After a long commute, with spotty cell service and more curves than I like in my roads, we pull up to an entrance. If you didn't know what you were looking for, you'd miss it.

"This is as far as I go," the driver says, putting the car in park, and glancing up at the sign.

Welcome to **The Emerald Canopy Lodge** *drop-off area*
For assistance, call the front desk.

"What do you mean this is as far as you go? I don't see an entrance," I lightly press the driver.

"That hill is too steep for this car. This is the drop-off area. You call the lobby and someone will come pick you up in an off-road vehicle," he replies while getting out of the car and popping the trunk. He struggles to get the awkward bags out.

"I'll skip the off-road vehicle. I can take care of it from here." I reach for the luggage, preparing to get a handle on all of it. The idea of asking anyone to help me get inside a building makes my skin crawl. I can handle this without inconveniencing anyone.

"Suit yourself. Have a good one," he says, his face kind but full of speculation.

As the car pulls away, I stare up at the hill, and down at my Manolo Blahnik pumps.

I love these heels. Yes, they're Manolo Blahniks but they're also a celebration purchase. I bought these, after careful deliberation and research, to recognize a substantial merit raise. They're a symbol of my stubbornness—Jack pointed out, passive-aggressively, how ridiculous it was to spend so much on a "basic pair of shoes."

He teased me every time I wore them, pulling at the lightness and pride I had when thinking about being able to do something like this for myself. To finally afford something like this, even if it was a one-off purchase, made me feel accomplished. My internal reaction outweighed Jack's poking fun.

I can't scuff these heels. I'm sure I can make it to the lobby—it might be slow but I'll get there.

In the first minute, it's clear I've made a mistake. Hell, it was probably less than that. There's a sidewalk but it rolls with the hill, making it difficult not to trip. It feels like I'm pulling a car behind me. My luggage is awkward and remarkably heavy. The incline is a nightmare.

My heels snapping onto the stone are met with sounds of birds and rustling tree branches. I don't hear or see anyone else. Beads of sweat form on my forehead and my breath is becoming louder than I ever approve of in public. I stop and take a short break, trying to get myself together. My legs are burning in protest like they do when I choose a Tunde Oyeneyin ride on my Peloton.

Finally, I see glass doors and a "Welcome to The Emerald Canopy Lodge" sign. My shoulders slump in relief knowing the end is in sight. I look down and focus on the pavement and make quick work of the rest of the walk. The automatic doors swoosh open. My legs are unsure about getting into the lobby.

"Goodness. You didn't make that walk in those shoes, did ya?"

Caught off guard, mostly trying to remember a time when I could breathe, I find a woman at the front desk, wearing a green sweater and what looks to be a pine cone brooch. She has white hair sleekly pulled back in a bun.

"I certainly did. I'm here to check in. The name is Ivy Lawson." I do my best not to breathe too loud in the quiet space.

"What a pretty name, Ivy. I'm Beatrice but everyone calls me Bea." She points at a name tag underneath her brooch. "You know someone would've picked you up at the drop-off so you didn't have to haul all that luggage up? In my twenty-six years at the lodge, I've never seen someone trek that hill in shoes like that." Her eyes crinkle with her giggle.

"Thanks for the tip, Bea. I made it just fine." Trying to convince myself and anyone else in this lobby that my statement is true. Luckily, most people aren't paying attention to me and my bald-faced lie.

"If you call huffing and puffing in those stilt-like high heels fine, then I guess you're right, Ivy Lawson." She laughs as she checks me in.

I look around the lobby and am reminded I'm not at a high-end hotel. Missing is the bustling of hotel employees zipping through the lobby, loading luggage on carts, offering bottles of water, and mentioning the spa down the hallway. I long for a spa down the hallway.

The open space greets me with soft quiet. There are a few people in the sitting area, but they seem to be content gazing out the towering windows, an abundance of trees, mountain views, and lakes in the distance. Everything is so green here: the paint, the views, Bea's sweater.

The smell of coffee makes my mouth water. I haven't had any yet and I'm itching to get my hand on a cup. Or a carafe.

"I see you're here for the Bliss4ful event. You'll find a welcome gift in your room with a map, agenda, and notes. Quite fancy. This group… Are you here with Jack Wright? I see him on the same reservation."

"Jack isn't here. He was supposed to cancel that room. His head must have been… elsewhere." I screen my insult and paint a fake smile on my lips. Bea looks like she might pass out over her pine cone brooch if I said what I wanted to.

"You won't be able to get a refund for that room, Miss Ivy." It's clear Bea has done her fair share of fighting with customers over this very issue.

"Don't worry about it. It's a business trip." I try to reassure her and wipe sweat from my brow at the same time.

"Whew! Okay. Your room is on the sixth floor and you'll want to take the elevator, not the stairs." Beatrice smirks as she peeks at my choice of footwear for emphasis.

"Great idea," I respond, thankful I don't have to walk six flights of stairs in these heels. "Quick question, my company sent a few boxes directly for the event. I've checked the shipping information and it shows they were signed for and delivered. Where can I get those?"

"Can't imagine you carrying anything else, especially in those spiky shoes, so it's a good thing you sent them. Let me take a look." She laughs at me, again, but it's genuine. She thinks my shoes are hilarious.

"I confirm we've accepted packages for your company. They'll be waiting for you tomorrow morning at your designated table. Now getting you to your room, I'll call someone to help with your bags. The elevator is down at the end of the hallway. It's a bit of a trek," she says as she picks up the phone and puts it to her ear.

"No, no, no. That won't be necessary. I'm sure I can manage. The walk is quite flat, yes?" I joke with Bea before she can finish dialing the number.

"Of course it's flat, but I insist. It'll give them something to do," she retorts, not getting my joke.

Arguing with Bea would be more of an inconvenience than letting them take my bags. I keep my personal bag but leave the others. I won't need them until tomorrow anyways. "Thanks for your help."

Almost to the elevator, I turn and give Bea a smile, as my Manolo Blahniks click-clack on the tile floor.

The room isn't what I expected, which was lots of log cabin wood, flannel, scratchy blankets, and a stale smell. With deep blues and beige, it feels soothing, with a minimalistic but modern vibe. Expansive windows overlook the main grounds and even give glimpses of the water and mountains in the distance.

When I get a few more steps in, it kind of smells like the outside. It's hard to put my fingers on it, until I see the fresh eucalyptus in the shower and cut flowers on the console table. The flowers are stunning. I can't help but dip my nose into them and breathe in. I'm not one for plants but I'm a sucker for flowers. They sit on top of a handwritten welcome note saying these were picked from the lodge's garden. Precious. I wonder if Bea writes these little notes.

I feel my cell phone buzzing with a text message. Jack's name stares at me:

JACK

Did you make it to TECL?

He can't even spell out the lodge name? A wave of mild rage and severe annoyance rolls through my body. How is it that the smallest of gestures can make my stomach turn—not in the this is a fun rollercoaster way but more so there's probably a serial killer in your backseat way? I make yet another vow promising myself I'll never date someone from work ever again. Ever. It's not worth it.

Unfortunately, I have to respond.

Yes.

Bubbles pop up, indicating Jack is typing.

JACK

See anyone from Bliss4ul yet?

I'll brief the entire team when I'm back.

And that's a wrap on this conversation and something I knew would happen. It's obvious that Jack still wanted to come to the event and he did his best to do so.

Turns out, it wasn't good enough.

CHAPTER THREE

HOLLAND

I'M IN MY OFFICE when clacking on the floor—clearly from someone's high heels—interrupts my thoughts. Soon, it mixes in with Bea's chatter. Not unusual, as of late, with the influx of guests here for the week. The smell of fresh coffee fills the room as I push down on the French press. My second carafe of the morning but the caffeine is a habit I can't kick. I'm not sure if it's the promise of fresh coffee or the fairly quiet lobby, but I pause and recognize the lull.

Before I know it, this place will be crawling with people.

The lodge is home to client events year-round, but no one is quite as demanding as Bliss4ul. Not complaining, especially because some hot-shot CEO is all about supporting local businesses and sustainability efforts. We've worked together on bringing in even more goods from small businesses in the area which always puts me in a better mood.

While I like the boost for our local businesses, I'll be relieved when this is over. The best part of my office is how it keeps me away from everyone. I can see a sliver of the lobby and that's it. Exactly how I like it.

I'm reviewing conference room layouts, shipping information, as well as our general staffing for the event. I'm off the next two days and I'd like to spend it with a clear mind. Best to get everything squared away now.

We're almost at guest capacity this week on top of being responsible for a packed event schedule. The team has been through each day's itinerary multiple times, discussing everything from logistics, to staff, and possible concerns.

Said list is more than a typical client event. Damn. I'm lucky to have the people I do. I'm grateful I'm not needed to work at any of the events.

I *would've* done it. Obviously.

These fucking events. Leave it to companies like this to jam-pack everyone's itinerary, like they do back home. Why can't it ever just be the event? When did we accept the networking, welcome breakfasts, scheduled breaks, and whatever else they think of? We wouldn't want people to have an actual moment to themselves or their thoughts, right?

I hate to say it, but this event is more proof that I'm not as necessary to keep this place running. It's bittersweet. I don't let myself dwell on it for too long. There's no point. I'm here and not leaving. That's how it is.

I read through the materials list and double-check everything is where it's supposed to be. I'm on my third call to the storage floor, checking to make sure we indeed were asked for and are ready to provide a ridiculous amount of dairy milk alternatives. They laugh and let me know it's not a typo and we're ready to rock.

Great news. Don't have to like what they ask for but give them what they want. Make fun of them later is my motto.

Bea's laughter breaks my concentration. No matter who comes in through those doors, that woman has a way with everyone. She's been a pillar to this place and I'm glad she's chosen to work for as long as she has. It's no secret she doesn't need the money, but I joke she needs the words.

She speaks enough for the both of us. That's for sure.

The phone rings. Our order of local coffee beans is ready for me to pick up. The final errand to cross off on my to-do list.

I head out to the front desk to let Bea know I'm driving into town and that's when I see—and hear—her walking away. Her dark hair sways back and forth with each step. The shoes crack the air around her. Her body moves with a purpose, like she's on the way to one of the most important meetings to be held in corporate America.

She turns back and grins at Bea. Not just any old smile but one that reaches her eyes, all the way to the corners. I stop what I'm doing and take her in. Her lips are dark red, making her look even more bold. Confident. Bright. She looks like she has everything figured out.

"That one is all city." Bea laughs.

"Figures," I mutter under my breath.

After picking up and dropping off the last of the coffee and extra produce requests from the kitchen, I head back to my place.

Technically, it's still part of the lodge, but it's far enough away that guests don't stumble upon it. Often I'll use the twenty-five-minute walk to get some quiet. Not today. I drive the short five minutes instead.

It's supposed to be a cabin but it's much more modern than the word cabin insinuates. With dark green paint, it's part of the pine trees. Tucked in. There are barely any windows on the front to see inside, which helps with the allusion. The back of the cabin is almost completely made of windows. The view is nothing but lush green trees and mountaintops in the distance.

Hazel, my little sister, was the mastermind behind the almost hidden space. She wanted to be somewhere new and comfortable but still feel like she was in the woods. I know the contractor gave her hell on the window locations. He kept telling her, "No one does this," but she didn't care. She liked being a tad difficult with her request and overall vision. Hazel didn't budge, except to turn the front door into glass, allowing more light in, when needed.

She thrived when she was outside, the sun hitting her face.

I shut my truck door and hear Slate running from his bed, his feet not getting any traction. You'd think the dog would learn.

It's been just Slate and me for a while. Amazing he thinks someone else could be at the door.

"Hey, buddy. How'd the nap treat ya?" I bend down to greet the French bulldog. "Did you get your uninterrupted beauty sleep?"

On cue, Slate slumps onto his back, legs in the air, waiting for a belly scratch.

Before he can capitalize on the attention, he smells the peanut butter scone in my vest pocket. Slate immediately sits and puts his paw up—as if to shake—before I can get the scone, a gift from the coffee shop, out of its bag.

"You're not spoiled at all. Not one bit…"

He knows the drill, half for him and half for me. After practically inhaling his piece, he looks up before carefully checking the floor for crumbs.

By the time I take my boots off, Slate is retreating to his bed, his paws tapping on the hardwood floors. Tough life.

I walk into the kitchen and stand in front of the coffee pot. Having another cup is overkill but here we are. The coffee brews and I spend the five minutes it takes to clean the kitchen. My preference is to put everything away as soon as I'm done with it. It makes cleaning a breeze.

The sound of the dripping coffee, mixed with Slate's snores, is comfortable as I wipe down the countertop. Fucking sparkly quartz countertops. I shake my head, laughing to myself. Can't deny they look good in here but I never would've bought these. Another Hazel touch.

It's exactly how she envisioned it and I haven't changed a thing.

My watch tells me it's much earlier than I thought. I have a completely free afternoon. No work to complete, errands to run, or things to do.

"Slate… want to go for a walk?" Even though he was asleep five seconds ago, he almost slips running to the door.

CHAPTER FOUR

MY SELF-CONFIDENCE IS through the roof as I check my reflection. The combination of a black midi skirt and crimson top works perfectly with my red lipstick. Not just any top, but one of my favorites, with a chiffon tie at the neck, meant for a bow. My hair is down in loose curls and I'm having one of those superb hair days. The ones that show up out of nowhere and are like a mini miracle.

The Babbling Brook conference room—I wish I was joking about the title—is still being set up. But the vendor tables look ready, and I find mine. A single piece of paper with SPARKS WELLNESS and JACK WRIGHT in size 200 font sits on top of a bare table. I can't roll my eyes any harder at how Jack couldn't take six more seconds to include both of our names on the attendee list.

Glaringly missing from my vendor table are the boxes we had shipped. The ones I nervously checked as my flight prepared to take off, confirmed with Bea during check-in, and before I went to sleep last night.

"Don't freak out. Don't freak out. Don't. Freak. Out," I say aloud, even though it's only meant for me.

"Do you need something?" A lodge employee must've heard me talking to myself. Lovely.

"Good morning and yes. I'm looking for some boxes I sent. Are you still bringing those out… Brad?" I squint and read his nametag.

"Nope. Everything sent early is on the vendor tables. Sounds like you're missing some?"

"Yes. I confirmed they were signed for and delivered here a few days ago. It should be five boxes. My name is Ivy Lawson and the company is Sparks Wellness."

"Let me double-check. I'll be back in a sec," Brad says as he's already exiting the conference room. He can't be more than eighteen, but age doesn't determine capability or maturity. I cross my fingers that Brad is the best man for the job.

I do what I can with what I have. Focus on the task, and mini list, at hand:

- steam the tablecloth
- put together what I have of the display
- organize fliers and business cards

The tablecloth only covers half of the table, and the exposed section looks like a great opportunity for injury.

My heart rate continues to rise with each minute that passes. My smart watch is going to think I'm doing a workout which is a real slap in the face. You'd think we'd be able to differentiate between physical activity and run-of-the-mill anxiety.

Brad strolls into the conference room with no sense of urgency. This gives me time to see his wrinkled shirt, bedhead, and puka shell necklace. I'm losing hope. And quick.

"We don't see any boxes in the shipping area for you or your company. Are you sure they were delivered?" he asks without making much eye contact with his bloodshot eyes.

I pull in as much air as possible, a breath that reaches my ribs, before

I respond.

"Yes. I confirmed they were delivered from the tracking information as well as with Bea yesterday afternoon."

I pull up the tracking information on my phone and hand it to him. He squints down at my screen for far too long. There isn't much to see besides a tracking number and the large "DELIVERED" message.

Part of me wants to ask if I can look in the shipping area. I know I have a fixation about needing control. It's not new. I make progress and then something like this happens.

"Do you remember what you put on the label, as far as delivery details?"

There isn't enough air in the room to breathe in before the annoyance seeps through my response. I now get a whiff of Brad's stale boozy breath.

"Brad—I will *never* forget the details on that shipping label. Deliver to Point 3 - door 1, signature required. Time-sensitive—deliveries only accepted from 8 AM–3 PM," I spit from memory as a too big smile paints my red lips.

"Okay, okay, I get it. You read the instructions and followed them." Brad's the one who's annoyed now.

"What a concept!" I throw my hands up in a sarcastic "wow" expression.

Honestly, I don't like how I sound right now. I know Brad is just doing his job and I'm guessing many shipping mishaps occur because someone didn't read or follow the specific instructions. Also, he looks like he's nursing one hell of a hangover.

He pulls out a clipboard with what I'm guessing is some sort of vendor checklist. He looks like a kid playing dress-up and like he's not actually supposed to be in the workforce.

"I believe you on the label. I checked and no other boxes are waiting to be brought in. There's another place I can check but maybe you want to go talk with Bea?" He nonchalantly turns and doesn't wait for my response.

He might be trying to get rid of me, but I don't care. Some people may be bothered by this directive, but I'm thrilled there's something I can do.

"I would love to. Here's my card in case you find them." I pass my card to Brad.

I'm in the hallway faster than Brad can pocket the card and casually stroll to his next spot to check. The sun is coming up, but the lodge is quiet and still.

"Good morning, Miss Ivy," Bea croons when I'm about twenty feet away, her eyes still down on whatever it is she's working on at the front desk.

"How did you know it was me?"

"Click-clack, click-clack," she says with a head tilt for emphasis.

"Ah, the heels. First, good morning. Second, I'm on the hunt for the boxes I sent. Brad is also looking for them but suggested I check with you." I put my hands on the front desk.

"Well, that's unfortunate because Brad is a ding-dong and shouldn't be in charge of anything," Bea replies, giggling.

"Lucky me."

"Don't get me wrong—very sweet boy—but not very sharp. Kind of like his dad in that way. You know—" She's shifted her weight with a hand on her hip.

Before she can launch into some small-town lore, I bring her back to the task on hand.

"I'll pay to hear the story of Brad's ding-dong dad. Really, I will. But we have to find my boxes first. I need them for the event which kicks off in a few hours."

"I'd never take your money, but I *will* take you up on a drink before you go home. Let's find those pesky boxes." She pulls out a three-ring binder.

I laugh to myself, not wanting to distract her. I can't remember the last time I saw a binder, with paper, tabs, and ripped plastic on the front. Before I can get too nostalgic, Bea is on the phone, not caring how early it is. I leave my card on the front desk, pointing to my cell number, and she shoos me away.

On my way back to the conference room, I get a whiff of the marvelous smell of freshly brewed coffee. I'm convinced there's nothing better.

I grab a cup to go, because if the universe has given me a crisis this early, I'll never get through it without copious amounts of caffeine.

Back at the Babbling Brook nightmare, Brad is waiting at my designated table—still no boxes.

"I've looked everywhere I can think of and no luck. I've got someone else going down to the drop-off point to double-check they made it into the building. For now, you'll have to hold tight." He's bracing himself for my response.

In the few moments I take to gather myself, I notice how nervous Brad is. He might be a ding-dong, but it looks like he has lots of time to un-ding-dong himself. Honestly, he looks like a kid.

"I appreciate you taking another look and asking for more help. Bea's making some calls at the front." I try to reassure him.

"I'll call you once I have an update." He practically runs from the conference room.

Time flies as I frantically call the delivery company to gather any other helpful information. The missing puzzle piece is who signed for the boxes. What seems like a straightforward piece of information ends up stumping anyone and everyone I've been transferred to. It's something that should show on my end when I log in to view the delivery status on the app, but it doesn't, and no one knows what to do next.

Bea's been down to check on me—she's so sweet but I also don't think she's a fan of the heels in the hallway—and insists she has a few more ideas. The lodge is hosting several different events this week and is pretty popular so it's possible my boxes are with a different event.

Vivian encouraged me, reiterating the missing boxes aren't my fault. I texted her when I had been transferred to the third person who was trying to find anything else about the mysterious signature. She's resourceful and always good for a quick reality check.

No matter how many times she tells me, this feels like my fault.

The other vendors have made their way in and are setting up tables and displays, and getting prepared. I feel like I don't belong here and am unsure of what to do next.

What couldn't come at a worse possible time is a text from Jack.

JACK

How do the quarter zips look?

Of course, he'd want to know about the thing in the boxes that no one can find. I eye roll and tilt my head to the ceiling. Since this text is a question about work and is completely acceptable, I must respond.

> Small issue with the quarter zips but I'm on it

What kind of issue?

> The boxes were signed for by a lodge employee and marked as delivered but no one can find them

Have you called the delivery company?

> Yes, I'm all over it.

I know I'm almost out of time. Royce, the Bliss4ul CEO, approaches the glaringly empty table. He seems confused as he glances left to right, around the room, as all these other vendors are ready for the event to start while I am not. There's a small group of people with him.

"This is a different approach, Ivy." He reaches for a handshake and makes eye contact for a second before he's looking at the table. "Very minimalist, which is usually something I care for—"

"Royce! Good morning. I know, I know," I interrupt him before he can continue down the path of how this isn't what he expected. I shake his hand, even though my palms are sweaty. "We're currently on the search for all the boxes. Logistics situation. I've got it under control."

"The event starts promptly at 10 a.m., which is in fifteen minutes." He glances down at his watch. "We're expecting heavy traffic at your table around 11 a.m. I have some VIPs I brought to the vendor area early." He gestures to the unimpressed cluster of people around him. "What's your backup plan?"

"I'm going to ask everyone to share their email address with me, they can write it on the back of my business cards here. If worse comes to worst, I can send everything by hand, when I'm back in the city. Sparks would obviously cover the cost."

"While that's not a very environmentally friendly solution, it could work. Still seems like a lot to manage. Where's Jack?" Royce looks around for someone he'll never find.

"Jack had something come up and couldn't make the trip. No worries—everything's under control," I reassure him, proud of my ability to mask the distaste for my ex.

"It's a shame Jack couldn't make it. I'll check in with you in a bit—I have to deliver our welcome message." Royce's voice is stern, like when a parent tells you they're disappointed.

"I'm hoping we don't need the backup plan, but no matter what, I'll find a solution." The fake enthusiasm burns my cheeks.

The current pit in my stomach is something I go to great lengths to avoid. What was once a small divot is now a canyon of uncertainty.

Royce nods silently and walks away with the VIPs following. My skin is itchy and hot—this isn't what I'd planned. This also looks haphazard and reflects poorly on my team. The trip here was quite the investment for our company and the leadership was only on board due to the visibility our table would have.

Jack worked some magic regarding getting our table placed in a high-traffic area and including a few blurbs about our services during conference sessions. I know Royce won't want to do the last part if I'm sitting behind a table that could give you a sliver.

In panic level four of five, I pace outside of the conference room. People slowly move through the hallways in front of me. The welcome message is wrapping up and people are moving on to what's next on the agenda. I wonder what it must be like to be having a day like this... where you can just be and not deal with something that's bringing you actual stomach pains.

I should've checked the boxes yesterday. Physically checked. I should have touched the cardboard, opened, and touched the quarter-zips. Why didn't I do that? Why didn't I see this through?

I'm usually so prepared and I can't believe I let this happen. If I would've known this was an issue when I arrived, I could've found a solution faster and been ready for today. Why didn't I have a better back-up plan? I could've at least packed a tablecloth and branded notepads from the office.

My hands are sweaty and my heart beats fast. Thudding rushes through my ears. This was an idiotic decision. I had nothing but time yesterday. Stupid, stupid, stupid. Careless.

Stupid and careless.

CHAPTER FIVE

HOLLAND

THE BEEP OF THE two-way radio wakes Slate up from his precious slumber. The dog loves to sleep.

I must've left the radio on after I had coffee. Sometimes, even on my day off, I listen in to make sure everything is going smoothly. It's easier to get a hold of me on the radio than my cell phone. I'm always forgetting to charge the dumb thing.

"Cool it. It's just the radio." I pick it up and put it towards him to sniff. He stops barking when he realizes there's no intruder to protect me from. Oh, what would I do without the big bad French bulldog?

On the other end, I hear Brad mumbling about missing boxes for the Bliss4ul event.

Shit. I've only met Royce once but he's someone I'd like to have minimal interactions with. When he came to walk through the lodge, to see if it was a good fit, he insisted on making a show of wiping down his loafers with Clorox wipes. I didn't understand it then and didn't want to ask and then have to talk to him about it.

It's better not to know. He seems like someone who likes to hear himself talk. Pass.

He reminds me of my old life in the city. Before everything. I hate it.

Guys at my firm were just like him. I could tolerate anyone to an extent, but even then, I kept to myself. I had a small group of friends for a few social connections.

Before I can respond, I hear Bea on the radio. "Holland—are you there?"

"Hey, Bea. What's up?"

"Hate to be a bother on your day off. Did you run around already?" This is how Bea jokingly asks if I went running yet.

"I'm that predictable, huh? What's going on?" I make a mental note to find another hobby.

"We're searching for some missing packages." She sighs. "Brad is the go-to this morning because we thought this would all be taken care of. We didn't think we'd need him for anything."

I hear what she's saying and what she isn't.

"I got you. Text me the details and I'll be over in a few minutes."

"Holland rescues The-Ding-Dong-Brad again!" she says emphatically.

"Quit calling my employee a ding-dong." I set the radio down.

Must be my lucky day. I find the missing boxes in the shipping elevator on the way down to start my search. Anyone looking for them has been in this elevator at least five times.

Damn. That's embarrassing. Maybe the lodge isn't operating as smoothly as I'd thought.

I load the boxes on the dolly and take them to the vendor area. I'm not sure who I'm looking for but hoping it won't be too difficult.

Before I start looking for who these belong to, someone pacing outside the conference room draws my attention. It really is my lucky day. When I get closer, I realize it's the woman from yesterday. Same high heels, her brunette hair long and tucked behind her ears, but this time she's talking to herself.

Not talking exactly, but giving herself a verbal ass-kicking. The more I hear, the worse I feel.

"Stupid. So Stupid. Careless. Ivy, you're so stupid. Why didn't you check…"

Gone is the woman with the strut from the front desk. She's replaced with a frazzled version of a woman with her head down and jaw clenched. She's rubbing her hands together, white-knuckled, and shaking her head. It's like the words aren't enough and she needs to be physically hurt.

This is painful. I can't take another minute. I stop the boxes right in front of her and noisily set the dolly down to get her attention.

"I'm guessing these belong to you?"

CHAPTER SIX

SOMEONE'S VOICE BREAKS through my panic.

"Are you Ivy?" He gestures to the boxes.

"Yes, I'm Ivy. Yes! Thank you so much!" Finally, I can breathe again until I get a full look at who the voice belongs to.

This man is definitely not Brad. His dark hair is doing that swoop-fallen bang thing that I feel like I've read about but have never seen. It looks like it's still wet. He's wearing jeans and a flannel button-up and his eyes are the color of rich coffee.

"Hello? Anyone there?" He waves a hand and leans in a little closer to my face. Close enough for it to be clear I'm being a creep and have forgotten how to function in society. I blame it on being surprised. Someone awkward and young, like Brad, is who I was expecting. I wasn't expecting *him*. He's taller than me, not by a lot, but enough for me to notice.

"Yes, I'm here. Just a little caffeine crash," I joke, but wonder why I can't act like a normal human who has conversations all the time. "You can put them on the table that looks like a splinter hazard." I gesture inside where the mostly empty table is mocking me at this point.

He carefully wheels the boxes to the table, dodging vendor displays and people. After unloading the boxes, he puts the dolly back where I had practically left marks in the carpet with my pacing.

He returns with a box cutter and starts opening boxes.

"What are you doing?" My voice comes out higher than intended.

"From what I understand, these boxes have been MIA all morning. I can help you," he says, still carefully opening the boxes.

"Oh, are you sure? You must have something else you should be doing." I start unpacking the boxes he's opened.

"Nope, Bea called me in to help," he shares. "I'm not on the schedule today so I have nothing but time." His voice is deep and scratchy in a way that immediately makes someone more attractive.

Even though he's offering to help, I feel bad. My hands—still clasped—are pressing on my lower stomach. The man's eyes peer down, taking me in. I'm lost in the way he seems to almost look through me. My skin prickles with awareness.

I don't want to be a burden but I don't even get a chance to protest.

"Based on that verbal beat down you were giving yourself, it seems like you could use it," he says, wiping a little bit of sweat off his forehead.

My chest squeezes and my cheeks burn. I must have been *actually* talking to myself while I was pacing. Nothing like turning on the crazy when meeting new people.

And to top it off, the reason he's not in an Emerald Canopy Lodge shirt is because it's his day off.

Fantastic.

"You don't have to do that. I mean, I appreciate you at least finding the boxes, but I don't want to take up anymore of your—"

"Ivy. It's fine," he interrupts and says it in a way that's final.

"Thank you... I just realized I never asked your name." My cheeks flush hearing him say mine. My skin color probably resembles a beet at this point. I have no chill.

"It's Holland."

"Like Tom Holland?"

"No, like *me* Holland," he says, hands on his chest, reiterating his point.

"Is your first name Tom?"

"My first name is Holland. Like your first name is Ivy. When's the last time you did this whole introduction thing?" He looks at me, almost skeptical, but still making progress with the boxes.

"I blame this on the caffeine crash, time zone difference, and response to the crisis this morning. Okay, Holland, tell me you were named after the best Spider-Man of all time."

"I doubt that, since I'm thirty-four, and was born before Tom Holland," he exclaims, matter-of-factly. "And easy with the best Spider-Man of all time label." He rolls his eyes.

"You *don't* think Tom Holland is the best Spider-Man of all time?" I fake gasp but am also interested in his response.

"Boxes first. Merits of each Spider-Man later," he says as he points to the boxes.

A little embarrassed, I nod and we get to work. Together we unpack and bring the long-awaited life to the table. We get the other tablecloth out, steamed, and on. After assembling the rest of the tabletop display, we arrange giveaway items.

I pack bags for the individuals I know will stop by. I want them to easily find their names and be on their way; people love a low-time commitment. Without saying much, Holland and I have an assembly-like line going; I write the names on the bags and add the plant-based pillow spray, collapsible water bottle, and reusable produce bags while he finds their quarter-zip size and folds it on top of the items.

Why could I watch this man fold sweatshirts all day? He does it neatly and carefully. They fit perfectly in the bags.

Conference attendees trickle in and I can't believe we've managed to get everything ready in such a short amount of time.

"That's my cue." Holland points to the groups of people making their way in.

"Thank you. I would've really struggled to do this on my own." That is an understatement.

"Glad I could help." He stands tall with his hands on his hips. "Anyways, I owe you a Spider-Man conversation. When's this whole thing wrapped up?"

"Tomorrow night. The networking event ends at eight," I say, unsure of where this is going.

"I'll be around. Drinks at the restaurant bar sound good?"

"Okay. Sounds like a plan. Thanks again, Holland, not Tom." I smile and prepare for the waves of people.

Holland turns and leaves. I'm surprised with myself. While I'm still disappointed I wasn't proactive enough for this hiccup, I'm no longer only thinking about how stupid I am.

Instead, I'm strategizing how I'll defend my Spider-Man.

CHAPTER SEVEN

HOLLAND

WHAT THE HELL is wrong with me? Helping with the boxes makes sense. Asking her out for drinks? The fuck. Who am I?

After helping Ivy, I return to the front desk with Bea. I pat my face, making sure I don't have a fever. Getting sick would help explain my recent change in behavior. Unfortunately, no fever. Damn.

"You say I can't make fun of your employees." Bea puts employees in air quotes. "But they had that poor gal in a fit." She puts her hands on her hips—a look I'm accustomed to. I find myself doing it sometimes as well. Embarrassing.

"Why have eyes in your head if you're not going to bother to use 'em?" She sounds exasperated.

"It's not great. I'll talk to them." Bea nods in agreement. "I helped her get settled. Whole groups were coming in to chat with her as I was leaving," I reassure Bea.

She turns to me, her eyes a bit wider than normal. "That was awfully nice of you, Holland." She overly enunciates my name. "I also offered to tell her my favorite Brad-is-a-ding-dong story after the event tomorrow night," she shares.

Of course she did.

"You might see me. I owe her a Spider-man chat," I say like it's something I do all the time.

Bea stops whatever she's doing. Her eyes are practically saucers. I know she's surprised. And I don't want to get into it. I hope my face is screaming that very sentiment.

"Are you telling me you willingly included yourself in a social event?" she presses.

Guess it wasn't screaming loud enough.

"It's not a social event. It's a drink." I try to reassure Bea so she'll stop looking at me like that.

"If you don't plan to be social, do that poor woman a favor and stand her up." Bea jokes.

I give her a side glance.

"Well, isn't today full of all sorts of surprises?" Bea laughs and answers the ringing phone.

Saved by the ring.

I get away from Bea while I can.

Slate and I are on the couch. He's snoring. I'm thinking.

About Ivy pacing and grappling with herself. And how it was completely out of her control. She was really letting herself have it. All over a work event. I'm wondering if my impression of Royce was a little more spot-on than I thought.

And then the way she looked at me when I stayed. Her expression was something like a mix of gratitude and relief. She still fidgeted enough for me to know that accepting help isn't her norm.

I can't stop thinking about one thing. Something specific.

In my thirty-four years of life, I'm not sure I've ever seen eyes that vibrantly green.

CHAPTER EIGHT

THE EVENT IS chaotic, busy, and a complete success. With Holland's help, I was ready for the first swarm of people. Some came to pick up their individually packed bags, pleased they didn't have to wait for their items. Hooray for a giant check mark in the win column of the wins and losses list I started mentally putting together earlier this morning. The poor win column was seriously lacking before this.

My favorite part of my job is collaborating with clients. Most of our work is done virtually, which is still rewarding, but it's much better in person. I feel energized with each person stopping by the table.

I even fielded a surprise phone call from Jack with nothing but grace, reassuring him that everything was back on track.

Besides those I planned to see, I had time with probably ten potential clients, some of who were in the VIP group that Royce had brought in earlier. My shoulders felt twenty pounds lighter, seeing some faces that looked at this empty table this morning and still came back.

I even chatted with a previous buyer, who is now at a different company. They saw the table and raved about how much they loved working with us at their previous job. Those kinds of interactions are the best.

One of my favorite parts of functions like this is hearing the chatter. It's rewarding when someone you had a brief chat with is talking about it with someone else.

I text Vivian.

> Crisis neutralized.
>
> All done and it was AMAZING

VIVIAN
I knew you'd kick that events ass

Boxes, schmoxes

There's no time between the end of the day one schedule and the networking event. I decide to stay in my current outfit, heels and all, and make my way to the outdoor space.

Logo-emblazoned lanterns lead me down to an outdoor sitting area, equipped with love seats and throw pillows. The contrast between the rough, tree-laden terrain and the furniture is something out of a modern architecture magazine. It looks like one of those viral aesthetic videos that circulate social media.

The networking event is practically perfect and a bit over the top—exactly what I'd expect. A personalized tumbler cup and Patagonia scarf were in my welcome gift, with a note to bring it tonight. I feel a little out of place with my heels still on, but the only other option was my slippers. Oh, the pros and cons of packing light.

The tumbler makes sense as the happy hour is centered around the most decadent, and boozy, hot chocolate bar I've ever seen. With five different options, no milk preference goes unfulfilled. I start with the oat milk base, said to have notes of butterscotch, and add from-scratch marshmallows. I top it off with a shot of craft butterscotch liquor.

At this moment, I drift to every eye roll and smart-ass smirk Jack would shoot my way whenever I ordered anything with oat milk. He loved to make jokes about "milking an oat." At the time, I thought this was in the realm of charming banter when in reality, I was giving Jack too much credit. He wasn't charming, he was annoying with bad jokes.

My shoulders relax as I take in a mostly laid-back group of people, enjoying their probably spiked cocoa beverages. Not a lot of company talk going on here and I love it. I prefer a low-commitment happy hour with the goal being to meet people instead of spouting your elevator pitch.

I come back to when a server, whose only job this evening is to walk around and top off everyone's drink with house-made whipped creams, asks again if I'd like any. When the question is "whipped cream?" the answer is always, emphatically "yes."

My game plan for any networking event, like this one, is to start by sitting alone. It's something I picked up after I heard someone complaining about the people who awkwardly jump into conversations. I find people who seek you out are much more likely to carry a decent conversation instead of forced small talk that makes you wish you had a sharp stick for your eye.

Before I can make a dent in the best hot chocolate I've ever had, Royce sits next to me.

"Ivy Lawson—so happy you could join us," he casually greets me, like we've been friends forever, and not like he was pissed at me earlier.

"Wouldn't miss it," I say as I try to remember the article I read a few weeks back. Royce is in his early thirties and worth something like four-million dollars. I immediately have the urge to ask him what's the deal with the number in the middle of his company name.

"I heard you were able to sort out your little mishap," he says with eyebrows raised, like it's some sort of gossip.

"Yeah, once the *lodge* employees found the boxes, we were all set," I say, trying to hide my mood which is plummeting.

"Those shipping details were tricky. Gotta follow them right down to the punctuation." He laughs and puts a hand on my shoulder.

I could melt into the ground. Is he insinuating that I couldn't follow instructions and *that's* why the boxes were lost? And also, his hand feels heavy and gross.

"Actually, I did follow the instructions. Not sure what happened but I'm happy we were able to deliver and have a great first day." I want this interaction to be over, so I don't elaborate on how ridiculous his passive assumption is.

"You're right, you're right." He smiles so big it's like lightbulbs could shine out of his front teeth. I hate it. "Now onto the fun stuff… will you be joining us for the morning hike tomorrow?" He leans forward, rugged hands on his knees.

My immediate reaction is to laugh but I don't think that will go over well with the CEO, at their event focusing on sustainability and the power of the "great outdoors." In my brain, the words "fun" and "hike" don't belong in the same sentence.

"Oh, you never know. Depends on how that time change treats me tomorrow," I reply, shrugging my shoulders, like there's a chance I'll show up for this pre-sunrise hike. I didn't even bring a pair of tennis shoes.

"Hoping I'll see you, but if not, definitely at the wrap-up event," Royce notes, lightly touching my hand, preparing to stand up.

"Sounds great," I say before taking a sip of my hot chocolate, aware of the touch. Huh? Maybe he's had too many hot chocolates.

"Do you have my cell number? Here it is, just in case." He slips me a business card with his number written on the back. Was this at the ready in his pocket?

Royce leaves his space on the loveseat, and I try not to look confused. That was a weird interaction.

Trying to shake off the awkwardness, I take in my surroundings. The Emerald Canopy Lodge name fits perfectly because I'm not sure if I've seen this many trees in my life. Quite literally, there are trees everywhere. Past the trees is an outline of mountains, actual come-and-climb-me-if-that's-your-vibe mountains, with a lake at its feet. Stars replace the familiar glow from city streetlights and traffic. I can't imagine how dark this place gets.

If you couldn't see the trees, you'd have no problem smelling them. I'm wondering if the scent will follow me back to my room.

But the thing itching my brain is how quiet it is. Right now, I hear the bustling of people moving around and enjoying the event, but there's nothing outside of that. Gone is the buzz of traffic paired with lives you don't know, as you co-exist in the same place.

I've never been one for the outdoors. Sure, all the studies I've read say it's supposed to be beneficial, but I despise it. I blame it on a string of family camping trips going insanely wrong. Everything from second-degree burns, to the flu, to crashing my bike has blurred any of the happy memories that occurred.

Once you throw up for four days inside a tent, where you can't take a hot shower without shower shoes, you hit your quota for tent experiences for your entire life. Trust me.

I stay on the loveseat for a few more minutes, wanting to make sure I'm seen and available if anyone wants to chat. On my way out, I grab a refill on my hot chocolate with more butterscotch liquor, and extra whipped cream.

I check my phone and see missed calls from Jack. I'm sure he wants to know how the first day went but I don't have it in me to call him back.

While walking back to my room, I reluctantly think about Jack. How he wants to get together. How he wants to "talk." I've held strong thus far. Mostly because I don't care what he has to say. There's nothing he could tell me that would make me feel better, but there is the opportunity for him to make me feel worse.

When I caught him, it would've been easier if he'd told me he was in love with Misty. I wish he would've screamed that she was his soulmate. Instead, he pleaded for me to stay. To hear him out. He repeated how it was a mistake. He grabbed my hand with both of his and put a kiss on my palm, the sweetest gesture he could think of.

He couldn't even give me the luxury of a clean break.

Jack manages partner relationships at Sparks, so unless I change roles—which I'm not doing, because get fucking lost—our jobs are closely connected. We have to work together in a real capacity.

I open the door to my room; the smell of fresh flowers greets me. Just when I think I've escaped the Jack roller coaster for the evening—worst ride ever—I get a notification about an apartment for sale on our favorite block. This one feels like lemon juice on a cut lip. I fall into the bed.

The memory of the two of us looking at places, holding hands, smirking as we counted bedrooms and discussed kitchen tile. We almost put an offer on a place a few days before I caught him with someone else.

I'm motion sick even thinking of the pivot. One day, we're trying to find more ways to entangle our lives and the next, I can't stomach being in the same room as him.

The shift is what hurts. Not just in what our future looked like, but my new view on the past. I thought Jack was sharp with a unique sense of humor. It was like he had all this extra time to come up with the perfect one-liners for any situation, ready to go at a moment's notice. I thought he was light and could bring laughter to any situation.

Now, when I look back at all those quick quips, I think about the strained smiles, sometimes a wide eye or two, and a dash of cringe. People were just being polite and tolerating him.

I feel like my brain tricked me because only after this shift was I able to see our relationship through a new lens. Clarity is easier with some space, but it has a knack for finding things that I once thought were charming and making me severely question them. I get stuck in this loop wondering how I could let myself fall for someone like this.

The split happened about three months ago and while I was shocked, and still have some moments, I feel fine. I'm a bit vengeful in the sense that sometimes I visualize shaving off his eyebrows or watching his barber accidentally make him bald to show off that terrible lump on the side of his head, but I think we all do this when it comes to a breakup.

If you ask Vivian, "my level of fineness" directly correlates to how Jack was merely taking up space as a companion. It wasn't true love. Spending two years with someone is sometimes more attractive than spending two years without. Viv thinks I was looking for a buddy much more than I was planning a substantial future. She might be right, but it still hurts.

The advantage Jack didn't know he had was my lack of relationships to compare. I've dated regularly but interest fizzled quickly, and it was rare for connections to get meaningful or at all serious. A lot of "you're great for someone, but that someone isn't me," kind of vibes. How many times can you receive a compliment followed by getting dumped before you question the compliment?

I wish I was home. I'd take this anxious energy and burn it on a brutal Peloton ride followed up with a bag of sour candy, because it's all about balance. Nothing quite like fatiguing your muscles and then testing your tolerance for tart gummy sugar in bulk—lucky for me, I've built up quite the threshold over my lifetime.

As much as I try not to cry, a few tears drift down my face, like little fucking traitors. My resolve is chipped, and I feel inherently worse about giving someone who respected me so little, something as powerful as the tears on my face. It's not that I don't cry, because I cry about everything—from perfect cookies to fictional characters to being hungry to thinking about sports teams winning any and every type of championship. It's more like being cornered into tears.

Needing to feel productive, I make a list. My mind jumps to the first positive thing it can and before I know what's happening, I'm creating a packing list for my trip to Salem with Viv. Since we've been wanting to go for so long, we have accumulated a few accessories and items we'd gift each other with the idea that we'd bring them with us, whenever we made it to Salem.

Once I've mentally packed, I feel better. Never underestimate the power of creating a list, crossing things off, and feeling like you can conquer almost anything.

The time change catches me as I'm riding the mini-high from creating the packing list. Sleeping when I'm not in my bed, and especially when I'm alone, is a challenge.

I wash my face, pull on my matching PJ set, and grab my sleep mask and glass bottle of expensive sleep spray. I think the spray is mostly lavender, but it seems to help. It's quite the ritual, but to be honest, it's the only way I can fall asleep some nights. Seeming a bit pretentious always wins over staring at the ceiling, with your body on the edge of sleepless anxiety.

The Emerald Canopy Lodge doesn't skimp on the bed situation. I feel like I'm floating on a soft, cotton cloud. I'm surprised the bed isn't too soft and it feels like a light hug. The sheets are crisp white and soft on my skin, unlike most hotel sheets that had the softness bleached from them a hundred washes prior. There are even two different types of pillows: down and memory foam.

I do my bedtime yoga poses and still laugh to myself remembering the first time my doctor gave me this as an idea. I was hoping to find more ways to cope with my anxiety and she swore by it. After I got over myself, it was clear the sometimes-silly-feeling-poses helped me drift to sleep faster.

I wrap up my night-time ritual with belly breathing. In for five and hold, out for five, and repeat. Each set of breaths slows my heart, in the best way, and my eyes become heavy. I find a stopping point for the breathing exercise and snuggle under the heavy blanket.

Sleep is within my reach when I'm suddenly aware of how quiet it is. Gone is the buzz of traffic, car horns, and conversations that aren't mine.

My heart squeezes for home. I'm probably one of the only people who craves the sound of traffic.

Anxiety picks at my skin and I know I won't be able to sleep in the quiet. I grab my earbuds and my sleep playlist: sound baths, white noise, light traffic. My body sinks into the mattress and it almost feels like I'm back home.

CHAPTER NINE

HOLLAND

I'M OUT FOR A morning run when I get the sense to stop. It's one of those mornings where the temperature is perfect, the sun isn't blinding, and the air is easy.

We got rain last night, thankfully after the Bliss4ul event. There's nothing worse than people panicking over something like the weather. One of the only things that no one can control. Doesn't matter how much money or pull you have.

My feet, hitting the dirt, create a natural rhythm. The ground is soft; the way it is after rain. Something I love about the rain is how it brings out the smell of pine, cedar, leaves, and grass. This smell always reminds me of home.

There's a river near the lodge, nothing too wild, but enough to kayak when it's warm. Water laps and crashes. No need to run with headphones when you can listen to the sound of splashing water and birds.

I've been a runner for as long as I can remember. I never joined the track or cross-country team because, as stupid as it sounded, I wanted to keep it for myself. Running is one of the ways I think something through or chill my brain out.

Or if I need to keep myself busy. Which has been frequent, as of late.

I stop at the clearing and look out over the water. I'll never forget the first time Hazel screamed at me about some damn soothing moment. We were out for a run when she was pretending she was a seasoned runner and could keep up with her big brother.

She couldn't.

"HOLL, STOP!" Hazel screams, and my skin immediately gets goosebumps. A wave of panic hits me in the gut, and I run back towards her.

"Hazel, are you okay?! What's hurt?" I'm next to her and she has her hands on her knees. My own breath is ragged. I'm checking her over, looking for a bone breaking through the skin or blood coming from somewhere.

She picks herself up, gulping in air. No bone. No blood. "I'm… okay…" She ultimately gets out between breaths. "I didn't want you to miss it," she says, with excitement at the edge of her voice.

"You can't do that! I thought something happened." I push her playfully, and she immediately laughs. "What the hell are you talking about? What can't I miss?" I'm looking around trying to figure it out.

"It's the moment. Can't you feel it? Stop and take a breath," she says with her eyes closed. "A real breath."

I follow her lead and once my eyes have been closed for a few seconds, I may not feel it, but I do hear it. There's water lapping somewhere close, birds chirping, and a light wind rustles the trees. It's like the perfect sounds of outside combined.

She reaches for my hand when our eyes are closed, and I don't flinch.

I don't know for how long we stand there. When I'm about to move on, Hazel squeezes my hand. "Holl, you can't always zip from place to place. You need more soothing moments." She emphasizes "soothing."

I wrap my arms around her shoulder into a fake headlock and we both laugh before she screams about my sweaty armpits.

It feels like I relive that entire memory while I'm stopped.

But then I remember about tonight. How I made plans. Why did I do that?

I've gone back and forth on whether I'll go or not. I could cancel, and by cancel, I mean just not show up and I'd never see this woman ever again. She'd go back to whatever city she's from and maybe mention the guy who helped her out but then ghosted her. Or maybe not? Seems like something I could live with.

But then her face comes roaring back. The one where she broke into a smile after pure panic. There was something there. It was genuine. Like she meant it.

My brain has gone to great lengths to come up with excuses and reasons I can't go to gatherings; but tonight, I offered myself up. To a complete stranger. Fuck.

I can't put my finger on it. But I know deep down I'm not standing this woman up. There's something about her.

And I kind of want to figure it out. Which scares the hell out of me.

CHAPTER TEN

DAY TWO OF THE event went much smoother than the first. I stare at the mostly empty table in front of me, relishing in this feeling of unexpected success, even after such a disastrous start. I have just enough time to take down the display before the wrap-up event. I pack everything up and throw the extras in my bag.

It's challenging to take care of everything by myself, but I do it. After dropping everything off to get shipped back to the office, and my bag back in my room, I head directly to the event. When I step outside, the first thing I see is a custom sign reading "Enjoy the NETworking."

A variety of hammocks—all shapes, and sizes—surround the outskirts of a makeshift bar in the center. There are even netted swings throughout. Small side tables nestle among the nets and swings—a perfect place for you to set your cocktail. Well done, Royce.

I stand next to one of the swings. It looks like a trampoline but made with tightly woven rope where you can sit with a friend or two. This is something the city definitely doesn't have. Connected to a strong branch above, I look up, amazed this can hang from a tree in this open space. My hands push the swing and I watch it move, back and forth.

There's no need for me to find the bar because servers move around the area, each equipped with a tray of craft cocktails. As the thought of looking for a drink crosses my mind, a server steps in front of me, showing off their options. A small sign calling out the local ingredients used in each one sits on the tray in front of the choices. I pick lavender lemonade, the mocktail option, and my mouth waters before I can put it to my lips.

The lemonade is tart but still sweet on my tongue. The lavender comes through, strong enough but not overpowering, at the end. Delicious.

Sipping my drink, I explore the outdoor space. Most clients and venues would never think to do something like this. Most event planners want to be as efficient as possible which usually translates into mediocre wine and beer in a ballroom. I'm not sure if I've ever been to an outdoors after-hours event.

The social butterfly in me pulls to the fringe of a group. It's mixed with people I'm familiar with and some new faces. Someone I know smiles at me, recognizing my presence, and I easily fall into conversation.

Almost an hour and another lavender lemonade later, the group breaks off and goes their separate ways. No matter how unconventional the setting, this event seems to hit the spot. Attendees all seem happier and relieved to not be kept inside all day. The chatting is relaxed, and laughs are many compared to the typical obligatory small talk that events like this usually produce. This has Royce written all over it and it's a great idea.

Hovering near the same swing that caught my eye earlier, I'm debating if I want to get on or not when someone says my name.

"Ivy, it's great to see you," Royce says from behind me. My mental compliment must've summoned him. Along with a large amount of his cologne.

"Great event, Royce. And an awesome turnout here. What a fun idea!" I say with an exaggerated look around the space. No matter what, I can schmooze with the best of them.

"Couldn't do it without vendors like you." He winks. "Do you get it…

NETworking?" He puts his hands up and looks around.

Nothing like needing to reassure the millionaire his pun hits. Everyone gets it.

"Clever." I nod. A single-word answer is the absolute best I can do.

"I'm bummed Jack isn't here. We always have such a good time at these wrap-ups. Something really good had to have come up to keep him away." He claps his hands and rubs them together like I have any idea what he's talking about. "Nothing like some bachelors kicking back after getting some work done."

My brain can't compute what's happening. I'm standing in front of Royce, brows arched, and words aren't coming to me. It's like the entire English language has emptied from my brain and all my energy is being used to translate what Royce just said. What the hell are *bachelor things*? This feels inappropriate and like he's ratting Jack out for cheating—or doing something close to it—when he'd travel for work. Jack definitely made trips for Royce's company while we were dating.

Before I head too far down the rabbit hole, I muster a response. "I'm *sure* there's nothing like it. If you'll excuse me, I'm going to get back. I have an early flight home tomorrow." I collect myself and reach for a handshake. Royce takes it upon himself to start with a handshake but then to pull me in for a hug. Our hands get awkwardly caught between us and there isn't a word for how uncomfortable I am. He somehow finds a way to make it worse. I can hear him smelling my hair and feel his hands low on my back.

This. Is. Gross.

"Still lots of time to bump into each other tonight," he responds with a wink.

My mouth is watering like I could literally vomit all over Royce. Real-life vomit wouldn't make this situation anymore disgusting. I hope my face doesn't give me away.

"See ya around, Ivy. Give Jack my best."

He can't hear my response as I've already turned away. I'm walking as fast as these heels will take me. "I will absolutely *not* be doing that." Even if I'm the only one that hears it, it makes me feel like I stood up for myself.

A shudder goes through my body. What the hell was that?

I don't want to look like I'm running away, or draw any attention to myself, so I grab a chair and sit for a few minutes.

Once Royce is wrapped up with someone else, I head inside.

One step into the lobby and I hear Bea. "Sweet Ivy—it looks like you could use a drink or maybe a snack. You're as pale as a sheet." Her timing is impeccable, and she's spot on.

I do need a drink.

CHAPTER ELEVEN

HOLLAND

THERE ISN'T MUCH work for me to do at the lodge. It's been like that for months. Some days, it makes me feel useless. Like today.

No matter how little work there is, the pull to this place is something fierce. I'll never leave it behind.

I turn my cell phone on and see a missed call from my mom. Not unusual. We're close and talk at least three times a week. She and my dad are trying to book a trip to the lodge for a few days.

The house I grew up in, and where my parents still live, is an hour away, but I don't go home much. My preference is to have them here instead, as often as possible.

My parents have been dropping hints about how I should hire a general manager. This would allow me to focus more on big-picture decisions and less day-to-day management. Whenever they bring it up, my chest feels like I'm under a stack of bricks. They mean well but I can't go there.

If I were to go that route, I don't know what else I'd do to fill my time. These last few years have been focused around one thing and one thing only: the lodge. Outside of that, I'm not sure what else there is.

I owe it to my family. Most importantly, I owe it to Hazel.

Instead of staring at the lack of work, I go back home and take Slate for a walk. He was meant to be a city dog, so walks are short. If you take him too far, he'll eventually plop on the ground and refuse to move. I learned this the hard way. Everyone loves it and I despise it.

We take a trail on the outskirts of the lodge. The sun shines but when it's about to be too warm, a cold breeze shuffles through. Damn near perfect walking conditions.

The seasons are in limbo. Most days are still warm but the edges of the leaves are changing. Some have already fallen and litter the walking path. They don't crunch yet, but it's only a matter of time.

I used to think these were kind of useless, having a trail so close to the main grounds, especially when I was a kid.

My grandparents opened this lodge over sixty years ago and it's been passed down through each generation. When I asked how they came up with the name, my grandpa told me it was because of my grandma. When he used to stare into her eyes, it felt like he was in an emerald canopy. He couldn't imagine a better name for this place. I used to fake a gag when he told that story but I secretly loved it.

When my parents were ready to step away, Hazel took on the lodge responsibility, like we all knew she would. I remember when she was brainstorming ways to get more people to use the trails. She wanted to put picnic tables and other sitting areas along each of the trails, encouraging people to stop and have a snack or take it all in. I wasn't sure it was worth the effort.

Slate and I stop for a few minutes at a table. It's strategically placed to still see the lodge but also mountains and the river. No surprise: Hazel was right.

Bea will scold me if I don't bring Slate into the lodge for a quick hello. The networking event is well underway. Now is the perfect time to sneak into the lobby.

The trail will hopefully let us fade in the background. People can't help themselves around Slate. If I'm not careful, we'll be in a makeshift circle with people kneeling, petting, squealing, and asking me too many questions.

My nightmare. I'm not a recluse by any means but I hate forced interactions with random people.

I'm almost to the side door when I see Ivy and Royce. She's standing near one of the netted swings, almost like she's thinking of getting on.

We're too far away to hear any of their conversations but close enough to see Royce getting closer and closer. Ivy looks uncomfortable leaning away from Royce.

Can't this asshole take a hint? I can see her trying to get away from here. She continues to rub her hands together, like earlier. She fidgets and tries to put more room between them.

Finally, Royce leans back, and it looks like they're shaking hands. Ivy's body is stiff, and her shoulders almost touch her ears. Then Royce is pulling her into a hug, but with their hands awkwardly stuck between their chests.

For fuck's sake.

I've stopped and Slate pulls at the leash. That isn't the only thing pulling me. My jaw is clenched. The hand not occupied with the leash is in a fist.

I'm not entirely sure why I'm having such a strong reaction. I've met this woman once. There have been lots of women I've met and have never thought about again. In my defense, none of them had eyes as green as the trees.

I can't really explain why, but I hate seeing her uncomfortable.

After a few seconds too long, they separate. Ivy doesn't get on the swing but turns towards the lobby instead.

She doesn't go inside right away but drops into a chair. Her tapping foot is the only thing that moves. The rest of her looks like it's made of stone.

Slate sits, looking up, waiting for our next move.

"Sorry, buddy. No Bea visits today." I lean down and give him a treat from my pocket like he cares where we go next.

"I have somewhere else to be."

CHAPTER TWELVE

THE MORE SPACE between Royce and I, the better I feel.

Bea gestures for me to follow her. We end up in the lodge restaurant. Again, I'm pleasantly surprised. The inside features cozy booths and tables next to massive windows, mountains in the distance, without any tacky dead animal decor. I get closer to the windows and can see the networking event still in full swing. My body shivers.

"Here's a list of local ciders." Bea hands me a menu. I'm more of a cocktail and wine girl but a complete sucker for local brands.

"I don't drink much cider. It's usually too sweet," I try to explain. But when Bea insists, pointing at the dry cider selection, I pick one. My hand is slow to bring the glass to my mouth. If I hate this cider, I'll act like I actually love it and then stomach the entire pint. I'm a people pleaser down to my bones.

I take a sip and am surprised when it's the perfect balance of fruit and tart.

"Told ya! I knew you'd like it," Bea brags, taking a drink of her craft beer.

"You have no idea what I like." I laugh as we sit across from each other.

Bea jumps in and tells me story after story about Brad and his family.

This definitely has the feeling of small-town lore, where everyone knows everyone, some way or another. She's laughing as she says parts of sentences, and the story gets lost in translation. It's mostly broken words, giggles, gasps for air, and maybe something about a cat in the tree with a kite. Her belly laugh is contagious even if I have no clue what's going on.

"I'm going to have to ask you to keep it down," Holland says as he approaches the table, clearly joking. The bar is empty besides the three of us. He's still in his flannel and jeans from earlier.

"A joke? From Holland? What's the special occasion?" Bea asks.

Holland shrugs her off and acts like he does this all the time. It feels like he doesn't. He rolls up the sleeves of his shirt and then pours his own drink from behind the bar. The bartender barely notices he's there.

He sits down next to Bea and across from me. Holland brings the drink to his lips. Our eyes catch and my cheeks feel hot. It's like he caught me staring.

"I was just telling Ivy about my favorite Brad moments—"

"Bea. Leave the poor kid alone," Holland interrupts.

"He's not a kid. He's a man. A grown adult. If someone doesn't playfully make fun of him, how will he ever change?" She says it like she's doing him a favor.

I laugh under my breath and take another sip of my cider. Bea sounds serious.

"I mean, he is eighteen, right?" I interject.

Holland looks at me, mouth slightly open, seeming a little surprised I jumped in.

"Yes. He's *technically* an adult," he says, still looking at me. "But not really." He emphasizes while turning towards Bea.

"When will we cut the cord?" Bea asks and dramatically looks up to the ceiling, her fingers spread out in exasperated fashion.

Holland rolls his eyes. I bet they do this all the time.

"Remember when I kept signing the guest room notes with LOL, thinking it meant lots of love? You finally asked me about it and laughed so hard when I told you what I thought it meant." She claps her hands and sets them both down on the table. "Ivy. He ran to the first open room, grabbed the note, and brought it back."

"I had to!" Holland says. He's fighting a smile on his lips. His jaw is clenched. What is it about a man trying not to smile that is so attractive?

I'm holding back my own laugh because I don't want to interrupt this exchange.

"He then proceeded to read it aloud to all of the staff present—"

"You were signing the notes with '*Enjoy your time at the Emerald Canopy Lodge. Laugh Out Loud.*'" He laughs as he explains. But then, it's like he catches himself and pulls it back.

"I thought it meant lots of love!" Bea is louder now, giggling at herself.

"Even if it meant that, it was still weird." He takes a long drink.

"Agree to disagree but you made fun of me, and I stopped. I swear, we're doing Brad a favor," she says matter-of-factly.

Bea playfully bumps her shoulders into Holland, drinks what's left of her drink, and gets right into the next story.

After another cider, I glance at my phone to check the time. I'm stunned when I realize Bea's been in story-mode for over an hour. Time's flying.

When I look up, there's Holland. His lips turned up in the smallest of grins. He wears an expression that makes me feel like I've been caught red-handed.

But I don't stop. I like the way he's looking at me.

My face feels hot. I don't know if it's the drinks, the laughing, or this man's almost smile.

The longer we look at each other, with Bea still talking in the background, I can't help but grin.

I know we're busted when Bea stops, glancing between the two of us.

"Well, look at the time. I should get going." Bea finishes her dark beer. Not subtle at all. "It was so great meeting you, Ivy. If I don't see you tomorrow for checkout, safe travels."

She moves to sit beside me and pulls me into an actual side hug. The few seconds we're there feels wholesome. It's nice. Quite the contrast from the unwanted attention from Royce earlier. I hug her back. She gives Holland some sort of look—I can't put my finger on it.

"Don't worry, Bea. There's a scheduled Spider-Man discussion." Holland comes back from the bar, drinks in his hands, and takes Bea's place across from me.

I wave at Bea and smile at her as she leaves the restaurant. Without our very own chatterbox, the restaurant is quiet. Many other guests have left and it's mostly sounds from the event in the distance. After a long few seconds, Holland clears his throat.

"These are on me, for the whole box fiasco…" He picks up his glass, tipping it towards me.

"Thanks for the drink and thanks again for finding those. Any idea what happened?" I slide the cider closer.

"It's a classic tale of someone not checking the boxes in the shipping elevator, waiting to be brought up. Anyone looking for them had to ride the elevator next to them… but never looked at the label." He grimaces.

"You're kidding me." My mouth drops open. "That hurts to hear."

"Believe me, it hurts to say. And I'm not kidding. That's why I brought more cider. Those boxes must've been passed at least ten times." He covers his eyes, avoiding eye contact, in dramatic fashion.

"Wow. Brad is sincerely a ding-dong," I say before taking a sip of the new cider which is just the right amount of cinnamon sweet, like apple pie.

"You've been talking to Bea too much." Holland smirks and takes a drink of his own cider. "I'm glad she called and I was able to help."

"Ugh, I forgot it was your day off. I'm sorry you had to come in. What'd you do; draw the short straw?" I look at him over my cider glass.

"Quit doing that… saying sorry when it's not your fault," he says. Before I have a chance to respond, he continues. "I sort of run the lodge." His voice is so nonchalant. "Plus, I'm local and the usual go-to person for things like this. I live close by." He runs a hand through his hair, dark and still doing the swoop thing you only read about.

Doesn't seem like he's going to give me much more than that.

"Ah, okay." I nod in understanding. "Well, thanks again. Not sure what I would've done." I know damn well what I would've done, which is panic. Well, panic even more. The anxiety would've been so heavy it'd last for days.

I need to change the subject.

"Believe it or not, I'm sick to death of thinking or talking about those boxes. Let's get to the main event… defend your Spider-Man… and go." I drumroll my hands on the table and Holland dramatically sucks in a breath.

"With all due respect, Andrew Garfield walked so Tom Holland could run. He's the superior Spider-Man." He leans back in his chair like there's simply no other explanation, with his hands behind his head. His muscles make parts of his shirt tight.

"That's not much of a defense." I lift my hands off the table with a but-that's-none-of-my-business expression. "Tom Holland is the best Spider-Man and also has the strongest Aunt May and funniest M.J."

"I speak the truth and also the facts. No need to defend." He lays it on thick with a smug laugh. "We can both agree that Tobey isn't at the top of our respective lists."

"Agreed." We tap our glasses together for a cheers.

"What are your thoughts on Tobey?" I prompt him.

"He crawled through the end of his franchise," he says, eyebrows raised. "Tobey did the best with what he had."

We sit across from each other, drinking local cider, highlighting the merits and traits of our favorite Spider-Man.

I look around the restaurant and see Holland and I are the only ones left. The bartender has cleaned up the tables, put the chairs up, and is on his way out with a wave to Holland.

"Ivyyy," a voice squawks from somewhere close. The door to the outdoor seating area is open and there's Royce, in all his glory, clearly having had too many drinks. He's got a woman on his arm—one of his clients—who also looks like she's had *all* the cocktails.

"Closing it down, I see. Looks like the networking was a success." I force a smile.

"Yesss… not like when Jack is around, but it was a blast." He looks down at the woman on his arm. My stomach turns because this is kind of inappropriate and another somewhat gross interaction to add to the list. "Stacy here knows Jack reaaaal well," he slurs.

My mouth is dry. The nausea is back.

Royce looks at Holland and back to the woman, who I'm guessing is Stacy, and stumbles, "You know, our girl, Ivy almost had a really bad day yesterday. Almost lost the entire reason for her and her company to be at this event! Would've been a mess." He stammers his words, bookended with drunk giggles, but they pack a punch, nonetheless.

Extra cringe points are awarded for the "our girl, Ivy" comment.

Not sure what to do, I manage a nervous laugh, and stare at my almost empty cider. Each word made me shrink further into the booth. I feel like I'm almost eye level with the table.

"Think it's time to head back to your room, Royce? The bar is closed." Holland jumps in, with a stern but still professional voice.

"Why? You two are still here." Royce gestures to us, like a question, with his cocktail, as he spills some on the floor.

Holland's eyes follow the spill to the floor and then back up to Royce. "Yeah, we were just leaving. I'll follow you out and lock the door behind you." Holland gestures towards the door.

Surprisingly, Royce and Stacy do as Holland asks. Holland locks the door behind them and then comes back to the table.

He reaches his hand out to help me out of the booth, and I grab it. It doesn't matter that my palms are sweaty and I'm a bit shaky.

Holland pulls me to my feet. His other hand steadies my waist as I stumble a bit getting out of the booth.

"You look like you could use some air."

CHAPTER THIRTEEN

BEFORE I KNOW IT, we're walking toward the hammocks and tree swings. My hand is in Holland's and he's gripping it tightly. Thankful is an understatement.

The lights used to decorate the event are still on and a few staff members are cleaning up the bar area and side tables. Chilled air nips at my skin. We get far enough away from the main building, right on the edge of where the NETworking event took place, before Holland brings up Royce.

"Wow. That guy was wrecked." His voice has an edge to it.

"He was something," I reply.

"Are you guys friends?" The question seems loaded.

I snort and immediately cover my mouth. My hand slaps my face and the sound makes Holland flinch.

"No. Not friends." I reiterate using my hands. "Our companies work together."

Holland nods in understanding. He stops next to a tree swing and asks me to wait a minute. I watch as he walks over to one of the staff and they have a quick chat. After a few seconds, he comes back to me.

"What's going on?"

"I let them know they could head home after they pack up the bar. The hammocks and swings can stay. It's supposed to be nice outside for the next few days. We'll take them down later." He says it with such ease. I know he said his family owns the lodge but it sounds like *he* owns it. "It's been an event-heavy week. I'm sure they wouldn't mind leaving early."

"Everyone loves going home early." I think about how rarely this ever happens to me. Stella is always the last one at the office and has a bit of a problem managing her own work-life balance. She's not aware of her employees' balance most days. I can't remember the last time I took a day off or went home early. Vacation is calling my name.

"Now, let's get you on this swing." He grabs the base of it and pulls it in front of me. Not sure what he's getting at, my expression is one of confusion and questions. "I saw you earlier… standing in front of the swings, checking them out, before Royce started talking to you. It looked like you wanted to get on one. Now's your chance."

I choose not to address the part where he saw me at the event or how I like the thought of his eyes on me.

"These shoes, and the whole outfit, really aren't meant for swinging." I glance down at my heels, which have crossed into torture territory, and my midi skirt. While this is the perfect business outfit, it's not meant for much swinging or movement in general.

"See, the cool part about shoes is that you can… wait for it… take them off," he says as he takes off his own. "I'll help you up."

I look around and see that no one is paying attention to us. It's just Holland, the twinkly lights, these empty swings, and me.

"I don't know." I hesitate.

"Baby steps. Why don't you take your shoes off and set them over there?" He gestures to the space next to the swing. "And then I'll help you up."

Pausing for a second until I see Holland's face, eager and hopeful, I finally take my shoes off. I let out a groan and rub my toes. Is there anything better than the moments of relief after taking your heels off?

Holland smirks and stands next to me, reaching out a hand. "May I?"

My stomach tightens when he asks for permission. He acts like he didn't grab it earlier.

I nod and take his hand. He holds the swing with one hand, keeping it stable, and holds my hand in the other as he helps me get on. I can feel the strength in his hands alone.

Still unsure about this whole thing, it takes a little bit for me to get on the swing and not feel like I'm going to tumble off the edge. There's no sense of urgency or rushing. He's patient and seems to have no issue with me being almost laughably slow. I go from crouching awkwardly to my knees and then sitting with my legs out.

"Are you good?" Holland asks once I've gotten myself comfortable.

I don't know if he's asking about my swing position or the whole thing that happened with Royce.

I nod.

He gives me the "one minute" gesture and walks away. He comes back with a blanket from the crates strategically placed around the space.

Before he gets on the swing, he looks at me, like he's looking for the green light. I give a small smile. He wraps the blanket around my shoulders. The gesture is sweet and brings a smile to my face. He slowly arranges himself on the swing, sitting next to me, careful not to jostle or move me around too much.

The swing is much bigger than I realized, with enough room for probably two others to sit with us or for both of us to lie across it. Holland's feet would probably hang off the edge, or he'd have to bend his knees but it's definitely meant for more than one person.

"I have a confession… I love these things," he says. "I'm glad we have people who ask for them. We usually take them down right away. The employees never get a chance to enjoy them. Plus, it's hard to be bummed on a swing."

"To be honest, I haven't thought much about swings. It's not really a common occurrence in the city."

Hollands kicks his leg off the ledge of the swing, giving us a little momentum.

"You probably aren't able to see these in the city much either." He glances up at the sky, black and damn-near glittering. It's as surprising as it is stunning.

"No. We don't." I carefully lay back so I can take in the sky. Holland does the same. I'm surprised our shoulders don't touch. It looks like silver flecks are dancing on the richest black.

My heart has always belonged to the city. The buzz. The rush. I weirdly love the sound of traffic.

We're quiet. I don't know if it's been thirty seconds or minutes. I can't peel my eyes away from the sky.

"If you don't have views like this, what's your favorite part about the city?" Holland breaks the silence with a question.

That's easy.

"The sound. The feeling like there's always something happening or about to happen. And the potential of that something." I rub my hands on my arms because it's a little cold, but it feels good. "I'm not sure if that makes sense."

"It does. Just an interesting take. People are typically selling me on the food, abundance of cabs, and their tiny apartment. The usual."

"Not a fan of the city?"

"It's complicated. I grew up here, so I kind of stuck around for the most part," Holland says.

"Complicated?" I press for more details. I'm a bit surprised by my bold reaction to the vague statement. Holland's voice speaks in a way that feels final but I push my luck.

He pauses and takes a breath. "A few years ago, I lived in the city. Did the whole thing. It just... didn't work out," he answers with finality.

We stay like this, lightly moving the swing, not saying much. Did I seriously meet this guy yesterday?

I'm a bit surprised at how calm I feel. Anxiety thrums under my skin, it's always there, but I almost have to look for it now. I'm aware of how quiet it is out here, but it's fine. The silence is... okay. There's a breeze and it brings the smell of things green and fresh.

"Can I ask a question? If I'm overstepping, you don't have to answer." Holland turns his head to face me, almost stumbling over his words. I nod, especially because this feels like a compromise. He continues, "Who's Jack? I saw your face when the drunk-trust-fund-bro brought him up."

"One, that's what I'll be calling Royce, behind his back, for the rest of time. Two, Jack is my ex. We were together for about two years. We still work together. I'm aware that I'm a total cliché." Avoiding eye contact, I look back to the stars.

I try to not sound bitter and annoyed but I'm not sure if it's coming through as I fill him in on the details. "I'd rather do the workload of two people than spend any additional time with him."

When Holland doesn't interrupt me or my cliff notes version, I look at him for any sense he's heard enough. All I see are his coffee-dark eyes, almost blending into the night, and feel him waiting for me to continue. I keep going, sharing all the unseemly facts of how it ended.

"And apparently, he and Royce are *best bros*." I put a gross enunciation on the best bros. A small wave of shame and embarrassment floods my cheeks. "It's partly my fault. I shouldn't have dated someone I worked with. It's like corporate etiquette 101."

My brain and mouth have ganged up on me and I'm sputtering words at this point.

"I wish you'd stop doing that," he interrupts. "Stop taking the blame for things that aren't your fault. People cheat for a lot of reasons and that's on them. It's probably not even partly your fault." He says it like he'd been thinking about it for a bit.

This is unexpected. I had no idea Holland noticed my change in demeanor when Royce continued to dig at me about the mishap this morning, and found another way to bring up Jack, like my presence and contribution weren't satisfactory. I'm speechless on this swing in the middle of the night.

"You're also not stupid or careless. I heard you giving yourself quite the talk outside the conference room yesterday morning," Holland continues. "I mean, maybe you are…" He laughs. "But not when it comes to those boxes." He's clear, to the point, and calm.

"Also, Royce is a dick." He crosses his arms.

Taken aback by the kindness and compassion shown by someone I just met puts tears behind my eyes. This feels like a Vivian rant, even with one of her favorite words. She's usually calling me out for doing things like apologizing when an apology is unnecessary or taking blame for anything that goes even a little amiss.

Holland looks over to see me wipe my eyes and his face crumples with concern. "I'm sorry. Shit, I didn't mean to make you cry. I don't know why I brought it up. I'm a jerk—"

"You're not a jerk. And to be honest, I cry a lot. Almost burst into tears when Bea hugged me earlier." I dab my eyes and look over at Holland to see him intently listening and like he's a little afraid to move.

"I'm crying because you're being so kind. Also, because I wanted to cry earlier about the chaos, and for Royce constantly making me feel like I'm not competent." It's so easy to think of all the things I could've cried about so I keep going. "I could've cried when you found my boxes, and again when you helped me set up my table. The list goes on and on."

I have this nostalgic feeling that hits me. Almost like when an unexpected night or encounter would happen when you were a teenager. Staying out too late, sort of breaking the rules, or meeting someone new. No matter what it was, it felt like you'd always remember it. Nothing could wreck the memory. That's how I feel right now.

He turns and catches my eyes. We don't say anything but we're still telling each other secrets.

CHAPTER FOURTEEN

HOLLAND

I WOULDN'T HAVE put this on my daily bingo card.

Ivy and I are sitting with each other, in complete—but comfortable—silence, enjoying each other's company. This isn't like me, socializing by choice, but I couldn't just wrap it up in the bar.

Especially when Royce made her react like that. I hated how he talked to Ivy. Hated how her face drained of color. I knew this fucking guy was going to be an issue.

I break the silence. "When do you head back home?"

"Tomorrow morning. I'm leaving for vacation the day after," she answers and I can hear the joy in her voice.

Ivy chats for the next five minutes about her friend, Vivian and where they're going. About how she's going to finally take their "spooky sisters" vacation.

What the hell is that? Sensing my unanswered questions, she fills in the gaps. Sounds like they've been trying to take this trip for a while. I don't feel like I totally get it but I can feel the excitement rolling off her.

A cool breeze comes through and leaves goosebumps on my skin. I love that feeling. It brings me back to nights in our backyard when I was younger. We'd sit on the deck and stare at the stars. My parents with their wine and bourbon and Hazel and I with hot chocolate.

I acted like I was too old for hot chocolate but it was a lie. I'd take the mug, reluctantly, and scoff at the mound of whipped cream. Honestly, it was one of my favorite family traditions.

The city had a lot but it's never had this. The stars. The nostalgia.

"I should get to bed," Ivy says as I'm reminiscing. "And you probably have someone waiting for you at home."

"Oh yeah, sure do." I joke. "I'm sure Slate has taken himself to bed already."

"Slate?" Ivy's voice is higher.

"Yes, Slate. The spoiled French bulldog who has a nicer bed than I do."

"You have a Frenchie?" she exclaims. "I love Frenchies. Wish I was sticking around to meet the little guy." She's swooning.

For a second, I think about inviting her to meet him but I quickly dismiss the thought. I met this woman yesterday. Not a good idea. For probably more reasons than that.

I get off the swing slowly, trying not to bump into her. She puts her legs over the edge and I reach out my hand. When Ivy attempts to put both feet on the ground and reach for it, she stumbles. Directly into my chest. Her soft brown hair is under my chin and some of it touches my face. She smells good. Like a smell you know but can't place.

Instead of her hands, I'm holding her elbows. Her skin is chilled under the fabric. Our bodies are close. Her green eyes snap up. I hold my breath but see hers. It's the only thing between us. My hands are on fire, burning to touch her.

I finally exhale and Ivy steps away.

"Thank you." She smooths out her top, looking down at her bare feet.

After she puts her shoes on and I put the blanket away, we make our way to the lobby. We don't say anything. There's nothing but the sounds of crickets, the breeze, and rustling tree branches. If I had it in me, I'd ask her to stop and soak in the moment. But I don't.

"Thanks for everything." We're right outside the lobby door. She turns to me and waves. "Really—the boxes, the cider, tonight in general, everything with Royce…" Her voice fades away and she's back to looking at the ground. "I wouldn't have seen the stars if it wasn't for you," she says as her eyes catch mine.

The lights reflect off her eyes but they remind me of the sky we spent tonight staring at.

"Don't mention it." I can tell how uncomfortable she is bringing up Royce. *Dick.* "Also, quit with the thank-yous," I say jokingly… but I mean it.

Before we go in our separate directions, I decide to say what I've thought about since I saw her earlier. "Listen, do what you want with this, but anything that could go wrong isn't automatically your fault." Am I crossing a boundary? Probably. But I feel like she needs to hear this from someone. "Even if you've picked the wrong Spider-Man to defend." I attempt to lighten the mood and stick out my hand for a handshake.

"I appreciate the ability to look past my flaws with superhero preference." She laughs. She shakes my hand. Her skin is like velvet.

We stay here, for a few seconds too long, but neither of us seems eager to let go. My pulse quickens and I pull away.

"Good night, Ivy. Safe travels tomorrow." I put my hands in my pockets.

"Night, Holland-not-Tom." She waves.

"That is a terrible nickname." I turn in fake exasperation and walk towards my truck.

The lobby door shuts and I look back to make sure she's safely inside. A few steps in, she stops and glances over her shoulder. She smiles at me. And as much as I don't want to go, I make my way to my truck.

I feel a little weird thinking this is the last I'll see of her. We didn't exchange phone numbers. I don't know her last name. I could get it from

Bea, but I wouldn't.

    Would I?

CHAPTER FIFTEEN

HOLLAND AND I are back on the swings. No one else is outside. I'm not sure how we got here. This time, the swing is really getting some air. We are flying. Like I'm afraid we're going to make a full circle. My belly flips as we go back and forth. Each time we're getting closer to the stars. They glint and shimmer across the black night sky.

All I can do is laugh. Kind of like when you're riding a rollercoaster and it finally drops. Holland and I are both laughing. He seems to have more joy in his eyes.

The swing finally loses momentum and comes to a stop. Our gazes meet. We're both breathless. Then he makes a decision. I can see it in his face. He reaches his hand for the back of my neck, hesitant at first, and then pulls my head towards his.

I can feel his breath. His somewhat rough fingers on my skin.

My phone chimes repeatedly, waking me up from a damn good dream.

It's not even 6 a.m. The only notifications allowed to come through this early are from the airline app.

"*Your flight has successfully been rescheduled.*" The notification reads.

Huh? That's not right.

I read the email to see that my flight for today has been rescheduled for a week from today. I'm dialing the number for the airline when I get a text from Jack.

JACK

> Need you to stay at the lodge for a few more days.
>
> Royce wants a meeting and the cheapest option is to have you fly home a few days later. Call me if you want to discuss.

I lay my head back on my pillow and curse past Ivy who had no problem dating a colleague. *What was wrong with her?* Before I can get too deep into the scolding, my brain catches up and reminds me of my trip to Salem. Jack must've forgotten. I immediately dial his number.

"Hey, Ivy. What's up?"

"What's up is a few days is not a week. And I can't stay either. I'm on vacation starting tomorrow."

"I know, but Royce is trying to set up another meeting. We kind of need you to take one for the team."

Take one for the team? I already did that when Jack blatantly didn't follow through on this event. He thought I'd cave instead of taking on the additional stress. He was wrong.

I wait for the punchline. After a few heavy seconds, it's clear there isn't one.

"This won't work. I'm not staying here. I have a flight tomorrow and I'm headed to the east coast. I can't take this meeting," I say through clenched teeth. My body is hot with rage. My face gets more and more flushed with each word I say to Jack.

"If you would've let me tag along, I could've stayed for the meeting and you could have gone to Salem, but that isn't how it panned out…" He has the nerve to sigh before continuing with his bullshit.

"Stella and I both agreed this was the best decision, instead of telling

Bliss4ul we couldn't swing it. We know how much you value opportunity," Jack croons into the phone, a heavy emphasis on *Stella*. "I thought you'd be thankful."

"This is a joke, right?"

"You can obviously continue to work remotely while you're at the lodge. You won't miss out on any pay."

This worthless excuse of a human continues to one-up himself.

"Are you made of human parts?" I can't believe I was ever in love with this guy. "Do you mean to tell me I'm supposed to *thank* you for having no boundaries and canceling my vacation?" I'm almost yelling and I don't care. "This isn't professional. If you want to take the meeting so bad, you can fly here today."

"Can't incur the extra cost," he says flatly. "Stella approved this."

I'm contemplating my next move but there's nowhere to go. I feel like I'm trapped. If Stella wants me to stay, it must be worth it. She wouldn't ask me to cancel a planned trip. I could call her but I don't want to be a burden.

"You are unreal. In the absolute worst way." My resolve is chipped and I don't have words to describe how much I detest him.

"Ivy, you bagged the meeting. Quit being dramatic." His voice is rough on the other end.

Anger runs through my body. I'm immediately reminded of all the times I've missed dinners and drinks with friends all while handling the crisis of the week. My brain flashes to a highlight reel of each time I've said, "I wish I could" or "maybe next time."

"Dramatic? How's this… I'll stay but I'm not working. Royce has my number, he can correspond with me—and only me—on when he'd like to meet." I feel like I'm on a roll. Not entirely sure where this confidence came from but I go with it. "This will be *additional* paid time off since you've sabotaged my trip. And, listen closely to this next part, I'll still have all my vacation days to take when I return."

"That isn't realistic, Ivy—" Jack scrambles.

"Oh, I think it is." I cut him off and hang up before he can utter another syllable.

I sort of can't believe I did that. Making sure my phone is turned off, I slump back into bed, whip the covers off because I'm too hot, and let the tears flow.

After a quick cry and a nap, which I'm certain can cure almost anything, I'm back to strategizing.

First, I call Vivian. I cry when I tell her the news and I'm comforted by the familiar insults she uses to describe Jack. I'm pretty sure she's come up with her most creative insult to date: *cock nosed dick-weasel*. She's pissed but trying to console me. Another reason why I love Viv.

Next up is clothes. My suitcase holds a backup business casual outfit and that's about it. I made it a point not to bring anything extra so I wouldn't need to check a bag for such a short trip. I guess the joke's on me.

For the next seven days that I'm stuck here, all I have to wear, that isn't luxe business casual, is my matching pajama set. There's no way around it—I'll have to get some clothes.

Not sure how considering this place is in the middle of nowhere. I don't remember passing any stores, or even any streetlights, on our way here, but I did see a shop on the main floor. I haven't been inside, I'm unsure what kind of shop we're talking about. Stale novelty candy or things that will be helpful? Only one way to find out.

I put on my event outfit from yesterday and go downstairs.

Luckily, the lodge is quiet and most people are still in their rooms. I walk into the gift shop and am surprised at how much is here. Different local candy and treats, craft beer and cocktails by the can, luxury bath bombs and oils, and your standard souvenirs.

There's a small section of clothes and I'm thrilled when I find a few options that will work: two pairs of black leggings, a tank top, cozy socks, a crewneck, and two tops that I think are meant for yoga and hiking, all emblazoned with The Emerald Canopy Lodge logo.

I'm easily holding $500 worth of stuff when I walk towards the register. The company policy is that any purchase over $300 needs to be approved prior. They can get lost. I've never thought less about following a rule or not. No one consulted me before canceling my vacation.

The register is unattended. I leave my items on the counter and continue to browse.

Next up is the snack area. I haphazardly grab a few local chocolate bars, my stomach growling since I haven't had breakfast yet. The flavors range from spicy chocolate, to crème brûlée and blueberry muffin. I grab them all. Thank you, Sparks Wellness.

"Miss Ivy. Good morning!" Beatrice chirps from behind the counter. Her eyes are bright like she's been awake for a while. Gone is the pine cone brooch from yesterday and instead, she has a headband that looks like tree branches in her hair. On anyone else, it'd be the wrong kind of quirky but not Bea. It's almost like it'd be weird if she *wasn't* wearing this.

"Are you an early morning gal?" she questions.

"Mostly a sugar gal." I hold up the blueberry muffin chocolate bar with an OMG expression. The word gal feels funny on my lips.

She nods, approving my chocolate choice. "I took a call from a very persistent man about extending your stay." Beatrice gives me an opening to explain. "Do we like him?" she asks like we've been friends forever.

"Some work stuff came up and it looks like I'm staying for the next week." I force a weak smile. "And we absolutely *do not* like him."

Bea nods in a way that says *Team Ivy*. "An extra week with the click-clack-queen herself? What a treat!" Beatrice squeals without sarcasm. She starts ringing up the mound of things I've placed on the counter. With each item, she picks it up, evaluates it, and gives me several winks and "I love this" expressions.

"Looking to commemorate your time at the lodge?" a deep voice says from behind me. One I didn't expect to hear. Holland.

He's bringing in boxes, probably inventory, and he's carrying them like they're full of feathers. Why are there always boxes? A rush of nervous energy fills my empty stomach. I know I'm dragging out the silence. Any longer and it will be awkward.

Come on, brain. Get moving.

"Ah, not really. Apparently, I'm staying another week." I finally sputter out a reply.

"But what about Salem? Your trip?" Holland asks with sincere concern in his eyes. He sets down the packages from his arms. "The scary sisters... or whatever?" I know we only talked about it last night but I'm a little shocked he remembers. And Holland looks surprised that he asked.

"Jack strikes again. Something came up with a last-minute meeting and it makes sense for me to stay here out west instead of flying out again in a few days." The explanation streams out of my mouth like a robot. If I say it enough, maybe it would make sense. I try not to sound too dismal.

"So, you're telling me your ex-boyfriend extended a work trip, right over a long-standing vacation, that you've been wanting to take for years... and that's that? Just like that?" His hands are on his hips, showing the size of his broad chest.

Caught off guard is an understatement. I know my wide eyes give me away.

"None of my business." Holland puts his hands up.

"You're not wrong. I'm really surprised my boss let him get away with it, to be honest." I look down at my feet. "Jack loves to suck the happiness out of anything and everything, and this is no exception." My voice is flat and I try to hide the unexpected crack at the end.

"Let me give you the employee discount on all these goodies," Beatrice interrupts, reminding me it isn't just Holland and me. A normal person would feel uncomfortable, watching this play out, but not Bea.

"No. Absolutely not. This is a work expense and I'm paying full price," I reassure her. Beatrice grins as she checks me out. It feels great to be defiant this morning.

"So, what's your plan?" Holland asks.

My plan? I haven't made it that far. Anxiety buzzes under my skin. I need more of a plan than getting clothes.

"Haven't really thought about it. Maybe I'll catch up on Netflix." I try to make it sound not as sad as it is.

"You can't stay in your room the whole time. There's a ton of stuff to do here." A touch of excitement radiates from his voice. I'm paying a ridiculous amount of attention to his mouth.

I can't watch this gorgeous man list all the outdoorsy activities that I have zero interest in. It's too early and I need coffee.

"Let me stop you there. This may be tough to hear but I hate the outdoors," I interrupt. Holland squints like he's trying to figure me out. "I know it sounds ridiculous but it's just not my thing."

The number of times I've tried to explain this. The camping horrors roar back to me and I could gag. If I'm overly antsy in the city, my anxiety is on steroids when I'm out in the middle of nowhere. I wish I had the gene which experienced silence and felt some sort of calm or peace, not crippling questions and scenarios rolling through my brain.

"You aren't really planning to stay in your room for a week, right?" Holland asks with eyebrows raised.

My silence answers his question.

"I'll make you a deal," he says and my eyes automatically roll. "Let's go on an easy hike—"

"There's nothing you could offer that would make me take that deal."

"I think there is," Holland says and the way he says it makes my stomach flip. "We'll bring Slate."

That does it. I'm defeated. He went for the dog. My weakness. I bet he knows it too.

Holland senses my hesitation. "This hike is practically a walk. You know how to do that, right?" His lips pull into a smirk. "I think I saw you doing some of that as recently as yesterday."

I didn't picture him to be so sarcastic. This morning is full of surprises.

"My footwear choices are these heels or slippers. I couldn't be more ill-equipped to take a walk." This isn't a lie.

"Ivy already tried to hike in those heels." Beatrice claps her hands, laughs, and even throws her head back. Seems like my painful trek into the lobby is a core memory for more than one of us.

"We'll get you some real shoes and anything else you might need over the week." He continues to surprise me. "I know you have nothing better to do," Holland teases with his arms crossed.

His arms. Again, I'm noticing the evident muscles hidden beneath his shirt. How did I miss those shoulders yesterday?

He's right. I have nothing planned. There's only so much TV one can consume. And my desire to see the dog is a bit stronger than my nervousness about hiking. Also, did this man just offer to shop with me?

"I can take an Uber. You don't have to take me shopping. I'm sure you have things to do." I ramble.

"No, you won't. There are no Ubers here. My schedule is flexible and open. Lucky you." I swear there are gold flecks in this man's eyes that make my knees quiver. He's playful.

I can't believe what I'm about to say.

"Fine. I'll trade an extremely easy walk-like-hike in exchange for a date with Slate," I say, much faster than anticipated.

"Look at that. She click-clacks *and* rhymes." Beatrice jokes as she puts everything in a bag.

Holland looks at Bea then back at me, with a fake eye roll. His eyes are dark; like the coffee I desperately need.

At least I'll have another week of Bea. She's not what I expected at all.

"I can take you into town around eleven. Does that work for you?"

I hesitate and look for Bea. I barely know this person.

"He's not a serial killer. A big grump but he won't kill ya." Bea does her best to reassure me. Oddly, it works.

"Sure. I'll meet you in the lobby," I answer and grab the bag, the clothes, and snacks from Bea. This feels weird but I don't feel uncomfortable. It's ridiculously nice for Holland to offer to take me somewhere to get anything.

I don't want to be a nuisance, but he offered. He offered *and* insisted.

"If you need coffee or breakfast, there's some quick options in the restaurant," Bea suggests.

I wave to Bea and Holland. On my way out, I swear I can hear her giggling.

CHAPTER SIXTEEN

HOLLAND

IVY IS A JOLT to the system. I didn't expect to see her again, especially not this morning. The second I heard her talking to Bea, I moved a little faster. Had to make sure it was her.

She was fresh-faced, no makeup to be seen—it's not like she needs it though. Her dark hair was sort of messy, like she'd just woken up.

Fuck. Why is an image of her sleeping the only thing in my brain right now?

Last night was easy. It didn't feel awkward or forced. She listened. She shared. I listened and more surprisingly, I shared a little. This is the reasoning I use to justify offering to take her shopping.

Her ex seems like a real ass. Who reschedules someone's travel plans without asking them first? I don't have all the details, but Ivy's voice cracking and glassy eyes told me everything I needed to know.

Why does this bother me so much? As she was explaining, my skin was getting hot, and I was getting more and more pissed off.

It felt like the least I could do was offer to take her into town to shop for what she needs. Shopping is not my typical activity. And could I have offered at a worse time? Bea already has too many opinions.

I act like my cheeks aren't getting red and this is something I'd offer most of our guests. Standard hospitality. Bea and I both know I'm full of shit. My shopping habits are typically waiting until the last minute, and I spend a chunk of time getting everything I need at once. Or order it online.

The less time spent in town, the better. People talk too much.

I'm pretending to not watch Ivy walk away when Bea interrupts.

"Holland is going shopping?" Bea laughs and throws her head back. It fills the entire space and it's usually something I like. My preference is that Ivy be further away before Bea throws her barbs at me.

"I felt bad." I keep my eyes anywhere besides Bea. She'll see right through me.

"You felt bad." She uses finger quotes around the word "felt." Bea's known me for almost my entire life and she's not going to let this go.

"Yes. She had this vacation thing planned with one of her friends and her ex just—" I can hear myself rambling so I cut myself off. My heart is racing a bit and each word tips Bea's chin closer to her chest. She stares at me with these knowing eyes, like when you're telling your parents a lie as a child.

"You seem to know quite a bit about a guest that's been here just a few days," she shares with a self-satisfied smile. It's a rhetorical response, as she heads back to the front desk.

Bea is right. I don't usually act like this. I have acquaintances that work at the lodge or the businesses we support but it's rare that I make plans. It hasn't always been like this but that's how it is now.

I don't have anyone to make plans with. I've been so focused on the lodge.

"Also, your mother called while you were out. Call her back when you get a chance," Bea says, moving on to her next task. I nod in understanding.

I unbox what's needed for the gift shop and go back to my office. There's little to no work to be done. I mostly shuffle papers around, organize my desk, and clean up my inbox.

My mind wanders to Ivy. She was a different kind of bright when talking about her vacation. For a minute, it made me question the last time I was that excited about something. I can't recall.

This entire interaction makes me think. She's interesting.

That's it. That's why I'm about to go shopping—a hated activity—with someone I hardly know.

Why do I feel like I'm in trouble?

Ivy shows up promptly at 11 a.m. She's wearing a rendition of the business attire I saw her in yesterday. She wasn't joking about not having anything else.

It's like she's reading my mind.

"It was this"—she gestures to her outfit—"or my pajamas." She laughs.

The shirt she's wearing is dark green which matches her eyes. Her hair is dark but catches the light through the lobby windows. My mouth is dry.

Did I just realize she has shiny hair? Am I staring? Get it together, Holland.

"All good," I somehow manage to grumble. We head out to my truck.

"How long is the drive?" Ivy asks.

"About thirty-five minutes." I start my truck and gesture toward the radio. "If you want to connect your phone to play music, it's all yours," I offer.

Her head tilts in surprise. "You're offering up the radio?" she says, her brows furrowed in confusion.

"It's music, not a marriage proposal."

Ivy stares out the windshield for a few seconds. I can't read her face. Not sure what's happening here.

"Do you care what I play?" she carefully asks.

Unsure if I'll regret it or not. "Nope. Don't care. Whatever you want."

She connects her phone, confusion replaced with a grin. When normal music plays in my truck, I'm pleasantly surprised. Based on her reaction, I was expecting her to turn on something weird. Like a chorus of cats meowing in the background or something off the wall.

Ivy glances at me, almost waiting for me to tell her to skip the song or something. But I don't. I nod, put the truck in drive, and drive off.

Her music selection is unique, but not bad. She plays some pop hits that everyone knows and filters in other genres. There's everything from nostalgic boy bands to staple 2000s emo tracks and what I'm guessing are smaller indie artists.

It's a nice day. I roll down our windows halfway and look over at Ivy. She's mouthing the words to the song playing. When she sees me looking at her, she nods and rolls the window all the way down.

The sound of wind whips through the truck. I turn the volume up. Ivy looks at me and is smiling. Like, really smiling. The kind that goes ear to ear, pushing her cheeks up, creating delicate lines in the corner of her eyes. It's like her cheekbones could touch her long lashes.

This is the kind of smile that makes me smile. Because it reminds me of Hazel.

Warm air continues to flood the truck and I smell lavender. We're nowhere near any of the local farms. It must be Ivy.

CHAPTER SEVENTEEN

I'M IN A REMARKABLY good mood. First, there was the drive with the windows down and the music loud. I typically walk or take public transportation at home so this whole experience is rare for me.

Second, Holland let me play whatever music I wanted. Truly. He didn't make fun of me or make any snide comments as the playlist went song to song—another rare occurrence.

Plus, I've wrapped up one of my most successful shopping trips to date. Nothing felt better than swiping my company credit card in the smallest act of "take that." Even though no one will probably question my receipts, it feels good.

Holland even took me to an indie bookstore. I love visiting local bookstores when I'm traveling to a new city.

I should be set for the next week, and then some, because why not? Holland even had the brilliant idea to get another suitcase, since my small carry-on won't be sufficient with my new haul. Smart man.

We're at the last store to get some hiking things. And since I know literally nothing about what I could need, Holland takes the lead. After asking for my shoe size, he comes back with a few hiking boot options.

"They have these colors in your size. What's your pick?" Holland lifts shoes in blush pink, black, and gray.

The answer is easy. "Pink."

Holland hands me the shoes to try on. Surprisingly, I like shopping with this almost stranger.

The blush pink boots fit perfectly. Holland nods in approval.

"Okay, down to the last of the list. There's a wall of waterproof jackets." He points. "Pick one out and I'll grab socks." He spins away from me in the opposite direction only to turn back. "Do you have a sock preference?" he questions as he puts the boot back in the box with its match.

Again, I don't know what I'm supposed to want or not want from hiking socks. "No preference. Use your best judgment but don't be afraid to pick out something fun," I call after him.

He gives me a thumbs up. "Meet me at the checkout when you're ready." He tilts his head to the front of the store.

There are so many jacket options, I'm instantly overwhelmed. Instead of spiraling over something I'll only use a handful of times, I pick the first black jacket I find in my size, and try it on to make sure it fits.

I remember my phone is on *do not disturb*. A little wave of panic rolls though as I peek at the notifications. I double check that Stella hasn't tried to contact me. She hasn't. It's mostly Jack. I delete all the notifications and take a harmless mirror selfie for Vivian.

I click send. Almost immediately, I can see Viv is typing.

> OUTDOORSY IVY AT YOUR SERVICE

VIVIAN

> WHAT IS HAPPENING
>
> ARE YOU BEING HELD AGAINST YOUR WILL

> HA! No, I'm good.
>
> Trading a hike in exchange to see a dog

> Okay okay that sounds like my Ivy

>> I'll send you dog pics

> You better

> Who are you hiking with?

Whoops. I forgot to mention my time with Holland last night. I didn't think to bring it up because it was a one-time thing. Or maybe I didn't want to get into it? There's no time to examine my own thought process before more texts come in.

>> He works at the lodge

> Serial killer?

>> Don't think so. A colleague convinced me he was safe.

> What's his name?

>> Holland

> You're going hiking with someone named after your favorite Spidey?!

>> I can hear you shrieking from here. It's nothing.

> I love nothing. I want deets later.

I send a black heart emoji and put my cell phone back in my bag. Holland is patiently waiting with not even a faint sense of annoyance when I bring the jacket to the checkout. I'm used to doing things with Jack and when it wasn't exactly what he wanted to do, he'd sometimes pout and act like I was asking for a kidney.

When the cashier rings up all my hiking gear, I see the socks Holland chose.

"You picked out leopard print and otter socks for me?" I ask, almost in a teasing tone, attempting to hide my pure joy.

His cheeks go pink. "Ugh, I guess? You said fun, these seemed fun," he says defensively.

"You're right. Those are fun." I clap a few times and the cashier snickers. "I love them." I mean it.

Holland dips his face in understanding. His cheeks are still flushed and it seems like he's trying to hold back his expression. Perhaps he might be embarrassed. The whole interaction warms me from the inside out.

We finish checking out and walk out to the truck.

"I'm starving. Want to get some lunch?" Holland asks.

CHAPTER EIGHTEEN

HOLLAND

THIS WOMAN. Her clapping skit—over some hiking socks—made my stomach flip. All because she was genuinely happy and didn't expect it. This has been my favorite part of the trip into town.

The shopping was alright. Easy. The worst part was when I stayed in the truck when she asked to go to a lingerie store. I faked having to make a phone call because there was *no way* I wanted to step foot in a place like that with this gorgeous woman.

The window was full of lace and see-through lingerie. It'd make sense she'd need more than what she brought. I did anything I could to not think of her touching lacy things and trying them on. I turned on the local news radio to keep my mind under control. It didn't work.

Now, my stomach is rumbling, and we need lunch. We could head back to the lodge, but since we're already here, it makes sense to grab something while we're out. Plus, she'll get enough lodge food over the next few days.

She nods in agreement when I ask about food.

"You into burgers?" There is a solid local burger spot a few minutes away.

"Love burgers!" She exaggerates with hands on her chest. "What's the place called?" she questions.

Ivy seems excited about almost anything. It doesn't annoy me because it feels genuine.

"The Bun Room," I reluctantly say. If the food wasn't as good as it is, I'd keep my money in protest of the terrible name. Pretty sure the owner named it once he was too many drinks in. Or he lost a bet. Both stories have been circulated.

"The Bun Room?" she questions as she types something into her phone. "Is this it?" She shows me a menu.

"That's it," I confirm. It's odd she's looking it up. "I should've asked—do you have any food restrictions?"

"No allergies or anything," she answers while scrolling. "Just have this thing with menus. Kind of like to scope it out before I get there." Her voice gets quiet as she explains. "I know, it's a bit much." She turns to me, eyes struggling to meet mine.

She seems kind of jumpy about the menu. People do all kinds of things. It's not up to me to decide what's crazy or not. "Not at all," I say, doing my best to reassure her.

We're sitting across from each other when I try to recall the last time I had lunch away from the lodge or my house. Nothing comes to mind. When's the last time I went on a date?

Hold it. This isn't a date. More like a favor with a caloric reward.

Ivy's knee bounces, slightly shaking the table. She's intently reading through the menu, flipping from one side to the other.

"What are you getting?"

"Cheeseburger and fries. Can't go wrong." I knew what I wanted when we parked.

"My mouth is watering." She pretends to wipe drool from her mouth. All this does is draw attention to her full, pink lips. Gone is the bold lip color from yesterday. I kind of hate that I notice it.

"I should get a salad," she says in the way most people lament about food.

A salad? This woman was just drooling over the burger menu.

"Good choice. If you want a salad…" The question is implied. Her green eyes peek over her menu and catch mine. "Do you want a salad? You're at a place called The Bun Room. Not sure of the salad quality." I know her answer but ask anyway.

"No, not really." She sighs. I can see the wheels spinning. She's thinking through something. "I rarely want salad," she says quietly under her breath. I can barely hear her.

"Me either. What *do* you want?" I press.

Ivy flips the menu back to the burger section and is biting her lower lip. That lip.

"Ah!" she practically shrieks. "The peanut butter bacon cheeseburger. And fries!" Her voice is higher and vibrant.

"I've never had it. Sounds good though."

The server takes our order, clears our menus, and it's just the two of us, in a mostly empty restaurant. We've come right between the lunch and dinner rush. Ivy leans her back against her chair, stretching her arms up and over. Her hair flows over the chair and I swear I get another whiff of lavender.

"Peanut butter on a cheeseburger… who knew?" She beams. "I love peanut butter. I swear, I could eat PB&J sandwiches every day." She's rambling but it's cute.

"I love peanut butter too. There's a local coffee shop that bakes peanut butter scones from scratch. One of Slate's favorite treats," I divulge.

Her chin is propped up on her hands and I swear she has heart eyes talking about peanut butter.

"I think Slate and I will get along just fine," she says.

"I don't doubt it."

We talk while waiting for our lunch. She tells me a little about what she does for work. At times, it's hard to keep up because she talks so fast. Ivy also uses this time to tell me she's nervous for our hike, which we're planning for tomorrow. It makes me smile a bit, being able to share a new experience with her.

It's clear that she's a planner. Before I know it, she's got her notes app open and is asking questions about what trail we're going to take, when we'll leave, how long we'll be gone, and checks the weather. She doesn't lose any steam and the questions don't stop. I do my best to answer them.

When I tell her we'll have to put Slate in a sort of doggy backpack, she screams—loudly. Like, everyone in the restaurant looks over at her.

She laughs and tells me, "That's the cutest thing I've ever heard."

I can't help but smirk back at her.

Our food is dropped off and her heart eyes are back with a vengeance. She moans when she bites into the burger, with peanut butter stuck on the corner of her lip. I need to rearrange myself. *That moan.*

Ivy is completely oblivious to the spot of peanut butter. I lean over and pause with my hand near her mouth, waiting for some sort of green light. She looks down at my hand and I brush it away with my finger, touching her bottom lip.

I need a minute before I can do anything else.

CHAPTER NINETEEN

DID I MOAN in public while eating a cheeseburger with peanut butter dripping off it? Yes, I did. And I'd do it again.

We've been doing this wrong. Cheeseburgers are meant for peanut butter.

I can't remember the last time I ate something like this in public. In the past, men have made me so self-conscious of what I was going to order or how much I was going to eat. Jack wasn't so bad. He'd scoff at real pasta or beef burgers, coaxing me into zoodles and turkey burgers. Other guys I went out with were much worse.

I take a brief trip down memory lane, back to the guy who called me a horse when I finished a teeny tiny steak and an even smaller portion of mashed potatoes. We were at some fine dining spot where it was hip to serve snacks masked as entrees and I'm certain everyone left hungry. Not only did he call me a horse—while the server was at the table—he dumped me ten seconds later.

Holland encouraging me to order what I really wanted was the healthy push I needed. How many salads have I scarfed down, while I drooled over real food? There's nothing wrong with a solid salad but it never hits the spot like when you're craving a salty, carby, burger.

My mouth waters.

We're headed back to the lodge, with the windows down and my hair whipping around. Holland hasn't asked to take the radio back yet so I'm currently blaring a Phoebe Bridgers song. I sing loud enough for Holland to hear.

He doesn't grimace, or side-eye me, or sigh in annoyance. He drives and smirks when he feels me watching him. With one hand on the wheel, flannel unbuttoned and rolled up a bit, I'm thinking about those arms. How his forearm flexes when he turns the wheel. What it felt like to fall into him yesterday. How he touched my lip at lunch.

Before I can fantasize anymore about a man sitting right next to me, a Britney Spears song is on.

"I love this song," I shout over the music.

"Everyone loves this song," Holland replies.

I laugh when I imagine Holland singing along to a Britney Spears track. I cover my eyes for dramatics.

My shoulders do a small shimmy and I'm really going for it when the chorus hits. I'm singing into a fake microphone and there are choreographed head whips.

Jokingly, I put my fake mic in front of Holland. He stares, not a smile in sight, before looking back at the road.

Before I pull the mic back, accepting my solo-lip-syncing career, Holland playfully grabs my wrist.

He sings the chorus of "Baby One More Time" into my fake microphone. His voice is barely loud enough to be heard over the music. I gasp and can't control a belly laugh. Holland keeps saying the lyrics until he's also cracking up and can't get anything else out. We're both hysterical in this truck, with bellies full of cheeseburgers, and a solid shopping haul in the back seat.

I don't know a ton about Holland but I know this much:
1. He likes burgers
2. Seems like he hikes regularly
3. He knows Britney Spears, and he's not above scream singing in the car
4. Leopard print and otters are his definitions of fun
5. He has *nice* arms.

We're almost back to the lodge when I notice the sky. The sun is about to set and it's stunning. My chin rests on my hands as I lean forward to the windshield, trying to get a better look.

I can feel Holland's eyes on me. My skin prickles and heart picks up. I love that he's looking at me.

"This is something the city doesn't have." I continue to stare up through the windshield.

Holland nods and stares ahead. From the side, it looks like he's fighting a grin.

"Do you have somewhere to be or do you have time for a detour?" Holland asks.

"Definitely have time."

It's a few minutes before Holland parks. When I step out of the truck, Holland's already there, his hand out to help me out of the truck.

"Come with me." He gestures for me to follow.

We walk in comfortable silence. Holland leads us to an opening in the trees. It's like the forest abruptly stops and we're standing just past it. It's all mountains, lush bunches of trees far out on the skyline, and a cotton candy sky for as far as my eyes can see. Trying to capture the beauty in front of me, I take a few pictures with my phone. I know they'll never do the real thing justice. It's remarkable.

With the sun going down, a breeze, and fluffy clouds, I pause and take it in. Smell the dirt and trees. Stare at the scene in front of me. It's so beautiful it doesn't feel real.

I sneak a look at Holland and he's standing so still, his eyes closed, and his chest rising and falling with deep breaths. His shoulders are strong but relaxed. He looks peaceful. Content. His lips turn up a tad at the corner.

He opens his eyes and catches me taking him in.

"Want to know something?" he asks, pretending I wasn't awkwardly staring at him. The definition of a true gentleman.

I do want to know something. Alarming how much I want to know.

"I try to get out here once a day, at sunrise or sunset." He looks around the space, avoiding my eyes. "It's pretty, but that's not the only reason why." He shifts from one foot to the other. "My sister taught me this thing. At first, I thought it was stupid but she called them soothing moments. And you basically stop and take in what's around you." He sounds unsure of himself, voice trailing.

That is not what I thought he was going to say. It doesn't sound stupid at all. It sounds lovely.

"Just like we're doing now." His eyes peel up from the ground and lock on mine. The peaceful look from a few seconds ago shifts and he looks kind of sad. He fidgets and I get the feeling this is a part of himself he may not share often. I try my best to thank and reassure him with my own look. He makes me want to wrap him up in a hug, chest to chest.

I close my eyes and do box breathing, like I do when I'm trying to go to sleep. Instead of focusing on heavy limbs, my ears reach for the sounds around me. The wind gives me goosebumps. I realize I can smell the salt water and smoke in the distance.

When I open my eyes, I feel an immense wave of gratitude. Or maybe it's awareness. My body is trying to capture this moment to take me back to later. My eyes behold the sky, still painted pinks, lavenders, and blues. The sun—closer to its set—is still burning orange.

Holland and I stand with our shoulders inches apart. My skin buzzes with being so close. The sun falls behind a mountain, a little at first and then all at once.

I want to thank him for this. All of it. My hand falls to my side. I realize I'm holding my breath and blood pounds in my ears. The rhythm is heavy and getting faster.

Looping my pinky with his, I let out a slow breath when he doesn't pull away.

Holland doesn't look at me right away. He squeezes my pinky with his before slowly catching my gaze. My skin tingles from the unexpected reaction. The wind has picked up and blows through his hair. Even with the coolness in the air, it feels hot, and I feel like my entire body is covered in goosebumps. With my pulse thudding in my ears, my breath is hard to find.

"Thank you. For all of this. This was one of the best days I've had in a while." I'm intentional with my words—wanting him to hear me. "And I know that's something people just say, but I mean it." My own hair circles around me. What would it be like for Holland to take his hands and use them to pull my head closer to his? So that our noses almost touch, his eyes—intense and dark—looking for mine.

His response is a nod, with the faintest of grins. It's nothing and more than that. We're still holding pinkies like we're in elementary school, but my skin pricks and tingles. There's some sort of pull here.

I pick up our hands. "I swear."

Back in my room, my skin tingles thinking about Holland and I standing so close together. He didn't flinch when I reached for him. In all honesty, I wanted to hold his hand but thought that'd be too bold. Instead, I channeled my inner middle-schooler and grabbed his pinky.

What was that? My cheeks feel flushed. It's a wave of "I can't believe I did that," with a dash of awareness and need.

My dry spell is embarrassing. I haven't been with anyone since Jack so it's been months on that front. How long has it been since I've had sex? And if you're counting *good* sex, Jack definitely doesn't count. Being with him was nothing to brag about. If I could describe it in three words: lazy, vanilla, unfulfilling. Typically, I'd have to take care of myself afterwards. He'd finish and be on his way to sleep, or to shower within seconds. It felt more like it was Jack having sex and I was just there.

Instead of spending any more time thinking about Jack and his lackluster appeal, my mind goes to Holland. Reserved and patient. And the kind of man who owns a backpack specifically to take his dog hiking. The image of him reaching to touch my lip during lunch replays in my head.

CHAPTER TWENTY

HOLLAND

I DROPPED IVY off at the lodge with the intention of getting some work done. I walked her in and we said our goodbyes in the lobby. The employees pretended not to notice when we walked in together. They know better. Well, everyone besides Bea. But luckily, she was gone for the day.

Ivy picked up her pinky and sort of waved with it. Odd but fitting. With her hair pulled back so I could see her neck, I couldn't help but look at her. The leggings accentuate the curves of her ass and the strength of her legs. She looks strong. A definite turn-on.

I thought throwing myself into work would help. When I try to think of something else, I keep coming back to her. About the way she moans when she eats. How she grabbed my fucking pinky as we watched the sunset, and it made me feel like I was sixteen-years-old. Or how she always seems to smell like lavender or how her ass looks as she walks away flashes in my mind.

Should I be thinking of her like that? Maybe. Probably not. A man can only take so much.

A pinky-swear. That's a more wholesome thought. I haven't thought of that in years. When she lifted our hands up, her eyes sparkling from the setting sun, it felt like part of me was thawing. Not quite warm but trending in that direction.

It almost felt like relief.

A damn pinky-swear. Who am I? I'm in a heap of feelings all over something so small. The logical part of my brain takes over and writes everything off from today. Ivy was being polite, and I was accommodating. I can't dissect or read too much into this.

This whole thing is a fluke. She wasn't supposed to stay here this long, and she'll be going back to her real life soon. I'm guessing she'd get tired of being the ray of sunshine in a forecast of storms—which is me and all my bullshit.

My office line rings. I'm thankful for the interruption.

"This is Holland," I answer.

"Holland," my mom says on the other end. "I've been trying to get a hold of you. Bea said you were shopping?" She says it like it's a question.

Here we go.

"Of course she did. Yes, I was shopping."

"For what?" she prods.

I bet Bea shared more than where I was. I wouldn't put it past her or expect anything less. And if there's one thing to know about my mother, it's that she will not relent until you've divulged enough information.

"A guest needed a ride into town. She shopped. I basically drove her around."

"She?" My mom's voice is happy.

There it is.

"Yes, mom. She." I wonder if she can hear the small smile I'm fighting. Mom usually can. The logical part of my brain is nowhere to be found.

"Okay, okay. I can take a hint. The reason I called was I think we landed on a week to stay at the lodge. Have time to look at your schedule?"

My body relaxes and I'm thankful for the sidestep into more comfortable territory.

"Always have time for you, Mom."

CHAPTER TWENTY-ONE

SLEEPING IN IS something I haven't done in forever. I went to bed later than planned last night. First, I checked my email as promised, and immediately felt better. Besides the frantic emails from Jack, demanding I call him back, there wasn't much there.

It's unlike me to not be connected to my inbox throughout the day.

There's a quick note from Royce saying he's finalizing details for our meeting, and he'll call when he's sure.

Part of me wishes the meeting would fall through. Whenever I think of Royce, I picture the sloppy-drunk version. We all have our bad nights but it seems like quite the move at a work event. I closed my laptop for the night and called Viv.

Our check-in turned into hours on FaceTime. I might've lost sleep, but it's one of my favorite ways to pass time.

She told me about her most recent dating disasters. A man who couldn't stop saying bro, from last week, and a woman who spoke in baby talk this week. I don't know which is worse. I can always count on Viv to have some wild story about something that happened to her. Only Viv would have interactions like this.

Sometimes I'm jealous of how Viv approaches dating. She's confident and cool and able to talk with anyone. I envy how she doesn't beat herself up when it doesn't work out. She's excited for opportunities and getting back out there, no matter the most recent disaster.

Actually, I'm jealous of how she approaches life. She seems to rarely second guess her decisions or plans. She doesn't seem to overthink or run through all the possibilities of what could go utterly and terribly wrong. I wonder what that's like.

I would have no idea what to do with my brain if it wasn't for running through fake scenarios whenever I had a moment of downtime.

We also may have found a way to salvage our vacation. Well, sort of. She's going to try to reschedule her flight and stay here at the lodge for a couple of days. It's far from our ideal vacation but it would give us the chance to spend some time together. It might only be for a day or two but that's better than nothing. I make a mental note to check with Bea on a possible room.

After eating a "decent breakfast," in Holland's term, I do some light stretching. He told me to eat more than I would on a typical morning. You don't have to tell me twice. I'm ready to carb up for this hike/walk. No matter the nerves, I'm looking forward to moving my body. I'm used to taking a spin class almost every day and the lack of movement has made my muscles tight.

As I stretch, my mind goes over what I should expect for today. I looked up as much as I could about hiking this specific trail. And everything I found echoed Holland—it's almost a walk, and perfect for beginners. Seems like, overall, that hiking is walking with different levels of roadblocks and difficulty.

I check the weather a final time and change into my hiking attire. I grab everything Holland asked me to bring and check them off in my notes app.

I head down to the lobby a few minutes early to chat with Bea.

"Miss Ivy! Look at you," she squeals. This woman always seems to see me first.

"Do I look the part?" I do a quick spin.

"You look very outdoorsy!" She beams.

"Can you do me a favor? I have a friend who might make a last-minute trip out while I'm here. Do you have any available rooms?" I'm not sure what my expectations are. This place is buzzing with people. Holland mentioned multiple events this week. Even if they don't have any open rooms, Viv could stay with me.

"We for sure will have a room for them! Is this a girlfriend or a loverrrr?" She says lover in a fifth-grade teasing sort of way. She's a bit nosy but I kind of love it. She's funny. Wholesome. But nosy.

I notice a small gold clip in her hair that looks like a dragonfly. How many themed hair accessories does she have?

"A girlfriend, not a lover. My best friend and I were supposed to go on vacation, but I had something come up for work at the last minute." I give her a little more info.

"I'm sorry you're missing your vacation. Working is just one part of this crazy life. Make sure to have some fun." She nods to the door.

Holland is a few steps into the lobby. He's wearing a gray form-fitting long-sleeve shirt and navy shorts. My eyes drink him in from top to bottom. I blame it on his shirt choice showing specific bulges, dips, and details. It's also the first time I've seen him out of a flannel button up.

"Hello?" Holland interrupts my mental checking-him-out session.

Bea laughs in front of me. She knows exactly what I was doing.

Why am I so embarrassing? I'm sure my cheeks are red. Like maroon. No hiding it. Again, I blame it on the not-flannel-shirt.

I finally scrape out a "hi" that comes out sounding weird and kind of like a question. This isn't what I would call bouncing back.

"Ready to hike?" Holland asks, pretending like I wasn't so deep into check-out mode my brain didn't register he was speaking to me.

Not trusting my mouth, I emphatically nod my head yes. He walks out to his truck and I follow.

I turn and wave to Bea. She sends me off with a wink.

She's not helping.

Holland's place is not what I expected. It's modern, but still completely cabin-esque. With a long driveway and green exterior, it's part of the trees. An interesting camouflage. It's beautiful.

There's not much time to swoon over the house because I can hear a dog barking as soon as we shut the truck doors.

Holland leads us to the front and opens the door. Slate greets us, nose first. He's a gray French bulldog, with white markings on his chest, the cutest face, and his tongue out in excitement. It kind of looks like he's smiling.

I melt. His wrinkles. Matching gray eyes. Paws on my legs, jumping up for attention. I can't even muster words. At this point, I'm making those noises we use to talk to dogs and babies. It doesn't help with Slate's excitement but I don't care.

"He'll calm down in a minute," Holland reassures.

"Are you kidding? I love this!" I sit down in the middle of the entryway and let Slate lick my face and put his front paws on me, standing on his back legs. "He's so cute!" I proclaim as I pet the now drooling dog.

I look up and Holland is looking down at us with a faint smile and he turns away with a fake eye roll.

"I just need a few minutes," he says as he moves further into the house.

Slate is immobilized by a belly scratch. He's leaning the side of his body on my front, kind of side-sitting, one paw up, and his head tips up to me in complete bliss. Dogs are the best. I appreciate the boost of serotonin.

I tilt my head to see more of Holland's place. I peel myself from Slate, stand up, and take off my hiking shoes, lining them next to Holland's.

My mouth drops when I get past the skinny entrance area. I'm looking straight through the entire place, which is an open floor plan. The back wall is completely made of floor to ceiling windows, which delivers an amazing view. I can't put my finger on what I was expecting but it wasn't this.

Taking it upon myself, I quietly walk through the house.

It's small, not categorized as a tiny home, but comfortable enough for a few people. The high ceilings make the living space feel open and airy. There's a leather couch, the color of caramel, and the type of deep where you know falling into it would feel heavenly. A darker colored chair is near the couch, with an ottoman and side tables. It's not cluttered but simplistic.

Matching blankets go a step further to tie the room together. I have a weakness for blankets. The limit doesn't exist on how many you can have.

The kitchen is sleek and functional. There's no formal dining table, but instead a bar with a few stools and a bistro table for two. A few oranges and apples are in a bowl on the counter, and there's a coffee cup in the sink. This place is put together. Clean. Everything flows, almost effortlessly.

Me and my lovely but chaotic apartment can't relate.

It's not that I'm messy or can't keep it clean but more so that I have a unique set of preferences. I have lots of particular things that go in specific places. My place is full of color and texture—rich, fluffy rugs, statement furniture, mirrors to make it feel bigger, and books throughout. In my opinion, almost anything can be a bookshelf.

When I get to the wall of windows—letting in all the natural light anyone could ever want—I look up and see a loft. That must be where Holland's bedroom is. My cheeks get a little hot. Why am I thinking about this man's bedroom?

Trying to reel it in, I focus on the view. Mountains. Trees. Sky. This would be quite the spot to drink coffee in the morning.

I hear Holland coming down the loft stairs, interrupting my poor attempt at not picturing his bedroom.

"So, we should tape your feet…" Holland says, with no other explanation. Seeing my confusion, he realizes I have no idea what he's talking about. "You didn't get a chance to break in your new shoes. You don't want blisters." He sits at one end of the bistro table.

Makes sense. Also, very thoughtful. I sit in the other chair and take off my otter socks.

Holland scoots closer to me. Casually, he reaches for my first foot. He gently sets it in his lap and the world slows down. He rips a piece of kinesiology tape from the roll and slowly places it on my foot. My pulse picks up as he rubs his fingers along the tape, setting it.

He lifts my foot a few inches, taping behind my heel. His hand lingers on my ankle. His fingers are a bit rough on my skin.

I like this way too much. What is it about a man rubbing your feet? Enough men haven't massaged my feet.

I'm jolted back to reality when I remind myself what this is. This isn't a foot rub but a preventative measure to limit open sores on my body. I better pull myself together before this hike becomes even more frustrating.

Slate interrupts my thoughts when he whines, looking for attention. I reach down and pet him while Holland tapes my other foot.

Note to self: When I get back home, I need to reactivate my dating apps. It's been too long.

CHAPTER TWENTY-TWO

HOLLAND

THE TAPING WAS necessary but problematic. Her skin was warm and smooth, and my fingers were damn near shaking. Had to remind myself to breathe. When I did, I quickly remembered how she smells like lavender.

Slate gets extra bedtime treats for being my wingman and distracting her.

We're almost ready to head out. I've got Slate in his bag, on my back, with water for both of us. Since I'm hiking with Slate, I packed a bag for Ivy to carry.

It felt familiar to pack one of Hazel's old bags last night—an activity equivalent of a cozy, warm blanket. She loved being outside and would always bring a pack, but was notorious for forgetting essentials, like water. Even when we were older, I made it a point to check the pack and make sure she had everything she needed.

"Since I'm going to have to carry Slate for most of the hike, do you think you can carry this?" I hold the bag out to her. "I want to make sure you'll be comfortable."

Ivy eyes light up. "It's pink!" Her face drops as she puts the pack on. "I can't imagine this cute pink bag is yours. Did you scrounge through your dating lost and found?"

I don't even know what she's talking about.

"What the hell is a *dating lost and found*?"

"You know—all the stuff women you've dated have left behind." She's waiting for the lightbulb to turn on. "You either don't see them again to return or it's too painful." She mimics stabbing herself in the stomach. It catches me off guard and I scoff.

"No dating lost and found here." I'm hoping she leaves it at that. "Let me get those," I say as I step close and adjust the straps. I find myself almost holding my breath.

Ivy goes to situate the bag on her back. Before my hands are off, our fingers touch. I hope I don't visibly jump but the air could crackle with energy.

"Good? Not too heavy?" I grumble, acting like I'm not wondering what it'd be like to touch other places.

"Yes. It's fine," Ivy says, seemingly unfazed. "I can definitely handle this."

I don't doubt that. Her leggings give away all her muscles and curves. Ivy might not hike but she does something to keep her body like that.

"Sunscreen?" She gestures to the bag.

"Yes."

"First aid kit?" she quickly retorts.

She wasn't kidding about wanting to be prepared. She's going through her own mental checklist of what we should bring hiking, even though this is her first time.

"Yes."

"Water?" She's not being critical and I can't help but smile at her.

"Yes. And before you keep going, I promise we're prepared." Her shoulders sink a little. I can't tell if she's relieved or a bit defeated. "The weather will be clear. We have everything we need for a few hours and I know this trail like it's in my backyard." I give her a side-eye, trying to be light. I'm not good at this.

Ivy smiles at me, getting the joke. I must be better at this than I think.

"Okay, okay. I trust you."

She has no idea the weight those words hold.

The first twenty minutes hold nothing but silence. The trailhead is fifteen minutes from my place, so I usually tack it onto the beginning of the hike. I notice her staring at Slate in his pack several times.

Even though we're walking, Ivy looks like she can't move enough. She swings her arms back and forth, occasionally pressing them together and cracking her knuckles. Every few minutes, she turns to look behind her, and then back at me to see if I saw her. I act like I don't but can see her out of my peripheral vision.

This hike starts with a slight incline but it's a solid beginner spot. I don't ask if she's okay—she seems like the kind who would let me know otherwise. She's slightly behind me until I feel her pick up the pace.

I'm surprised when she lightly touches my arm. "Did you know Slate is sleeping right now?" she quietly asks; her face close to mine, clearly not wanting to wake him up.

"That sounds about right. Hard life." I give her a sarcastic eye roll.

"Is he able to walk any of this trail?"

"Yeah. This breed isn't meant for long stretches of activity. He doesn't do so hot with the inclines. We'll put him on a leash once it levels out."

"I've heard that about Frenchies. It surprised me when you said you had one."

She's right. Slate isn't a great breed for this type of environment. He was a gift when I was living in the city. A low-energy dog was the responsible choice. I wanted a dog that would be comfortable in my apartment and okay with the limited time I'd have to take longer walks. It's ironic because Slate never spent a single night in my city apartment.

I clench my jaw, the typical response for when I think back to a different lifetime. And what pulled me from it. Instead of getting into the real details, I do what I always do when it comes up. I lie.

"I've always wanted one. Just couldn't resist." I put on my fakest of collected expressions. The one I've worked on and perfected throughout the years. It looks easygoing and honest, but really, it feels like my skin is tight and doesn't belong on my bones.

Ivy seems convinced when she doesn't ask for any more details.

We're at a good spot for Slate to walk. We wake him up, get him on a leash, and keep going, leaving the story of Slate behind.

The sun is out but the air is still refreshing and crisp. A breeze moves through the trees and reminds me of one of my favorite hiking perks. The smell of the outdoors. Petrichor. Hazel taught me what that word meant. Basically, it's the smell after rain hits dry soil.

I hated the smell of the rain back in the city. Gone was the richness of dirt and grass and replaced with garbage and car exhaust. Instead of rustling leaves and raindrops hitting the lake, it was screeching tires and people screaming about traffic.

Never thought I'd miss the smell of dirt and rain but I did. When you're chasing the corporate city job, no one tells you about things like this.

We're coming up on a shallow stream. One of Slate's favorite stops.

"Ready for a break?"

I peer over at Ivy. Her cheeks are flushed and she's sweating a little. She looks up and nods. Honestly, this is going much better than I anticipated. I put Slate's pack and my light jacket down on a patch of grass—another reason why this is a perfect stopping point.

"Slate loves water. Want to see?"

Ivy answers with an emphatic nod.

I keep him on the leash, but we walk right up to the edge of the stream. He's getting restless so I give him some slack, which is the green light to enter the stream. Immediately, he's splashing and doing what resembles a hop. He doesn't ever want to go far, but loves his feet in the water.

"Stop. This is so cute," she croons. "Do you mind if I take a video and send it to Vivian?"

I shrug, letting her continue.

Ivy kneels and says his name, so he'll look at her. She makes kissing noises and Slate tilts his head. She laughs and he runs to her, putting wet paws all over her. Instead of pushing him away, she holds him to her chest and lays back. Slate licks her face and Ivy continues to laugh.

There's that sound again. Her laugh.

Her phone is on the ground next to her. I pick it up, stop the recording, and then pull Slate back to the water and off Ivy. I'm laughing now too.

"Come on, Slate. No tackling." I pull him back towards the water where he's happy to be back in the stream.

Ivy stands, wipes the dirt off the back of her legs. She catches me watching her and the eye contact reminds me how long it's been since I've felt like this. An easy day with someone else, not much stress and not forcing myself to do something I pretend to like. It's not bad.

"For never doing this before, you're a natural. It's nice to see you've mastered the stream tackle," I joke as I sit down next to her in the grass.

"Well, I must thank my good friend, Google. I did some research before the hike." I wait for the punchline, but there isn't one.

"Research?" I ask like I don't know she's serious.

"Yeah, I wanted to know what to expect. Things to watch out for. And I read a little bit about this area." She glances down at her shoes. "Kind of like when I look at menus before I go somewhere new. It makes me feel better. Prepared."

The vision of her scolding herself comes to me. This makes more and more sense. An unchecked box on her many lists, stresses her out. She likes a plan. Damn, this week must be a nightmare for her.

"I know, it's not normal." She sucks in a deep breath. Her eyes are glued to the ground while her hands fidget. Her voice is a touch faster than usual.

"My parents always told me there's no such thing as normal." It wasn't my parents; it was actually Hazel. Another white lie.

"That's a nice way to grow up."

We're sitting shoulder to shoulder and Slate's still splashing and pouncing.

"It was. So, I take it you're not the spontaneous type?" I jokingly ask, wanting to change the topic.

"Nothing good comes from spontaneity," she says. Her lips in a straight line. Those pink lips which match her cheeks, flushed from the hike.

"Come on, you don't really believe that?"

"You're talking to someone who prefers to read menus before she steps foot into said restaurant."

"Not being spontaneous and saying nothing good comes from it are two different things." I laugh but her face is still as serious as ever.

"I've never had anything good happen from just going out on a whim." She throws her hands up in a dramatic fashion. Her green eyes are vibrant, like her facial expressions.

"This hike was kind of spontaneous…" I say, lightly, and wait for her to respond.

I like when she pushes back.

"Was it? With a whole day notice and a specific shopping trip?" She laughs while crossing her arms.

She's kind of right but I don't want to let her win. Not yet.

"Okay, okay. Maybe you're right, but if you would've asked yourself last week if you would be here with me, on a hike, you'd never have believed it. Right?"

"We didn't even know each other last week!" she exclaims, her face in a full smile.

"That's my point. How fast things can change."

Right here, at this moment, I'm sort of thankful for her moron of an ex. Without him overstepping and being a complete asshole, I wouldn't be with her right now. Not that I'd confess that to Ivy. Ever.

"You and I seem to have different opinions on change. Agree to disagree." She runs her hands along the grass. The only sound is Slate's splashing. "Any chance you brought some snacks?" Nice pivot.

Kind of ironic—her and I out on this hike. She's the queen of planning and I gave it up a long time ago. It never mattered how closely I followed the meticulous blueprint; all it takes is a second for everything to go up in flames.

My lips are pressed together and I'm looking at my feet when Ivy gently bumps into me, pulling me back to the moment.

"Of course. Let's get a little further on the trail. We're close to one of my favorite stopping points." Another tip I've learned from Hazel—and hell, any other woman—is that you never go anywhere without snacks.

We coax Slate out of the water, dry his paws off, and put him in the hiking pack.

CHAPTER TWENTY-THREE

Ivy

I'M IN LOVE. With a French bulldog.

The hiking isn't bad either. I've never been more thankful for anxiety meds and my coping mechanism of research. Holland makes this so easy—he's patient and prepared.

Gone is the typical anxiety when being around someone new. Instead of constantly wondering about his perception of me, my actions, and my words, I can enjoy our time together. It's refreshing.

Since I'm not analyzing every single thing I'm doing, there's space to focus on Holland.

He's also like a puzzle. I'm getting pieces to click but it's not enough to see what the collective is. He's closed off and I wish he'd open up a bit more. It seems like he has his life semi-together. I wonder what's keeping him back.

Even without Holland talking much, the sounds are my favorite part so far. Sometimes it's birds in the distance, the chatter of other hikers farther along the trail, or flowing water. I was concerned it was going to be ridiculously quiet—an anxiety trigger—but it's like nature's very own white noise. I make a mental note to find some nature playlists. Might be something to throw into the mix for my bedtime routine.

After the break at the stream, we hike for a longer stretch before we get to the stopping point Holland mentioned. There are a few picnic tables off to the side. My mouth is watering thinking about any sort of food.

He takes my pack and pulls out collapsible bowls for Slate. He fills one with water and the other with dog food. Slate stays on the leash and Holland loops it around one of the table legs.

Holland hands me a sandwich, sets one down in front of him, and opens a bag of trail mix between us.

"I would've double checked what you liked, but I realized I didn't have your number," he says, unwrapping a classic peanut butter and jelly sandwich. "But I remembered your peanut butter and jelly sandwich comment."

"You're right. I love 'em." My mouth waters along with my eyes.

This is a real time example of how I can cry over anything. Hearing how Holland thought about what I'd like and taking that time to prepare it, makes me feel good. He remembered an off-hand comment. I blink away the tears.

Eating means less talking and I'm thankful for the break. My brain tries to make sense of my strong reaction to a slightly squashed peanut butter and jelly sandwich. Is it really this rare for someone to think of me? To be considerate of what I'd like? This is something to unpack with my therapist at our next appointment.

We sit and eat our sandwiches, taking turns grabbing handfuls of trail mix. Before I know it, I hear Slate snoring. I look down and see him curled up next to Holland's leg.

"He won't be doing much more walking," Holland jokes.

"How much longer is the hike?"

"Are you ready to be done?" he asks sincerely. He's not teasing.

"No, no. I'm good. Just the whole thinking ahead thing." I reassure him. I *am* feeling good. Not that I want to hike for another eight hours but I still have some energy.

"Here's the cool thing. You can pick how long we stay out." He watches me, waiting for a reaction. "The shortest option is ninety minutes. The longest is probably three hours." He pauses, packing up our bag. I'm fixating on the cupid's bow of his lips. "What do you think?"

I'm thinking I don't want to rush back, even as the fatigue starts pressing on my muscles.

"Not the shortest option," I say, trying to be confident.

He smiles and nods his head in agreement.

I look at the patient man in front of me. He planned all of this—took me shopping so it was even a possibility, and he packed us food which he's now cleaning up. Jack sucked for a lot of reasons, but not sure he has even one of these qualities or abilities. The worst part is I didn't realize this was something I was missing.

"Hey, I don't want to be weird, but would you mind taking a picture of me?" I hand my phone to him.

After taking my picture, he surprises me again.

"What about the two of us? I want it documented that you went on your first hike and I was there to witness it." He moves next to me, already putting the camera out for a selfie. He seems unsure, and a little awkward, like he never does this.

I lean in and he meets me halfway. Our shoulders bump, the smallest of touches, which immediately jolts nervousness into my bones. I'm thinking about his arms. Holland reaches out with the phone and takes our photo.

"I'm also betting Vivian would love to see it."

He's not wrong.

Before he gives my phone back, Slate wakes up from his nap and is right by my feet.

"And you need one with Slate."

This man.

CHAPTER TWENTY-FOUR
HOLLAND

SLATE SNORED IN the pack while Ivy and I chatted throughout the rest of the hike. She seemed more relaxed and I'm guessing she was finally comfortable and knew what to expect.

She confessed to having a significant sweet tooth, which I already knew, and she asks where we get the chocolate that's in the gift shop. I promise to take her to the local spot before she heads back home. We talk about how I'm a runner, how she never could be, but she likes to do spin and HIIT workouts.

That's where she got those fantastic fucking legs from—spin class.

She wanted to know my connection to the lodge. I gave her the short version—my grandparents started it, my parents ran it until they were ready to pass it on, and now in my hands it sits. I left out the Hazel part.

I almost didn't and that screams volumes—it pulls my stomach in a weird way. Not many people know that story.

She shares a few details about her own family, which is small. She's an only child. She has a single aunt on her mom's side, who never had kids. She has no cousins. It seems like she has a good relationship with her parents but they seem to do their own thing and are traveling ninety percent of the time. For example, they just left for a four-week vacation in Africa.

Honestly, it makes me sad thinking of her as an only child. Thoughts of her parents not being around tug my heart a little lower. I wonder what her holidays are like.

We're almost back to the trailhead. Even though we spent hours together, I'm not ready for our time to end. We're walking up to my place when I decide to put myself out there.

"Any chance you're up for a movie or something?" I ask, probably too fast.

She smiles and replies with no hesitation. "Yeah. That sounds good."

I wipe my face before she can see the grin taking over.

Back at my place, I take Slate out of his pack and get him cleaned up. He's walking to his bed when I realize I need a shower. The hike wasn't that difficult but we were moving out in the sun for hours. Lugging around a twenty-five-pound dog on my back didn't make it easier. I probably smell disgusting.

"I'm going to take a quick shower and then the loft bathroom is all yours. There's a small half-bath right here, but if you want to shower or anything…" I stumble my words.

She nods in understanding.

I did not plan *this* part. Idiot. Completely forgot about the whole post-hike situation. "Do you want to hang out inside or on the patio?"

"Patio," she replies, surprising me.

I show her out to the patio.

"Wow. Your place is something." She spins in a circle, arms out wide. "Open, modern. It's nice."

The exact way Hazel wanted it.

"Thanks. It was built and almost one hundred percent furnished when I moved in."

"You still chose to live here," she replies.

That's not true. None of this was my choice. Taking over the lodge, this place, even Slate—were all chosen for me. One day, I was living in the city and the next I was here. And I've stayed.

"Feel free to grab something from the fridge. There's water, local ciders, seltzers." I need a change of conversation. "All up for grabs," I say as I reach for the door.

For a few seconds, I pause. Ivy stands on my patio. She closes her eyes and tips her head to the sky. She pulls her shoulders back and lets her arms dangle at her sides. Her dark hair is pulled back, and her face is sun-kissed. The way she looks right now, carefree, looks great on her.

This feels natural. Slate sleeping inside. Me, leaving Ivy out on the patio, headed in to take a shower. It certainly doesn't feel like I met this woman days ago.

Taking off my clothes and getting in the shower is the best feeling. Hot water runs down my body. Rinsing the tension off my tight muscles. I hear Ivy's laugh come from downstairs.

Fuck. Me in the shower. Ivy here, laughing like that.

That laugh. I can't get enough of it.

My body groans in a different type of frustration. I force my brain to focus on literally anything else besides Ivy. My dick barely gets the memo.

I'm chalking it up to the self-imposed drought. I haven't been interested in going out, making plans, or spending time with anyone besides the casual after-work drink with employees at the lodge. I can't remember the last time Slate met someone new. This is risky. Borderline reckless.

I turn the water to cold and it helps. A little.

When I'm back downstairs, I see Slate outside on Ivy's lap. She doesn't stop petting him but acknowledges me with a look through the window.

"He's got you wrapped around his paw, huh?" I say as I step outside.

"I hope it's fine I brought him out. He woke up, saw me, and ran headfirst into the window." Ivy giggles and hits her forehead with a hand as the other stays on Slate.

Ah. The laugh.

"Totally fine. He knows all the tricks for any kind of attention." This damn dog. Can't blame him though. "I set out some stuff for you in the bathroom upstairs." I gesture to the loft. Slate and I'll start with the food."

My eyes so badly want to watch her walk up those stairs and think about her in my shower.

Don't do it, Holland.

Ivy has settled in on the couch, after taking a shower, and Slate is already resting his sleeping head on her thigh.

I sit near her legs and turn the TV on.

"I have to check my work email quick," Ivy says, phone in hand.

"No problem. I'll find something for us to watch," I reply like I don't know what I'm going to play.

She lets out a loud sigh. Whatever's in her inbox has her visibly annoyed.

"Everything okay?"

"Yeah. Just Jack. Doing what he does best. Annoying me. I'm turning this off." She puts her phone face down.

I hit play and it takes a minute for her to realize.

"Oh look! It's the second-best Spider-Man franchise." She pokes fun but sinks further into the couch, and Slate snuggles in a little closer.

We get thirty minutes into the movie before Ivy is asleep. She's on her side. Her knees are pulled into her chest, where Slate also sleeps. I grab a blanket and drape it over her and the dog. She moves a little bit and ends up putting her feet in my lap so I make sure they're covered up.

I'm alternating between Andrew Garfield and sneaking glances at this woman sleeping on my couch.

Even though I shouldn't, I let my mind wander. I think about yesterday and how it seamlessly flowed into today. Effortless. Like she fits here.

Except she doesn't. She lives a thousand miles away and is going back home in a few days. I always knew this, but at this moment, it's important to remind myself. She has a life back in a place I couldn't bring myself to go back to. Anger creeps up my neck and my skin is hot. I hate how my mind jumps too many steps ahead.

I steal one more look in time to see Ivy readjust herself, pet Slate, and smile in her sleep.

Yeah. This is a bad idea.

CHAPTER TWENTY-FIVE

I HAVE NO IDEA where I am. My face is pressed into a leather couch, blanket around me, and a warm, gray body sleeps close to mine. My eyes dart around the space, trying to fill in the blanks.

Holland sits next to me, my feet in his lap and the last few minutes of the movie is playing.

Pretending my sleeping situation isn't awkward, I stretch my arms over my head. "Such a good movie," I say, careful not to disturb the still-sleeping Slate. My voice is heavy with sleep, and I wipe my mouth to make sure I didn't spend the last two hours drooling on this beautiful couch. The dog wakes up and stretches.

Holland laughs and I pull my feet back, setting them on the floor and sitting up. I can't remember the last time I took a nap. I used to love a quick weekend nap but somewhere along the way, I started feeling guilty for not being productive.

"I'll get you some water." Holland goes to the kitchen and brings back a glass of water. I practically inhale the first glass and he smirks before getting me another.

"I don't ever remember being this tired from walking." My muscles are tight from the hike. Or maybe the awkward sleeping position.

"I told you." Holland makes a tsk tsk gesture with his wagging finger.

I look at the clock. It's much later than I thought. "I didn't mean to monopolize your entire day."

He shakes his head like it's no big deal. Taking his phone out of his pocket, which is the first time I've seen him with it, he shows me the screen. It's a picture of Slate and I sleeping. It's adorable and my heart melts a little.

"Will you send me that?"

He gives me the phone so I can save my number. This feels like something. More than sharing information so I can get a picture. A few seconds later, the picture comes through.

I save his number in my phone as "Holland-not-Tom" and show him. He rolls his eyes like he doesn't like it. I can't help but grin.

"Don't be surprised if I don't text you back, right away, or whatever. I sometimes forget this thing exists." Holland stumbles over his words.

I put my hands on my cheeks and dramatically say, "Oh no! What will I ever do?"

Holland shakes his head and puts his phone back in his pocket.

"I can take you back to the lodge… if you're ready," he offers.

The truth is, I'd have no problem spending more time with Slate. And Holland. But I feel like I've already overstayed my welcome.

My mind checks off a mental list of all the time I've taken from Holland over the last few days. The day off during the conference, drinks, shopping, dinner, hiking and this evening. He doesn't seem to mind but it makes me feel a type of way. It's probably best if I go back to my room at the lodge and give this man some peace. We've spent all day together. He must have other things to do.

"Works for me." I don't confirm if I'm ready but give him the green light.

Reluctantly, I move from the couch and am met with more stiff muscles. I grab my stuff and give Slate some extra attention before we leave.

In the lobby, someone is leaning against the front desk, talking with Bea.

"Your ears must be burnin'. We were just about to call you," Bea says from behind the desk. The man walks towards Holland and they shake hands.

"Oh, man. I completely forgot you were coming today."

"That's okay. You're here now." The man is clearly unbothered by Holland's tardiness.

"I'm here, but that's it. I forgot to schedule any staff." Holland runs his hands through his hair before wrapping them around the back of his neck. T-shirts are a wonderful article of clothing. If he hadn't changed into said t-shirt, after hiking, then I wouldn't be able to see his biceps. What in the world does this man lift to look like that?

I wipe my mouth to make sure I'm not drooling.

"Well, who's this?" the man asks, looking at me.

"Erm, this is Ivy. She's a… guest." Holland sputters through a response while Bea stifles a laugh.

"Hey, Ivy." He reaches out for a handshake. "Great to meet ya. I'm Ryan. The lodge's drink guy."

"Ryan, I'm so sorry. Let me see if I can find any staff to join us." Holland's voice is uneasy and fast.

"Holland," Bea croons. "I'm sure Ivy would *love* to sample all the beer, cider, and wine Ryan brought. Doesn't that sound like fun, Ivy?"

"Ugh, yes. I definitely want to do that." I can't answer fast enough.

"Are you sure? Don't feel like you have to…"

Compelled to reassure him, I reach out to touch Holland's arm. I'm met with muscles and I do my best not to feel around in front of Bea and Ryan. "I'm sure. Sounds like some *spontaneous* fun." The corner of my mouth slants up and I wink at him.

Holland's eyes go to my hand on his arm and then back to me. My stomach flips when he locks his eyes to mine.

"Excellent!" Ryan says. "Let me get a few more boxes from my truck and I'll meet you inside."

"Crisis averted." Bea claps her hands together. "You two have fun and don't forget to eat," she says with a knowing tone.

---△ △ 🌲 △---

Ryan pours the final cider in my glass. It seems pointless, considering I said I've loved everything in the last forty-five minutes. You could say I'm a little drunk and everything tastes heavenly at this point.

Not sure what I thought would happen, but I didn't predict it'd be two hours of sampling alcoholic beverages. You're never drinking a full glass but it quickly adds up.

Holland ordered what felt like half the food menu but I'm still tipsy. Now, here I sit next to a beautiful lodge owner, pondering my empty hands. And how they'd feel better if they were touching him. Maybe without his shirt on.

He's not much taller than I am but it feels like he towers over me. Maybe it's the muscles from his shoulders down to his legs. Stealing glances at his calves during our hike generated the same fluttery sensation in my stomach. Not sure if I've ever looked at a calf as a body part that could or couldn't be attractive. This isn't normal. What kind of person swoons over someone's calves?

The same kind of person who couldn't stop thinking about him when he was in the shower. The man was in his own shower, in his home, and I was drooling out on the patio.

Pathetic.

For a second, I entertained the idea of surprising him in the shower. The potential rejection shut it down so fast. I'm not the impulsive type. I like to know the end result before I jump into anything. What if I'm tired of being cautious? What if the next part of my plan is something I couldn't account for? I balk at the thought before it fully forms. I've never been one to take risks. Even though I planned and prepared for everything I could think of, Jack and I still didn't work out. To be honest, there's nothing I could've done to make him a better person.

Maybe I can't plan for the next chapter.

And that's fucking terrifying.

"You don't have to drink that," Holland says interrupting my borderline-inappropriate thoughts.

"I want to. Everything is so gooooood," I reply while tipping my head to touch his shoulder. I rest it there for a minute.

Ryan laughs and shoots Holland a look. "I like her."

"And I like your drinks." I pick the small taster up and cheers Ryan. Both men laugh as I taste the cider. "And we end this adventure on a wonderful note. This is delicious." I set the glass down in front of me.

"Ryan, my good man. Tell me your favorite drink."

"Easy. I'm a big scotch guy."

"Scotch." I giggle at the word. My head is floating. My face hurts from smiling.

Something else I didn't expect was how often I caught myself staring at Holland. I swear, I'm not a creep. Really, I want to figure him out. I steal one last look and I'm caught.

With pursed lips and a slow devious shake of his head, Holland looks right back at me.

Busted.

CHAPTER TWENTY-SIX

HOLLAND

WHENEVER RYAN comes in with new drinks, I sample a few. His tap room makes up most of our drink menu and I know it's all good. But Ivy didn't take the same approach. She took a drink of everything he put in front of us which was not a small amount.

It's more of a formality—him bringing samples. I feel like he comes in to hang out and tonight, he got more than what he bargained for. Ivy was so into everything he was telling her. She had so many questions about the apples, the grapes, the hops. Her curiosity and enthusiasm are genuine, which made the sampling much more enjoyable.

Ryan's gone and now it's just the two of us again.

My brain replays how she moaned while eating the bruschetta dip. It could be possible she's caught on to the moan reaction because now she makes sure to find my eyes with hers. Every time.

She's torturing me. And she knows it. I have to adjust myself a few times throughout which makes her grin ear to ear.

Drunk Ivy has her head propped up with her arm, elbow on the table. She giggles for no reason. I remind her of the water in front of her. She finds this funny.

"Ya know what I just r'membered?" she slurs.

"What's that?" I play along.

"You're Spidey! My own Spider-Man!"

The way my stomach drops when she says, "my own."

"Sure, I can be your Spider-Man." I go along with it. It's my go-to move when someone is drunk, no use reasoning with them.

"Slate is your sidekick." She gasps. "Can we go see Slate? Pleaaaaase?!" She claps her hands to her knees. Some people may assume this is sarcastic excitement, but I know it's authentic.

Before I can answer, she picks up her drink and spills the entire glass all over herself.

It takes everything in me not to laugh at her.

"Whoooops. It's fine. I'm fine." She's fucking adorable. "It's not that much. I'm not even wet." She's trying to convince herself that she didn't spill a ridiculous amount of water all over. "Oh nooooo… your table!"

I'm definitely not bothered by the table. My brain can't get past her talking about being wet.

Get it together.

"Don't worry about it. And yes, we can go see Slate."

She squeals in excitement.

The minute I say it, I'm feeling kind of queasy. I don't want to leave her alone. And I'm not sure how it would look with me bringing her to her room when she's spilling water and laughing out of nowhere.

I eye the side door of the restaurant.

I guess she'll have to stay with me tonight.

"Thank you… good sir," Ivy says as I open the truck door for her. We're in my driveway and I loop my arm with hers to keep her steady. No way am I letting a successful hiking day end with a driveway injury. When she hears

Slate barking and scratching at the door, she smiles.

Inside, she struggles with untying her shoes for much too long. Obviously, she's still feeling the drinks.

"How does a snack sound?" I ask as I kneel in front of her. She puts a hand on my shoulder for balance as I take her shoes off.

"Good. Snacks are good."

In the kitchen, Ivy sits on the floor. She rests her back against the wall and puts her legs out in a 'V'. Slate is lying against her for attention and Ivy alternates between petting and resting her head on the dog.

I grab a banana, a piece of butterscotch cake, and a glass of water.

"I don't need that banana. But I will have all that caaaake." Her words drag on as she reaches for the fork.

"You'll need that banana for tomorrow. It'll help curb the hangover." It doesn't take much convincing because she's already peeling it.

Before I can hand her the glass of water, she's digging into the dessert.

"Holland. This cake," she says with her mouthful.

"Like it?

"Like it? I love it!" she exclaims with honest enthusiasm.

"One of my grandma's secret recipes. It's been on the lodge menu ever since it opened," I say with pride. When it comes to my grandma's recipes, I'm a complete sap.

She goes from banana to cake until both are gone. I get her another glass of water.

"How am I going to live without this cake?!" Her eyes are misty like she's about to cry. Please no. Drunk tears are rough.

"You don't have to. I'll give you the recipe."

"Isn't it a secret?" She acts as if I've committed a crime.

"I mean, kinda. But I trust you'll use your intel and power for good."

She sits back in triumph.

In between sighs, she says, "Today was awesome. I can't believe I went hiking!" A smile scrunches her face.

"You did that." I reach down to give her a high-five. "And today was pretty awesome." My chest warms at the thought of her enjoying herself.

Ivy leans her head back, eyes on the ceiling, her hands still petting Slate.

"There's one thing that would make it better…" she teases.

"And what's that?" I have no idea what she's going to say next.

She takes a few seconds to contemplate. Drawing it out for dramatic effect.

"A shower." Her eyes are mischievous and needy.

Fuck.

"You got it." I stand up and reach my hand out. She grabs it, stands slowly, and squeezes. We make eye contact. Her eyes remind me of trees in the height of summer.

I lead her upstairs. At least she's not walking in front of me and parading that perfect ass.

I get her situated to take a shower. I'd be lying if I said I wasn't itching to get in there with her. She doesn't need me coming on to her. Especially when she's drunk.

"Only one bed," she whispers. I swear she's smiling. I don't know how to respond, so I act like I don't hear her.

Once in the bathroom, she lets her hair down just to put it in a different messy bun on top of her head.

"Help yourself to whatever you need," I say, wanting to get out of there. I set a towel on the counter. She nods in understanding. "I'll be downstairs."

I shut the door and then find a change of clothes for her. I toss a shirt and a pair of gym shorts with a drawstring on the bed.

Need ripples through my own body every step I get further away from her. I don't know if it's the protective part of me wanting to keep her safe or something else. It's not because she can't take care of herself but because it feels like she's done it for so long.

I reach the bottom of the stairs when I hear a loud thud. The kind of sound a body would make when it falls in the shower.

Oh god.

"Ivy?!" I'm taking the stairs two at a time to get to the loft. "Are you okay?"

She hasn't responded.

My brain immediately goes through terrible scenarios: blood everywhere, her unconscious, a bone sticking out of her arm.

"Ivy. I'm coming in!" I announce as I step into the bathroom.

I pull the shower curtain back and see her on the floor of the tub. There's no blood, but she seems to be shaking. Is she having a seizure? I get a little closer and realize she's laughing. Ivy is hysterically laughing, naked, in my shower.

"What the hell happened?" I make sure to look at her face and only her face.

She pops her eyes open, still laughing. "I slipped but I'm fine. And then the water was pelting me in the face. And then I thought about what I must've looked like… have you ever seen a baby giraffe trying to walk?" She's crying now, from laughing so hard. Thank god.

"Did you hit your head?" A head injury is not how we need this day to end.

"No, I swear. It was more of a slip right onto my ass." At this point, she takes one hand and drapes it across her breasts and turns her hips away from me. Basically, showing me the side of said ass, making it harder to keep my eyes on her face. "Ah, it feels good to laugh," she says.

I exhale and my shoulders relax. I hang my head and shake it slowly, catching my breath. My heart is still pounding.

"What's the matter?" Ivy asks.

"I thought I was going to come in here and you were going to be bleeding from your head or something. But nope. You're just laughing," I say as I look around the bathroom. I'm looking for anything to distract me from a naked Ivy in the shower.

It's not really working.

"Aww, poor Holland," she teases me.

I give her a look and reach for the shower curtain.

"Wait," Ivy says, her hands still covering herself. "Why don't you come in here?" she asks, as smoothly as if she's asking for me to pass her something on the dinner table.

That is *not* what I expected her to say.

CHAPTER TWENTY-SEVEN

TO BE FAIR, I'm clumsy even when I'm sober. So the fall is no surprise.

I'm definitely still buzzed. Holland leaving was the last thing I wanted. But asking him to get in the shower with me? That's more of a Vivian move. I'm not sure I have moves.

"You're drunk." His voice is flat and hard to read. "Sort of against the rules."

Nothing like offering yourself up only for a hefty dose of rejection. This is awesome. "If you don't want to, you don't need to make excuses—"

"I want to. Are you fucking kidding me? Of course I want to," he interrupts.

His voice is like a jolt to an already charged system. And that makes me want him in here with me even more. His response turns my nipples hard under my covering arm.

"I'm not drunk. I'm buzzed. What are the rules for *buzzed* women in your shower? I feel like we can make this work," I say like I'm negotiating a deal.

He breathes in deep, eyes to the ceiling. With his lips pressed in a thin line and his hands on his hips, a look of determination tells me his wheels are turning.

"Ivy, are you sure?" He sounds exasperated and almost like he's pleading.

"I promise. I'm sure."

Holland and I hold eye contact. After some long moments, he closes the curtain. I sit up and pull my knees to my chest, unsure of what's going to happen next.

He peeks his head in the shower. "You're a hundred percent sure this is okay?"

"Yes," I reply. And it is. I'm trying to be serious but it comes out more playful than I hoped. I don't want him to deem me too drunk for him to get in here.

Less worrying and more doing. Out of all the ways this man makes me feel, the thing at the top of the list, is safe.

Holland steps into the shower, still wearing his boxer briefs. I can see his length pressed into the fabric. He wasn't exaggerating about wanting to get in here. He reaches his hands to me and effortlessly pulls me to my feet. Cautious and strong.

"You're still wearing clothes," I say.

"These are the rules. No sex. Not when you've been drinking."

I nod. I'll take something over nothing.

Holland puts both of his hands on my face, brings his nose close to mine where it's almost touching, and then stops. My heart drops.

"What's wrong?"

"Why do you assume something's wrong?"

"It's how I'm wired." I shrug with his hands still on my face. My arms awkwardly hang to my sides. A wave of doubt threatens to crash over me.

"Nothing's wrong. I'm just… taking this in." His eyes drift to my lips. And then he does this ridiculous half-smile thing. And I can't breathe.

This. Man.

I could melt. Or combust. Holland is thoughtful and kind, but right now, he makes me want to burst into flames. I want his hands all over me.

Hell, I want his smirking mouth on every inch of my skin.

When I think I can't take another second, he leans in and kisses me. Like *really* kisses me. His hands move from my face to my hair, lightly pulling, and then stop at the nape of my neck. After a few seconds, he pulls back and looks me in the eye.

The flutter that was in my stomach is now rattling in my chest. I swear, he can feel it, because he smirks and then puts his lips back on mine.

The water is almost scalding and the air is thick with steam. My mind is calm and full of need, all at once. Not sure I could've dreamed up a better first kiss.

I don't know if it's the drinks, but this is one of the first times I haven't felt self-conscious about my body. When was the last time I was naked, with the lights on, and not under a blanket? The way Holland looks at me helps—his eyes are filled with such adoration that I don't even second guess how I look right now.

He looks at me like I'm enough.

His tongue lightly grazes my bottom lip before he playfully bites it. I moan and I can feel his lips turn up into a smile.

This is better than I imagined.

I take my hands and softly press them into the ridges of his chest and abdomen. I lightly drag my fingers over the muscles, which are a pleasant surprise. Yeah, I knew he was fit, but I didn't know he was *fit*. Like, count-the-abs fit.

Holland must be ticklish because he flexes as I touch his sides with the tips of my fingers. He moves his arm just a bit and I see a tattoo on the inside of his bicep. It's a single letter: H. I didn't guess Holland was the tattoo type. My fingers brush it. Holland dips down to kiss my neck.

"Your own initial?" I laugh. "Someone thinks highly of themselves." I playfully point at his chest.

"Not my initial. My sister's."

He doesn't elaborate.

"It's a sad story. For another day," he says, clearly trying to change the subject. His body tenses with his response.

I don't ask any more questions.

Instead, I reach up and wrap my arms around his neck, pressing my breasts into his chest. He moans and the vibrations press into my skin. His length is against me, the cloth of his briefs, the only thing separating us.

I wish I was sober.

His skin on mine is perfect. More. All I can think is *more*.

He wraps his hands around my low back, his fingers touching the top of my ass. Those arms wrapped around me are the highlight of my day.

"Kiss me," I practically plead.

"Where do you want me to kiss you?" he asks, teasing.

Slowly, I press my fingers lightly on the side of my neck. I drag them down as Holland leans in and plants soft kisses where my fingers were a second ago.

My fingers dance along my collarbone. Each time his lips touch my skin, my center throbs with want. My body inches closer, bringing my body to his lips.

I swipe my lower lip with the tip of my finger. He was ready for that because his lips are on mine before I'm able to take my finger off. He opens his mouth and I welcome his tongue. I sink into him. Into this kiss. This moment.

It's like he's kissing away any remnant of anyone else.

I pull away and delicately scratch a path on the top of my breasts. Holland grins up at me before using his lips, and tongue, along the same path. First, he teases me by barely touching me with his soft lips. And then he puts my nipple in his mouth, sucking lightly, and flicking with his tongue. My skin tingles anywhere we make contact. I throw my head back, fully enjoying this experience which causes me to push my hips closer to him. I let out a groan.

He picks his head up, done with that spot.

"So, you moan over more than just food?" Holland jokes.

I nod and flash him a smile.

I feel weightless. Holland's strong body holds me up and my nerves help with the floating feeling.

Holland's hands glide down my body. He starts at the sides of my breasts, and my breath hitches as he moves his hands down to my waist, my hips, and ass.

My hands slide down from the top of his shoulders to the band of his briefs. I break our kiss and slowly pull the band towards me.

"Fuck, Ivy." His voice is low and deep. He puts his head back as I slowly take him in my hand. Nice and almost tortuously slow. On purpose.

I pull my lips into a wicked grin.

"Does this count for being spontaneous?"

CHAPTER TWENTY-EIGHT
HOLLAND

DARK STRANDS SPLAYED against my chest are the first thing I see when I wake up to the sight of Ivy's mess of hair. I'm on my back and she's draped across me. I breathe in. She smells like me—my body wash.

I look down and see Slate, snuggled against her legs, still sleeping.

Our shower make-out session ended when the water turned cold. It was fucking freezing. She was stroking my dick with those perfect hands and we still got out. That's how cold it was.

Getting dressed and into bed took even longer because we couldn't keep our hands off each other. There was no end in sight. Our skin was pruned, like when you spend too long at the beach. And when Ivy shivered, I put her in some of my clothes and she crawled under the blankets.

I offered to sleep on the couch or the floor, but she insisted on sharing the bed. It's a king so there's lots of room. We both danced around the boundary of "no sex" even after we were dressed.

I had to take care of myself last night. I couldn't help it. I snuck downstairs and fucked my hand like a chump, needing the release.

When I crawled back into bed, Ivy nestled her face and body to my side. She gave me a sweet, soft kiss on my shoulder, and it felt like I got punched. My heart—typically made of ice and stone—felt something.

Before I determine the next steps, I pause. I think about this beautiful woman in my bed. She's funny. And caring. And ridiculously attractive but I feel like she doesn't know it. She probably has never been with someone who deserves her.

Not saying I deserve her.

What would've happened if she wasn't drunk last night? Would she still have invited me into the shower? Was there a chance she'd have come back here to hang out?

Fucking hell.

This woman lives across the country. I'm getting too far ahead of myself. She has a life. Roots. And I have everything that pulls and keeps me here. She wants something that's going to last. I definitely don't fit into her plan.

I look at the clock: 9:30. Wow. I can't remember the last time I slept this late. To be fair, Ivy and I didn't go to bed until after 4 a.m.

When my thoughts are this chaotic, I usually go for a run. That's not going to work this morning. I don't want to wake Ivy up yet, but I don't want to leave her either.

From this angle, I can see her long eyelashes. She looks peaceful and happy, draped across my chest. I hate myself for being so sappy, but it feels like she belongs here.

Last night was comfortable. I wasn't second-guessing myself and everything just felt right. Even when she brought up my tattoo for Hazel. She let me deflect and there were no other questions asked.

My brain happily replays parts of last night as I lay with Ivy. I'm thinking about our tangled limbs, kissing her naked body while being partially clothed, her little moans. Also, I'm going to never forget the vision of her in my shirt and shorts. For fuck's sake. She can wear the hell out of some gym shorts.

But what I'm most surprised by is wanting to tell her about Hazel.

It also terrifies me.

When 10:30 hits, I'm no longer able to be in this bed. Ivy has shown no signs of waking so I do my best to get out of bed without jostling her or Slate. The last thing we need is Slate to start barking.

I'm able to be stealthy enough to get downstairs without waking either of them. I fill Slate's bowl with food and start a pot of coffee.

Caffeine is always the answer.

Next is breakfast so I throw myself into cooking. Can't go wrong with pancakes, hash browns, and bacon after a night of drinking.

I'm about to wake Ivy up when she pads down the stairs with Slate close behind her. When he sees me, he prances over for some pets before inhaling his food.

Before Ivy sits down, she wraps me up in a hug. I'm afraid to move or scare her off. She kisses my cheek and then sits down.

Seems like she's still interested when she's sober.

I pour her a mug of hot coffee. She cradles it with her hands, like it's precious, and blows on it.

"Good morning," I say with a level voice—trying to gauge if she's hungover.

"Morning," she replies with sleep still in her eyes.

"How'd you sleep?" I think I know the answer but still want to hear it from her.

"Great. You and Slate are good sleeping buddies."

"How are you feeling?" I flip the last of the pancakes. "Do you need anything for your coffee?"

"I'm a tad hungover. Black coffee is great... would be better if I could get it in an IV." She takes a sip. "Wait, are you making breakfast?"

"Yes. Thought it'd be better than going back to the lodge or having to leave. It's no big deal." I'm aware of how gag-worthy it sounds like I don't want to be without her. But the truth is, I don't.

Her eyes stop on me before she sputters out, "Do you always cook like this?"

She's staring at my bare chest. I haven't put a shirt on this morning. She makes me blush, but I don't want her to see so I turn and pretend to focus intently on the last pancake in the pan.

Her eyes are viciously green and peek over her mug of coffee. "I don't know the last time someone cooked me breakfast."

This bothers me. I hate how people haven't done the bare minimum for her.

"Is that bacon?" she asks and I nod. "Ughhhh, you're the best. Thank you."

I make our plates and by the time I sit down, Slate is already begging for Ivy to feed him food. He's shameless and knows she's an easy target. Ivy takes one look at him and laughs.

"What's your plan today?" She pours syrup all over her pancakes. "Do you have to work?"

"No real plan. And I just have a few things to get done at the lodge. It'll maybe take an hour or so. You?"

"How can you not have a plan? You run a whole business." Her voice is playful but curious.

"Things tend to work out."

Ivy doesn't say anything while she stares at me over her coffee.

"I mean... I have a plan some days... just not today." I take a sip of my own coffee. "Don't you worry about it.

We sit, eating our breakfast, like we've done it a thousand times.

"After breakfast, we could take a walk. Movement is good for a hangover."

Ivy groans and rolls her eyes.

"We'll bring Slate," I say, and I know I've said the magic words.

"Fine. I'm in," she replies.

CHAPTER TWENTY-NINE

THE WALK HELPED with the hangover but it's clear I still need a nap. And a gallon of water. And maybe some fries.

Holland brought me back to the lodge after we walked Slate. We didn't hold hands, he didn't kiss me goodbye, but the air between us was different.

I couldn't stop thinking of how he looked at me in the shower, his hands on my face, right before he kissed me. And then the actual kiss. He was intense. Sweet. Surprising.

Hell, I surprised myself.

In my room, the site of my laptop interrupts thoughts of Holland and me.

The intentional step away from my work inbox was challenging and made me feel a little uncomfortable. Me telling Jack I wouldn't work my entire time here was probably more detrimental to me than him.

Typically, my phone and laptop are like extra limbs. I'm always available and willing to help. Truth is, I don't want to miss anything. I do my best to plan for every scenario, with every client—no matter what stage the project is in.

I know I won't be able to take a nap without checking my email first.

Luckily, it takes a total of three minutes to skim my inbox for anything important, or client facing, and to delete any emails from Jack.

Success.

I pull the shades down, darkening the room, chug a glass of water, and crawl into bed.

I wake up courtesy of my phone ringing. *Royce Jones* flashes on the screen. I don't want to answer but I know I have to.

"Hello, this is Ivy."

"How's it going? It's Royce Jones." One of my biggest pet peeves is when people ask you questions they don't really want the answers to.

"All good here. What can I help you with?" To the point but professional.

"As you know, I'd like to sit down and discuss extending our contract with Sparks. We're thinking of a five-year extension instead of our typical three." Royce is all business right now and this is the man I'm used to working with. Not the slurring version from the other night.

Intrigued is an understatement. Five more years with Bliss4ul means lots of revenue and growth for our company. Promotions and new hires—if things continue to go the way they've been. No reason to expect anything different.

My mouth is open.

"This is great news. What works for you, as far as a meeting?"

"How about tomorrow evening? Seven? I've reserved the room off the restaurant at the lodge." At least I don't have to worry about going anywhere else.

"Works for me. Anything you'd like me to prepare?" Good thing I have no plans and could get something done during such a short turnaround.

"I'll send over the draft of the contract. Take some time to review. Just want to have a conversation on some ideas we have for the next five years.

I'd like to make sure we're on the same page." He sounds nonchalant while I'm borderline freaking out.

"I'd also like to keep this between us and probably your boss. It's still in the early stages and that means we won't be renewing some other vendors we work with. I'd like the time to get out in front of my employees, if you don't mind."

Jack would scream if he knew about this. It feels good knowing something he doesn't. I won't be able to keep it from him forever but that doesn't mean I have to rush to let him know. Especially with Royce's request.

"You got it. I'll only share with Stella."

"Appreciate your discretion. Look forward to connecting tomorrow."

The line is dead before I can utter a goodbye.

Not even a minute later and the contract comes through my email. I forward it to Stella.

Stella, see attached. I'm meeting with Royce tomorrow evening to discuss this extension. He'd like us to keep it between you and I for now.

Would you mind taking a look and let me know anything you'd like me to bring up tomorrow?

Appreciate it!

And then, a few minutes later, Stella's response pops in at the top of my inbox. Not surprising as Stella is old school and is a more frequent email checker than me. And that's saying something.

Ivy! This is exciting. I didn't read much into it yet but saw the five-year term and couldn't help myself. I'll review it right away and get my notes to you.

Thanks for staying a few extra days. This meeting will be worth it.

To see Stella use an exclamation point is startling. Not her style.

Before I can fully wrap my head around what just happened with Royce, my phone rings. This time it's Viv.

"I impulsively booked a flight that lands tomorrow at six and we'll only have like one full day together but that's better than nothing—"

I scream in excitement and jump up and down. My heart warms thinking of Viv being so pumped she word vomits instead of using any sort of greeting.

"This will work?" She's trying to talk over my screaming.

"OF COURSE IT WILL WORK!" I remember the meeting I *just* scheduled with Royce. No way am I letting two pieces of good news lessen each other. "I have a meeting at seven tomorrow night, but it should line up perfectly for when you get here," I share.

After running through the short list of logistics, she asks about my hiking experience.

"Wait, you haven't dished on the hiking yet! How was it?" She squeals but in the smoothest way. Viv is the coolest friend I've ever had.

"It was good." I'm short on purpose.

"That's it. It was good? Have you tried being any more vague?" she replies sarcastically.

"That's not it, but we can chat about it… tomorrow… FACE TO FACE!" My voice is much too loud.

"Fine, fine. You win this one. But you share all the details tomorrow, k?"

We say our goodbyes and I'm ridiculously excited.

The smile painted on my face almost hurts. Falling back onto the bed like a trust fall, I mentally check off the good things from the last few days:

1. Vivian will be here in less than twenty-four hours
2. Potential contract extension with Bliss4ul

3. One of the prettiest sunsets I've ever seen
4. A pinky promise
5. Holland.

I'm abruptly brought back to the moment when I think about Holland on my list. My skin tingles at the thought of his lips on mine. How he didn't flinch when I reached for his pinky the other night at sunset.

Before my body gets any tenser and frustrated, I need to get things in order for Viv.

First, I stop at the front desk and get Viv all set with a room, hoping we can be on the same floor or close to each other, but we'll take what we can get.

Second, I need to see if there's anything fun we can do. I ask at the front desk and the employee doesn't have anything to share, besides what's at the resort. I find myself wishing Bea was working because I'm not sure what I'm looking for. This won't be a Salem vacation, but we'll get to spend time together.

Again, we'll take what we can get.

CHAPTER THIRTY

HOLLAND

MY PHONE BUZZES in my pocket and it makes me jump. I usually never have this thing on.

I can't stop thinking about last night. My stomach flips but it's a mixture of being terrified and excited. At the same fucking time. Obviously, I'm attracted to Ivy. But what is this? Does it need to be anything?

I have no idea what I'm doing.

For years, I've pictured my life centering around the lodge. The idea of sharing it with someone else has never interested me.

The lodge has kept me running around, getting from one season to the next, for the last few years. It was natural for it to be my priority and focus. Is that all I want?

Maybe it doesn't matter what I want. Maybe I'm incapable of letting anyone else get that close? Is she too good?

Whenever women have been in my life, it's been tense. Calculated. A game I felt like I could barely keep up with. One where there were no real winners.

Ivy makes me tense for other reasons. Good reasons. The image of her sleeping on my couch—with my dog, wrapped in my blanket—is stuck in my head. I'm nervous. Could it be this simple?

A second buzz from my phone breaks my concentration. Text message notifications from Ivy show on my home screen.

Both messages are pictures of food: truffle fries and butterscotch pie. It looks like she's still in bed and taking full advantage of the lodge room service.

HOLLAND
> How are you feeling?

Better after cake and fries

> You're going to get sick of that

Highly doubt it

Does Slate miss me yet?

> He hasn't mentioned anything

WOW didn't expect you to be funny

Give him some love for me

Time for a walk tomorrow morning?

I stare at the message. Straight forward. To the point. Why can't I give her an answer?

I don't text Ivy back until morning. I turned my phone off and pretended it didn't exist.

My mind races from thought to thought. I definitely want to see her. Maybe that's enough? Does it need to be more complicated than that?

Typically, I run in the mornings before going into the lodge. My alarm went off much earlier than usual because I wanted to sort myself out before seeing Ivy.

When I text her back, borderline too early, I don't expect her to respond right away. Like she's done since our first interaction with a strong opinion on a superhero, she surprises me.

HOLLAND

> If you're still up for a walk, I'll be at the lodge until ten this morning. Text me and we can go get Slate.

> Yay! I'll text you after breakfast.

That was fast.

Ivy texts me, saying she's in the lobby. Whatever work I was doing can wait.

She's sitting in an oversized chair. If I didn't know her, I'd think she's one of the eager souls trying to get a glimpse at the mountains and outdoors. She's wearing one of the tops she bought at the gift shop with her hair pulled away from her face. Before she notices me, she pulls a chocolate bar out of her pocket, breaks off a piece, and puts it in her mouth.

I can't help but scoff. I'm in the presence of a legitimate sugar fiend. And that's when she sees me.

She shrugs and says, "I'm sort of on vacation, right?"

"Right," I reply, knowing I'd agree to almost anything she says.

Her cheeks are pink from the hike. We didn't wear enough sunscreen. It oddly brings out her green eyes and long lashes.

Stop. Staring.

"Let's go get Slate! I can't wait to see him." She walks towards the door, rubbing her hands together, like she's about to go on a treasure hunt.

She walks in front of me.

Stop. Staring. At. Her. Ass.

Once we get in the truck, it appears her phone is still connected from the other day. A Taylor Swift song immediately starts playing. I don't know a lot about new music but I hear enough at the lodge to know this song.

"Whoops! Sorry!" She scrambles to stop the music on her phone.

"No need to apologize. Turn it up." It kind of sounds like I'm joking but I'm not.

Her face goes from slightly embarrassed to excited. I look out my window so she can't see my almost-smile.

Why is it that the smallest things make her this happy? How does she make *me* this happy?

"Do you know this one?"

I do know it. It was overplayed a few years back and it's hard not to know the words. A type of song that everyone knows.

"I do."

"You don't." She's skeptical with her brows raised. A challenge.

I meet her with my own look, glancing from the road and back to her. She doesn't believe me. I turn the volume up as the chorus starts to "We Are Never Ever Getting Back Together" by Taylor Swift. I kind of hate how I know it.

I'm not exactly singing but it's more enthusiastic than the talking we did the other day. She's surprised and I'm right there with her.

Who am I?

I keep going and Ivy goes from shock to hysterical laughter. She's leaning back with her hands on her stomach, and truly laughing. The sound fills the truck, anywhere the music isn't.

And it clicks. I'm the guy who wants to make this woman laugh like that. My own personal mission. A tall task for someone who actively avoids being around others.

Once she can finally open her eyes, I see tears rolling down her face. She wasn't kidding. Tears on a dime. I hold my laugh in.

"I did NOT expect that," she exclaims, turning the music down. "Are you a Swiftie?"

"I don't know what that is, so I'm guessing no. But everyone knows that song."

Her face is full of joy.

"Aren't you full of surprises?" She stares forward with a small shake of her head.

We don't say anything else on the rest of the short drive. She basically runs into the house and opens the door—like she's been here a thousand times—to greet an excited Slate. I grab his leash, harness, and a bottle of water.

I take her past where we watched the sunset together. She's holding Slate's leash and he doesn't pull her. He's on his best behavior. Ivy can't get enough; she's radiant.

When she tells me about Vivian flying in today, I pretend like I didn't already know. I was in the office when she was making arrangements at the front desk. It's more fun listening to her share the details. She talks ridiculously fast and I'm trying to keep things straight.

"We're going to leave the swings up for a few more days. Good weather and all," I mention to her. "If you want to show Vivian and hang out. You can always get blankets at the front desk."

"Ah! I love that idea. Thanks for the suggestion." She beams.

The walk was short. Ivy talked almost the entire time. It's clear she's excited. When we're back at the lodge, she mentions how she wants me to meet Vivian.

"Viv will want to meet the person who convinced me to hike. Even if it's just for a minute." She's trying to convince me but it's unnecessary.

"Sure. Just let me know when you guys are around," I say nonchalantly, like I'm not excited to meet the person who makes Ivy light up.

I'm such a sucker.

CHAPTER THIRTY-ONE

I TAKE A BREAK from prepping for the Bliss4ul meeting and head down to the lobby. Bea's at the front desk and waving me over.

"Miss Ivy! How was your hiking adventure?" Her hair accessory of choice is a thin gold clip with a few delicate flowers. I haven't seen the same accessory twice.

"So good! Slate is adorable. Nice weather. Can't really ask for much more."

"Good company?" But before I can answer, she continues. "Slate is a lump! But he sure is cute." She giggles.

The company *was* good. And I have a feeling Bea already knows it. I bet she's one to gossip after a drink or two.

"I see your friend is coming to stay with us. How exciting!" Her attention is on the computer screen. "Now, this is no Salem, but here are a few things that might be fun for the two of you." Bea hands me a piece of paper, with a few business cards stapled to it.

It's a list of possible activities: tarot reading, psychics, candle making, and dinner suggestions. Next to each are the open times for when Viv will be here. My heart swells.

"Bea, this is so sweet." I mean it. Tears prickle at my eyes to no surprise of mine.

"Don't get all weepy on me. If you don't see each other often, it's important to make the most of it." Her smile is genuine. She's right.

"This all sounds fun but we don't have a car. I remember Holland mentioned there were no car services here." The planner in me immediately goes from gratitude to logistics.

"Don't you worry about that. Vivian will have a rental car."

"She will?"

"She will. It's better than scheduling a car service. We're so far from the airport that a flight change becomes a logistical nightmare," Bea says matter-of-factly.

When I wasn't planning for the meeting, I was overthinking everything with Holland. And before I knew it, time had flown and I didn't research anything for Viv and I to do, other than dinner. This is helpful.

"Bea, this is kind. And thoughtful." I put both hands on my chest and she reaches forward for one of them.

"It's no problem. And I can't speak to the quality of anything, besides the candle making. Here's my tip, don't grab more than four scents or you'll end up with a candle smelling like vomit or garbage." She squeezes my hand.

Seems like a solid tip.

"I'm going to get lunch and make some calls. Do you need anything?" There's the people pleaser in me, offering to help someone at a job I know nothing about.

"If you wouldn't mind, I'd love an iced tea." She gestures towards the restaurant entrance.

"I absolutely can do that."

As soon as I sit in a booth, in front of a massive window, I pause. I don't know if this counts as a soothing moment, but I'm immensely grateful. The thought and effort Bea put into this list may have been minimal, but it means something to me.

The sun is shining, glittering off the water in the distance. Truly, this is beautiful. I'm not someone who is eager to be outside, but these views don't suck.

The people also don't suck. My heart twinges at the thought of leaving this place and going back home. This is an example of a surprise which didn't turn out to be horrible. I'm thankful for the slow days and new experiences, like hiking. I'm not in Salem but Viv will still come to see me. Plus, I had the opportunity to meet Holland. And Slate.

But Holland.

How will I leave Holland?

I feel like a teenager. It was one night and we didn't even sleep together. There's no way I can be developing real feelings for someone this fast. Right?

The anxious wave in my chest tells me I'm wrong. I am. I did. And it's going to hurt. I've never been this person. Everyone I've dated has always been calculated; I only pursued people I knew who were already interested. It was more about me saying "yes" than anything else.

What should I do? Does it matter? Holland and I fooled around when I was drunk but that doesn't tell me a whole lot. I wish I knew what he was thinking.

Instead of anticipating the sadness that will come with leaving this place behind, I focus on something good. I order lunch, take Bea an iced tea, and make calls to schedule activities for Viv and I.

CHAPTER THIRTY-TWO

HOLLAND

I MAKE IT THREE steps into the lodge before Bea mentions Ivy.

"You missed your hiking buddy," she jokes with me.

"Has her friend checked in yet?" I ask like I don't know said friend's name.

"She should be here around six. The rental car is being charged to our account at the airport. And before you ask, I gave her the adjoining room and already comped it."

"Thanks." When all else fails, just say thank you.

When I overheard Ivy booking Vivian's room, I started researching some activities they might think were fun. I'm by no means a spooky sister or really grasp what the hell that really means, but I get the overall idea. I called around, found some availability for when she's here, and had Bea share it with Ivy.

Honestly, I thought it'd be more acceptable from Bea. I don't want her to infer that I'm overinvested.

Taking care of the room and car rental is no big deal. I've covered less for guests. The amount that Ivy dropped at the gift shop was enough to give her a free room. Or that's what I keep telling myself.

It has nothing to do with a laugh that brings me to my knees. Or how her green eyes dare to see right through me. Or her perfect fucking mouth.

Bea is staring at me with that look. The one where she wants to say something, but she wants me to read her mind and bring it up instead. I won't break.

She sighs. "Ivy was awfully excited about the list of things for her to do. She almost started to cry in the lobby."

"Yeah, she does that." I'm thinking of her big glassy eyes I've seen more than once.

"Holland." Bea faces me and says my name like an inquisitive parent.

"Beatrice." I match her name game, shuffling the random papers in my hands.

She rolls her eyes.

She closes the distance, takes the papers, and sets them on the desk. All so she can grab one of my hands.

"Holland," she says slowly and quietly without breaking eye contact. Her hands are gentle. Caring.

I look down because I'm not quite sure what to do. My throat is tight.

"Ivy seems like a good one." I bet she feels my body tense. "I can't remember the last time you smiled like this or went out of your way to make plans… like shopping and hiking. And an entire itinerary of things for her to do with a friend."

She's right. I don't know what to say to her. Bea is like my second mom and knows almost everything about me. She's been a pillar in my life ever since I was thrown into this. The lodge. After Hazel.

"Your sister would've liked her," Bea says with her own glassy eyes. She squeezes my hand knowing what she's done.

The five words hit me like a truck. They sting. Burn.

I know Bea means it. She'd never bring Hazel up if she didn't. It's somewhere we don't go unless we have to. I swear my legs almost buckle and I forget to breathe.

My thoughts of Hazel are always of me missing her. Everything she did and all she was. I rarely imagine her in the future tense. It's too fucking hard. It's unfair how she's missing out on all of this. Thinking of what she would've been or would've done breaks me.

I can't look at Bea.

"And Hazel would want you to fill yourself with as much joy and happiness that your rigid, closed-off self would allow." Bea's voice cracks at the end.

I look at her with my own watery eyes. Again, she's right. Bea has been gentle with me for so long and has tried to let me work it out on my own time. She's meticulous and intentional when it comes to advice like this. I'll give it to her—pushing me towards Ivy is bold.

"I don't… I can't…" My voice isn't more than a whisper.

"You can. I'm not saying you need to marry Ivy or think past the time she's here. It's a reminder that it's okay to let someone in." Her hands are warm on mine. She pulls me in for a hug. "Even if it's just for a few days."

I dip down to rest my cheek on her shoulder. Bea rubs slow circles on my back. Hazel used to do the same thing. I feel like I'm about to drown.

We stay there until someone dings the bell for the front desk. Bea uses her fingers to tip my face up.

"Are you okay?" she asks.

"I'm not right now, but I will be." And I'm being honest. These moments where I'm lost in all things Hazel happen when I least expect them.

I didn't expect a girl from the city—neurotic and constantly in a state of planning—would be the reason.

Bea goes to the front desk to help a guest and I head to my truck. I do what I can to escape the conversation. The Hazel-sized hole in my heart is burning and bleeding. I'd give anything to see her one more time, even just for a second.

So I do what I always do. I drive back to my place and make my way to a lookout for sunset. This time, I bring Slate with me. Few people are out on the trails tonight. To be safe, Slate and I walk to one of my favorite spots that's really tucked away.

When the sun peeks behind the mountains and I feel the warmth dim, I double check no one is around. When the coast is clear, I put my head in my hands.

And I cry.

For the first time in a long time.

CHAPTER THIRTY-THREE

I'VE PREPARED AS much as possible for a vague contract meeting with Royce. I read through Stella's notes and we had a quick call to review them. We're both feeling good about the meeting. And I feel even better knowing Viv is on her way to the lodge and I'll see her soon.

I'm so proud of myself for packing an extra business casual outfit. I'm happy I don't have to meet with Royce in leggings. Putting on my heels was tough; my feet were still sore from the hike and my new shoes. No blisters, though—Holland's tape did the trick.

When my heels hit the tile floor, I can't help but smirk and think of Bea. I look over at the front desk and see she's working. Her face shows she's absolutely heard me.

The hostess leads me to a room that doesn't give off professional meeting vibes. It's more like a perfect place to have a romantic evening with someone you care about.

Royce sits at the table and I feel the blood leave my face. The table feels out of place with fresh flowers and a bottle of wine chilling next to it. There's even a fire lit in the fireplace.

I'd love nothing more than to turn around and walk straight back to my room.

Before I have a chance to run in the other direction—or power walk, because of the heels—Royce sees me.

"Ivy, it's great to see you." His voice is like a purr that makes my skin crawl. "Wine?" He gestures to the bottle next to the table.

"No wine for me." I politely turn it down, although I'm sure alcohol would make this more tolerable.

If he's disappointed, his face doesn't show it. Instead, he sits down and encourages me to do the same. I awkwardly hold my laptop and notes, realizing there's not much room here.

"I've reviewed your contract and also have notes from Stella," I say as I open my laptop.

"We don't need to get into that just yet." He laughs and gently shuts my laptop.

We don't? Weird. I thought the whole purpose of the meeting was to exactly get into the contract.

"Okay, what would you like to discuss?"

"How's the trip been?" His smile is too bright, showing all his teeth like a shark caricature.

"It's beautiful out here," is all I can manage to say. The last thing I want to do, when Vivian is minutes away from the lodge, is have a friendly chat with Royce. However, sometimes you've got to play the game. It's bothersome but some people need to hear themselves talk. I'm getting the feeling that Royce is that kind of person.

"Have you done any activities around the lodge? I know that was one of the big pulls for Jack to get us to host our event here." He leans back, pouring himself a glass of wine.

I didn't expect our meeting to take this direction. Also wondering if I'll ever have the chance to meet with Royce when he doesn't bring up his *bro*, Jack.

"Actually, I went hiking—"

"Grim's Peak? Lucifer's Ledge? Crestview?" he interrupts, speaking so fast, I can barely catch what he's saying.

I laugh because of how those all sound like advanced trails or spots. "No, we actually did the trail that's about fifteen minutes from here. Not sure what it's called. It was my first time and I enjoyed it."

"That's not even a hike. It's a walk." He cackles at his own joke. "You'll have to let me take you on a *real* hike." He emphasizes real, making his stance on where we went very clear—it doesn't count.

"I'm a beginner so it was perfect for my first time out." I deflect his offer.

"There's no way you're a beginner. Not with those legs." He grins and tips his head down, to get a glance at them under the table. He might be trying to be playful but it's not quite landing.

My hands are clasped in my lap, my knuckles white. I laugh nervously because I don't know what else to do. So I try to pivot the conversation.

"Believe it or not, I'm a beginner." I throw my hands up in fake surrender. "Okay, you wanted to talk about some priorities and goals for the next five years. What's on your mind?" I do my best to take control of the conversation and give Royce an opening to talk. His favorite thing.

"Sure. Happy to get into it. Are you interested in dinner?"

Is this guy for real?

"I have a friend flying in and we haven't seen each other in a while. We're having dinner later."

That isn't the answer he was hoping for. The people-pleasing part of me wants to scream *yes*, grab a menu, and do exactly what he asked.

"You agreed to a meeting but it seems you've double booked yourself." His voice is flat. "I thought you were out here for work, but I may have my lines crossed." Immediately, he goes for the gas-lighting.

The part of me that can't stand that disappointed tone of voice, all self-abandoning and eager to accommodate others, wins. "I'm certainly here for work. The plans for her to come were last minute and she won't mind waiting a bit. Why don't we grab some apps and a glass of wine while we discuss?"

I don't want to do any of this, but this is an important client. It shouldn't be difficult. Especially since he brought the contract extension to us a year early.

The thought of going back to Stella and letting her know this meeting veered into a complete disaster makes my blood run cold. Panic and guilt surges, forcing me to comply.

He pauses a few seconds before nodding and pouring me a glass of wine. He gestures for the server to come over and orders appetizers.

I dare not bring out my phone to text Viv. I told her I'd get a hold of her as soon as the meeting wraps. She's not expecting me at any specific time. And because she's Viv, she'll get it.

Royce seems to be in a better mood but not like the version of him a few minutes ago. He's short, to the point, and a bit annoyed.

We drink wine, the appetizers come, and we've barely discussed the contract. He slips in the bare minimum amount of work appropriate topics while having this innate ability to drive the conversation back to himself. His homes. Upcoming vacations. Overall success. Upcoming press events. New products. With each minute, he's less annoyed and more vibrant.

Basically, ninety-five percent of this conversation is useless.

I play the part. I nod, wear a fake smile, eat some of the appetizers, and appear to be engrossed in his self-centered storytelling, and pretend to enjoy the wine that's too sweet—even for me.

When I look at the time, I realize it's 8:30 p.m. How has this man talked about himself for ninety minutes?

And for the first time today, I feel like I've caught a break.

"I had no idea it was this late. I guess time flies when you're having fun." He winks at me and I do my best to suppress a laugh. "If your friend is coming in tonight, I'm guessing you'll be around for a few more days?"

I absolutely don't want to share my travel itinerary with him. The last thing I need is for him to invite me to do something else when I'm trying to appease him.

"I'm free to meet the day after tomorrow. Does that work for you? I know you've got such a busy schedule…" I hate myself for saying it but at this point, this is a game. Royce doesn't know it, but I'm winning.

After looking through his schedule for the next two days and giving me more details about what's on his calendar than I could ever care about, he confirms it works for him.

"I sent an invite for 3 p.m. Same place." He looks around, avoiding eye contact.

"It was lovely catching up," I lie through my teeth, standing up and gathering my stuff. This is the only time I'm thankful to have my hands full. "I've asked the lodge to bill this to my room, as you're the client." I move some things around and place a *sarcastic to me but real to him* hand on my chest. I'm playing the gracious host.

"Oh, you didn't need to do that." He stands. I notice that he doesn't say thank you. Since my hands and arms are full, he puts his hands in his pockets. I'm grateful he's not expecting a hug or handshake.

I used to think Royce was attractive. Maybe it was the way he seemed collected and put together. Our interactions before were friendly but professional and he appeared to be generally happy.

Is this really the bar? Are we giving points to men for taking care of themselves? All I see now is a man desperate for attention and may be willing to go a little too far to get it.

"It's our pleasure. See you soon." My word choice is intentional—no way was this *my* pleasure. I nod at him in fake appreciation and turn to walk out of the restaurant. If I were to look back, I'd bet he'd be staring at my ass. No way am I confirming that. I do everything in my power not to run to the elevator.

When I go to swipe my room key, the door directly next to mine swings open and I see Vivian. We both squeal and she wraps her hands around me, as I awkwardly hold all my things to my chest. The stress from the meeting doesn't dissipate entirely but it's no match for the energy Viv brings.

Tears come to my eyes. I don't feel the need to hide them. I let my mascara run and my face gets messy. Vivian puts both hands on the sides of my face and kisses me on the lips. We both laugh because this is just how she is.

"It's so good to see you! I thought your meeting would never end." She is still holding my face like I'm a chubby-cheeked toddler.

"Ugh, you and me both." I roll my eyes. The meeting weighs on my shoulders.

"Tell me everything," she croons as she follows me into my room.

Where do I even start?

"I can't believe it," Viv says, her eyes wide and mouth open. "You, Ivy Lawson, are having your very own romp. Wait… a lodge affair!" she screams and lays back on the bed.

We're back from dinner, in our pajamas, and lounging in Viv's room. No topic at dinner went untouched, but I intentionally waited to drop the steamy shower details. It needed to be just the two of us. There was no telling what Viv's reaction would be.

"Who the hell says romp? And it isn't an affair!" I try to get her to hear me, but her laughs drown me out. "Viv. Come on!" Now I'm laughing.

Having her here, gossiping on the bed with me, is surreal.

"Why do I feel like a proud mom?" She sits back up and lovingly puts her hands on the sides of my face, scrunching my cheeks.

"Stop it." It's impossible not to smile when I'm around her. She makes my heart full, like it could burst—in the good kind of way.

"No. I will *not* stop. I'm legit proud of you. This is—"

"Nothing. It's nothing," I interrupt. My eyes stare down at my fingers playing with the fabric of my pajamas.

"I've known you for a long time… this isn't nothing. It's *something*." She reaches for my hand and holds it.

"He lives here. My home is on the other side of the country—"

"Quit with the logistics and the planning and the micromanaging of every detail. Just stop. Why are you already dismissing what *this* is without even exploring it?"

"But—"

"In all the years I've known you, I'm not sure you've ever once invited someone into a shower. Not even when you're *dating* the guy." She smiles but is still serious. "Throw out the planner. Take a risk."

It's hard to hear but I know she's on to something.

The thing is, I don't know if I can.

CHAPTER THIRTY-FOUR

BEFORE VIVIAN AND I start our day, I send Stella a meeting update. Instead of getting into details, I say Royce and I ran out of time and we're meeting again tomorrow. It's not a lie. I intentionally leave out the weird vibes because I'm not sure how I'd describe them.

I forward a few emails that someone else on my team can take care of. Other than that, there is nothing urgent here or waiting for me at the office. I confirm my out of office email auto-reply is on and close my laptop. Still a weird feeling, leaving work behind, but my skin isn't as prickly today.

Choosing not to stress about work is tough, but today is all about Viv and I. Thanks to Bea, we have a day packed full of fun and I can't wait.

First stop is the local indie bookstore. Bonus—said bookstore is right next to a bakery.

How do bookstores consistently feel so magical? It's like they all have this energy which makes your skin buzz and immediately better your mood. I love the idea of being surrounded by words, ideas, characters, and even some happily-ever-afters.

Windows line the front and back of the space, flooding it with natural light. The floors are a dark which highlight the bookshelves and tables.

Immediately, I'm looking for the romance section while Viv is already walking towards horror. Our love for books is equal but on different sides of the spectrum.

Scattered throughout the shelves are handwritten notes indicating staff picks. I breathe in deep and am hit with the smell of pages, covers, and a hint of sugar from the bakery next store.

You're not supposed to judge a book by its cover, but sometimes I can't help it. Is there anything better than browsing new books, letting a spine pull you in or seeing the most gorgeous cover?

After smiling at covers, reading blurbs, and exhibiting a strong amount of self-control, I decide on three books. Viv and I compare after we check out and while I'm convinced there's nothing better than a swoony love story, she holds books with blood on the front.

"Books, bakery, best friends. All while being in this quaint small town? Seems like we're starring in our very own Hallmark movie," Viv says as we walk into the bakery. She fakes gagging. "But, I fucking love it!" Her smile is massive and she catches me off guard.

I laugh way too loud in the small bakery. The woman behind the counter does something unspeakable—she smiles back at us and winks. Oh, the small town magic I've read about but haven't experienced until right now.

My mouth watered the second we stepped foot in here. The glass case—miraculously not covered in fingerprints—is lined with sweet and savory croissants, different breads, muffins, and an impressive collection of sugar cookies. The type of cookies with fluffy frosting piped into the cutest designs.

We ordered coffee and too many pastries. According to Chelsea, who insists we call her Chels, there's no such thing as too many. I only know the names of a few of my favorite servers in the city and that's because I tend to go to the same places.

The coffee is ridiculously good. We drank it black and could taste the notes of cinnamon and even chocolate. Viv and I both bought a bag to take home. We shared a croissant but saved the rest of the baked goods for later. I made sure to get an extra peanut butter scone for Holland and Slate to share.

The scheduled plans for today are a tarot card reading and candle making. Just enough structure for the two of us.

We may not be in Salem but we are definitely making the most of our time together.

I've always wanted to try a tarot card reading. Of all our plans for today, this might be what I'm most excited about.

Did I expect a wiry woman wearing a blue velvet cloak to do our reading? No. But I also didn't expect the woman in front of us either. Jane's younger than I expected—fresh-faced, and dressed comfortably in a flowing tunic, leggings, and flats. Her skin looks like it's honestly glowing. I make a mental note to ask her about skincare if the opportunity presents itself.

The space slightly surprises me. It's warm, dimly lit, and inviting. There are multiple places to sit. Each feels different enough to attract different people. Candles and crystals line shelves and ledges. It doesn't feel chaotic at all—I get the sense everything has a place.

Since this is my first reading, Jane gets us situated. She offers up throw pillows and blankets—anything to make us more comfortable. It takes me a few tries to get comfortable, like the tarot virgin I am. She also pours each of us hot tea.

Viv, on the other hand, knows exactly what she wants. She feels like an extension of the space, with her energy, and familiarity. It shows this isn't her first time.

"Tarot is all about seeking understanding where you are, in order to forecast a possible future. This future could be mere hours away or years." Jane would make a killing with guided meditations or as an audiobook narrator. Her voice is soothing like a cup of hot coffee on a cold morning.

"What we see today is not set in stone and you always have the power to make other choices. We must not forget the power of free will," she reminds me. "Please choose the deck that calls to you and knock on it three times."

There's a console table with a variety of decks—different colors, themes, and sizes. I choose the first one that catches my eye, trying to tap into that intuition.

"Excellent choice. The first thing the deck asks is to open and share your energy. You can do this by handling the deck—shuffling, cutting, shifting cards from one hand to the other." She gestures for me to sit at a larger table, where she sits across from me. "Please take your time."

I take the deck and start moving my hands through it. I knew this was coming. Last night, I brushed up on my tarot research, reading several "what to expect" type articles. Viv, knowing me better than anyone, asked if I had any questions before we made it to this part of our itinerary.

She gets me.

"While you're shuffling the deck, take a few moments to think about questions you'd like answers to or topics you'd like to explore."

Although I knew this was the purpose, my heart races. The idea of tarot always seemed like a blast, but I forgot most of the premise.

I feel like a cliché when the first thing that comes to mind is about relationships. Is there something wrong with me that I'm only capable of attracting people like Jack? Is there someone out there for me? I'm embarrassed by my own thoughts. Out of all the things to want to know about, why is it about men?

"It looks like you've thought of something. Would you like to share?" Jane lightly prompts.

"Ugh. Not really." My hands are still nervously going through the deck.

Jane continues. "There are no wrong questions. It's a good sign you've found something you'd like to explore. A sign of an intentional mind." Her voice could lull me to sleep. "It's difficult but try to be kind to yourself and honor these thoughts." She closes her eyes and takes in a deep breath. I do the same.

"But it's so basic and not worth talking about—" My judgmental and diminishing words barely make it out before Jane interrupts.

"Stop. Why are you putting yourself, your thoughts, and your questions down before we've even looked at the cards?" Her eyes are filled with compassion and an invitation to be open. "Ivy, take another few breaths. When you're ready, share what you'd like to explore." Jane sits still and tall across from me. Her expression is one of patience and openness.

The breathing helps. Even if these aren't the right questions, I'll never see this woman again. This is supposed to be fun and exciting. Vivian squeezes my knee under the table.

"I want to know about love. The last relationship I was in ended badly. After it was over, I started to notice all these things about him I can't stand. It's like I made excuses. I think my specific questions are: am I doing something to attract people like this? And is there an opportunity for love in my future? Am I worthy?" I'm out of breath. It's hard being vulnerable.

Jane keeps eye contact the entire time, nodding, and showing me, she's understanding. "Oh, what lovely matters to explore with you today. I appreciate you opening up." She means it. Or she's incredible at making me feel this way. "Is there anything else on your mind?"

"My ex still works with me. It's been difficult. I know I'm capable of overcoming hard challenges, but I'm interested to know if this is the right move for me. It feels vague, and I'm not talking down to myself, but that's what's on my mind."

Jane smirks when she sees the self-awareness showing through.

"Another wonderful adventure, Ivy. When you're ready, create three piles. Continue to breathe and let your intuition guide the direction. You may create these however you'd like. We'll use these to explore relationships in the sense of past, present, and future." She gestures to a possible placement for the cards.

After shuffling the cards a few more times, I cut the deck into thirds. I spend a few seconds thinking about each section: past, present, and future. I push the piles forward, indicating I'm ready.

Jane pulls the first card and pauses, like she's letting me take it in. The image of the card is someone being stabbed.

"Your past: The Ten of Swords. Wounds. Pain." She looks up at me. "You mentioned your previous relationship ending badly."

"He cheated on me, at work, while I was still there, in a room full of windows. Lots of colleagues saw."

Jane can't keep her face level when she hears that.

"Wow. Well, there's the deep sense of betrayal. If you think past your most recent relationship, can you recall any that served you positively? This doesn't necessarily mean it worked out, but maybe you had an amicable breakup or separation?"

I don't have to think much about my answer.

"Not really. I haven't had a ton of relationships, even fewer of them were serious. None who I'd view in a positive light, today."

Jane nods, letting me sort this out.

"What did you learn from these past relationships?"

What did I learn? I feel like I'm back in my therapist's office. I think I accepted more than I learned, when it came to myself. I easily looked at myself and thought how there must be something deeply ingrained in me that made me not a match with the other person. It wasn't much as self-reflection as it was coming to the quickest conclusion.

"Mostly, what red flags to run from." I cringe a little when I say it. I sound like a woman scorned.

"An important experience, even if it's not desirable." Jane's voice soothes and reasons with me.

"Okay, we'll come back to this card in a minute. I'd like to pull your present card if you're ready."

I nod as her hand hovers over the deck.

"For your present: The Wheel of Fortune, reversed." Her voice is as calm as ever.

"Does that mean misfortune?" I ask, panic on the edge of my voice.

"Perhaps. When we see this card reversed, it lends to bouts of bad luck and breaking cycles. Not necessarily misfortune. What do you think of the cycle element?"

"I mean, breaking cycles seems like it could be positive. Bad luck feels right." I laugh, taking the seriousness out of the room. Jane is quiet, waiting for me to elaborate. "Well, I'm supposed to be on a vacation right now and it was canceled due to said ex. The bad luck could also be falling into relationships with the wrong people at the wrong time?"

"All possible." Jane contemplates. "What about cycles?"

"The bad luck forced me to make some changes. I've set boundaries, tried new activities."

"Ah, this could also be regarding the relationship with oneself. It can also be romantic in nature."

"Is this good or bad?" I'm trying to boil this down to the overall message and meaning.

"This isn't an answer you'll like, but it could be both or neither. What is good to some, is bad to others. Instead of getting into that, I'd like to think about these two cards together. Any thoughts?"

The anxiety of the unknown buzzes as I try to keep an open mind. I know Jane's job is to pull cards, explain possible meanings, and let me interpret them.

"I can't explain it, but I like the idea of my past card catching up with my present. This could mean bad luck but a change in cycles, which could've led to the betrayal I've experienced in the past."

Jane nods, pleased with my observation. "Are you sure this is your first time?" She jokes.

"First-time tarot reading but long-time therapy attendee." I place my hand on my heart.

"Your reversed Wheel of Fortune could also mean changes are coming." She says it like it's a good thing. If only she knew how much time I spend preparing for the most basic of new experiences—reading menus, making sure I'm weather-ready, and my most frequent Google search history starts with "what to expect when…"

The idea of change makes the hair on my neck stand up. I know I can't be stagnant, but I prefer to be in control. Maybe tarot isn't for me.

"Let's pull your final card and the one I find is the most exciting." Jane's hand rests on the top card of the last deck. She flips it over. This has to be a joke.

Death. My future card is Death. I gasp and cover my mouth. All the color leaves my face, and a cold sweat breaks out over my brow.

"Interesting," Jane mumbles, looking at all three cards.

"You pull the Death card and all you've got is 'interesting'?!" My voice comes out higher than I mean for it to.

Jane laughs. "Contrary to popular belief, the Death card doesn't mean mortal death. I mean, it could, but all the other cards could as well. Surprisingly, this card plays nicely with your previous card. What I'm seeing is true transformation and transition."

"Please keep going. I know you're going to prompt a question for me to answer and I'm telling you now, I've got nothing."

Jane seems excited as she elaborates. "Your present card all leads toward change but your future card kind of cements it. You could view this as a life-changing experience that you take with you into your next phase or a new partner, adventure, hobby, or even a new job."

"How do you feel about change?" Jane reaches out and grabs my hands.

"Well, by the amount I'm sweating, I'm guessing you already know." I'm not trying to be funny but she still laughs.

"Change is difficult for all of us. But wouldn't it be harder to remain the same throughout our entire time on this planet? How wonderful we get to grow and morph."

Damn, she's good.

Jane is wise. Her and my therapist would get along, that's for sure. I don't like the word morph but can get behind the general idea.

We all sit in silence for a few moments. Jane is patient and observant, knowing I'm still reviewing the cards in front of me. "Do you have any other questions about these cards?"

"I don't think so, but would you mind if I took a photo of these?" I'm not sure if this is a tarot faux pas.

She smiles. "Not at all. But please remember, you still have your own free-will and can create the life you love and deserve."

A life you love and deserve. This hits me. It sounds so easy. It's *my* life and I should enjoy it. What a concept.

I take a photo while Jane rubs crystals between her hands and starts the process with Viv. She selects her deck and now I'm the observer.

Viv doesn't even need Jane. She opts for the same layout but pulls her cards and tells Jane what they mean, not the other way around. Her pulls take way less time and they end up talking about decks and complex layouts. It sounds like they've been friends forever instead of just meeting. It's not surprising, because this is how Viv's always been.

While they're wrapping up their reading, I'm browsing Jane's selection of tarot card decks and journals she has for sale. Ah, there's nothing like a new blank notebook. Pulling tarot cards may be fun. It feels like a solid souvenir to remind me of this time with Viv.

My brain is still reeling from my reading. I'm doing my best not to overthink but that's how I'm wired.

Before we leave, Jane offers to take our photo. We snuggle up on a couch in the corner and have her take a few.

We each buy a tarot deck and say our goodbyes. When Jane thanks us for coming, she pulls me into a hug. She smells like patchouli and flowers—what I *would* expect.

She quietly whispers in my ear, "Ivy, don't be afraid of change. I'd encourage you to spend time thinking about worth."

Her words are soft but pack a punch. They don't make me feel bad or immediately question myself.

I don't know what the change is, but I don't need to be afraid of it… yet.

CHAPTER THIRTY-FIVE
HOLLAND

I WALK INTO THE restaurant and hear Ivy and Vivian before I see them. Loud laughter. I could probably pick out Ivy's laugh in a crowded room. Their booth is easy to find.

"Holland!" Ivy yells, waving me over.

I walk over and sit next to Ivy. Our hips touch and I realize I'm nervous. Ridiculous.

"This is Vivian," she says with her hands out to the woman across from us. "Viv, this is Holland."

"Great to meet you! You have the cutest dog. Ivy was showing me pictures." Vivian reaches for a handshake.

"I meant to ask, do you have any pics of him as a puppy? I bet little Slate was even cuter," Ivy says enthusiastically.

A gut punch. I do have pictures but they're all of Hazel and Slate. There aren't many but they're special to me. Not because Slate is a puppy, but because they're some of the last pictures I have of Hazel.

"I don't. Was too busy adjusting to get many puppy pictures." The lie sounds ridiculous but I'm hoping they'll let me get away with it.

"Bummer!" Vivian says. I feel like we're in the clear.

"Before I forget, I have something for you." Ivy turns to a few shopping bags. It looks like they had a successful day out.

She hands me a small bag from my favorite local bakery. A peanut butter scone—the same one Chels always throws into the lodge's coffee order for Slate and I to split.

Ivy thought of me today and my chest warms at that.

"Thanks. I can't wait to split it with Slate later."

Ivy and Vivian tell me all about their day. I like hearing them get excited about the local spots they checked out. I do my best to hide my satisfied look.

They complement each other, both in the pieces of their personality showing and physical looks. Vivian is tall, and blonde with a pixie cut. Ivy seems to filter what she's saying, whereas Vivian doesn't even make an attempt. The energy of them together makes me miss having a group of friends.

In this moment, I'm trying not to stare at Ivy. She's something. I can feel the happiness rolling off her. How does she act like this is exactly what her and Viv planned? Instead of being disappointed, they made the best of it.

Wish I could do that.

"Did you end up doing the tarot thing?"

"How did you know about that?" Ivy pauses. Damn it. Before I can string together a white lie, she gives me an out. "Bea must've told you…"

Nope. Bea didn't tell me. Vivian shoots me a look.

Both women give me a tarot reading play-by-play. I know nothing about tarot besides there are cards. They both talk so fast; I'm trying to keep up. Even when Ivy tells me about the Death card, which sounds horrific, she sounds positive. They tell me all the things this Death card could mean, jumping from one theory to the next.

Ivy's passionate and it makes it fun to listen to her.

"Ah! We also made candles," Ivy says, as she sorts through a bag and pulls out a mason jar. She opens the lid and puts it in front of me, an invitation to smell. Before I lean down, I know it's something sweet. I look at the label and see "Butterscotch Cake" in Ivy's handwriting.

She and I share a look. It's quick. But it's packed with "I know what you did here." I'm fighting a massive grin.

I order the table another round of drinks and Ivy excuses herself for a bathroom break.

"So, when I checked in, my room was free. Zero dollars. Zilch." Vivian talks with her hands. "Do you know something about that? Or do I have to find a way to get Ivy to accept money?"

My face flushes. "That was me. No big deal. Really."

"Same thing with the rental car?" My lack of response is my reply. "Does Ivy know you did that?" Her brows are furrowed. She's trying to read me.

"No, she doesn't. I don't mind if you tell her. She was bummed about your vacation. This was something easy I could do. I've comped rooms and cars for much less."

"No, no. I appreciate it. I don't need to tell her. It's not my business." She lifts her arms up in a "hands-off" gesture.

I lift my beer, tip it to her, and take a swig.

"Does Ivy know you're the one who came up with the activity list?" My eyes go a little wide. I'm surprised she's calling me out.

"How did you—"

"I saw your face when she asked about the tarot. It gave you away," she interrupts with a smug smile showing. "Don't worry about it. I'm very self-aware and really into body language." She leans back and crosses her arms.

Busted.

"Not sure why you didn't bring it to Ivy yourself, but again, it's not my business."

I nod at her and then look down at my beer.

"Here's the thing. Ivy is independent to a fault. She'll take on too much for almost anyone, even the people who don't deserve it," she says, razor sharp. "She's the queen of spreading herself too thin and making excuses for people falling short." Her eyes are full of compassion. It's clear she loves her friend. I'm happy Ivy has someone like this.

It's also clear she was itching for Ivy to step away, leaving the two of us for whatever this is.

"When she told me how you helped her at the conference and got her away from that creep, I was surprised. It's hard for her to accept any kind of help, but it seems she's different with you."

"It was no big deal—"

She puts a single finger up and I immediately stop talking.

"Don't interrupt. I don't need to tell you to treat her with respect because you've done that time and time again when you were practically strangers. Just remember, it's hard for her to let people help her and stick around. The last guy she was with is a cousin of Lucifer himself, I swear. Do with that what you will."

"Not a big Jack fan, I take it?"

"No fucking way. He always found a way to take things from her. Like she dimmed the light, a little more each day, so he could be brighter. That guy is the worst."

To the point. Viv's no bullshit, zero runaround manner makes me like her. My heart tugs thinking about Ivy making herself smaller because of an insecure asshole like Jack. Glad I'll never meet him.

"All I'm saying is this behavior of hers is a deviation. And deviations from the list and task-oriented Ivy are not to be taken lightly." She winks at me and takes a drink of her old-fashioned. It's fitting that she's a bourbon girl. I should've ordered one of those.

"And, before she gets back, you're not fooling me. Not for a minute. And maybe you don't know it yourself, but the last thing I'll say"—she paints a wide grin on her face—"since Ivy is walking toward us right now, is that she's totally worth it."

And with that, she takes a sip of her drink, like a victory bow. She drops something like that, and I have zero time to react.

"What'd I miss?" Ivy asks as she scoots into the booth.

And without skipping a beat, Vivian jumps in.

"Nothing. Holland was just telling me about local breweries." She gestures to my beer.

I take a long drink. Luckily, Ivy and Vivian fall back into busy conversation while I'm an innocent bystander.

After finishing my drink, I decide to leave Ivy and Vivian to their own devices. Let them be without me.

"Vivian, great to meet you. Glad you could spend a couple of nights here." I go to shake her hand and she pulls me into a hug. Which, ironically, is exactly what I expected from her.

"Nice to meet you. Try to get Ivy on another hike before she's out of here." She winks at Ivy.

"Definitely." I gaze at Ivy to see her pink-cheeked, probably from the drinks, and radiant. "Your flight is tomorrow?"

"Yeah, tomorrow afternoon. I'm bummed I couldn't get more time here. The return flights were outrageous for me to stay any longer. But you take what you can get."

"I understand that. Safe travels," I say to Vivian before turning to Ivy. "Let me know when you're ready for another walk with Slate."

Ivy claps her hands in excitement.

"I'll text you tomorrow!" she says, her voice easy and like she's said it to me a hundred times. I love it.

After I take care of their tab, my brain goes over what Vivian told me.

I spend the rest of the night thinking about her comment, "Maybe you don't even know it yourself."

CHAPTER THIRTY-SIX

Ivy

SAYING GOODBYE to Viv is hard.

Our time together was entirely too short. We packed in as much as we could, including staying up way too late last night and breaking in our new tarot decks. It wasn't the witchy vacation we planned, but it had enough of the right vibes to scratch the itch. We'll get to Salem eventually.

Although she had her own room, we decided to have a sleepover. It felt like we were back in college, giggling in beds much smaller than this one, after a night of drinks and dancing.

There's something about sharing a bed with your best friend. It lead to staying up ridiculously late, talking about anything and everything, and having your cheeks hurt from laughing so much.

The adult version was just as amazing. It's one of those things that doesn't lose its shine as you get older. But the main differences are bigger beds, high quality sheets, plus expendable income for all the snacks and drinks you could dream of.

In the morning, my heart is full and my eyes are heavy. Nights with Vivian always leave me feeling like I can get through almost anything with her by my side. We never get enough sleep, but this is the best type of exhaustion.

We wait in the lobby for the off-road vehicle to take Viv to her car. We each have the largest coffee they sell at the restaurant. Viv also got a piece of the butterscotch cake to go. I told her it was a must, even if she only has a bite.

"Make sure to enjoy the rest of your time here." Viv prods. "If that includes handsome lodge owners who feed you cake, then so be it." She throws her hands up in sarcastic enthusiasm. "Casual sex should *not* be off the table." Her eyebrows creep up making sure I know it's a suggestion.

"Viv. I'm only going to be here a few more days—"

"Who cares?! Quit writing off good things just because they might not work out."

This isn't the first time we've had this conversation. Vivian is vocal about how she hates when I play it safe, sticking to what I know, and talking myself out of risks before I get a chance to consider them. It's hard to hear but I know she's mostly right. Sometimes I don't know that I'm doing it; I chalk it up to being efficient and plan oriented.

"I won't write it off."

"Plus, you have no idea what's coming next. No matter how much you plan."

This makes me uneasy, and she knows it.

"There's this massive world with all sorts of people and places. I hate to be the annoying cliché, but sometimes the universe puts us on specific paths. Think about it—Jack could've harassed Royce to have this thing anywhere, but he chose here."

The words flow off her tongue like she's been considering this for a while. She's confident and effortless in sharing her opinion, showing how much she cares for me, no matter how tough the conversation is.

And again, she's right. I could've been stuck anywhere, but here I am. It's a lot to take in. Especially because the disaster of Jack over-stepping has kind of turned into a wonderful experience.

"You're not wrong." I surrender this part of the conversation. I wrap her in the tightest hug. We hold onto one another in the lobby, swaying like it's a slow dance.

"Any other wise words?" I ask, tears in the corner of my eyes.

"I feel like a cliché even saying this"—she takes a deep breath—"I wish you could see the way he looks at you." She pauses, for a long second, before pulling me into a hug.

"That must've been hard… you really do hate clichés." I laugh into her shoulder, savoring these last few moments of us together.

She blows me a kiss and is out the door. Viv never lingers. I stand in the lobby, tears and all, until she's out of sight.

When she's gone, I take my coffee and slip into a massive chair, in the corner of the lobby sitting area. It faces the window with my back to the lobby. There's no one talking or being noisy in the connecting hallways or check-in area.

A week ago, this was something that would prick my skin and make me put in my headphones. Always running from the quiet. Not today. I do my best—no matter that it's a bit uncomfortable—and take it in. I sip my coffee and think.

First, the tarot cards. Well, the Death card specifically. Nothing like a nice jolt of panic while you're getting a little introspective. I'd be lying if I wasn't intrigued by the idea of change. Not sure how that fits with my desire to control absolutely everything possible. Something has to give.

And about what Viv said. *"I wish you could see the way he looks at you…"*

I do see it. Or I think I do.

The question is, am I willing to risk it?

CHAPTER THIRTY-SEVEN
HOLLAND

I'M FUCKING EXHAUSTED. I can't remember the last time I was up all night. My brain wouldn't turn off. Hopping from one thought to the next on an endless loop.

The coffee brews in my French press and the smell is the only thing keeping me going.

My phone is face down on the kitchen table. It looks like it doesn't belong there, out in the open. I grab it and go to my text messages. There are only four conversations to choose from but the one I want is at the top.

I tap on Ivy's name, opening the last message, and I freeze. The revelation hits me like a punch to the stomach.

I can't get enough of her. When we're together, I'm relishing in the sound of her laugh, the sight of her green eyes, and terrified at her ability to make me want to share. It's almost like I need her to know me. I want to share everything. And when we're not together, I'm wondering how we'll see each other next, or I'm itching to text her.

The phone in my hand is proof. Before I met her, I'd rather throw it in the river and now I'm wondering what to text Ivy. Is it too soon to text?

She came out of nowhere. This feeling, running around in my chest is hot. So massive it barely fits.

I want her. And not just for a few more days.

Fucking scary. This is terrifying.

How do I do this? *Can* I do this?

I worked from the shipping area today. If I would have seen Bea, she'd know something was going on. She'd then make it her personal mission to get me to spill my guts. I'm tired enough to know I don't have it in me to go toe-to-toe with her.

I brought my laptop down here, left my cell phone in my office, and made it look like I was busy enough so no one would bother me. Worked like a charm.

To be honest, I finished any actual work within an hour or two and just took up space for the rest of the day. I pretended to work and instead, my mind jumped from one thought to the next.

The thought of accidentally bumping into Ivy before I'm ready, was a great motivator to sort of stay hidden. Not until I sort out what I'm going to do next.

Fuck. Am I planning? The word feels weird just thinking about it.

A goner. I'm a goner. I'm also a fucking coward.

I need to do something. Talk to her. See her. Touch her.

Closing my laptop, I head for the elevator. I call a staff member who lives close to my place and see if they can walk and feed Slate tonight. Just in case.

The minute I make it to the lobby, I lose all my nerve. I thought I'd go to her room, knock on the door, and see if she wanted to do something. Instead, I practically run into my office and shut the door.

Now I'm sitting at the end of the bar. You'd only see me if you walked into the restaurant and were specifically looking for me.

Something I love about this place is that when I want a drink, the bartenders pour and leave me alone. They never judge me—at least not to my face—and make sure the glass is full. To show my appreciation, I leave substantial tips even though they're on my payroll.

Having a couple of drinks while you're exhausted and dealing with heavy feelings is always the best way to cope. Said no one ever. I know this is a horrible fucking idea but I have no other moves.

Bourbon never lets me down.

I throw back the last of my third old fashioned. The cherries sit at the bottom of the rocks glass. Dark red. The color of Ivy's lips the first time I met her.

She's everywhere.

Before I can change my mind, or it gets way too late, I take the elevator to the sixth floor. I can't get to her door fast enough but when I reach it, I stop. My fist, ready to knock, is a few inches from the door and I know if someone saw me, they would have questions.

I take in a breath and pretend my hand isn't shaking. I'm fucking nervous. But something Vivian said comes roaring back, *"you're not fooling me… she's totally worth it."* Like I didn't know it already. Sometimes you need someone to say something you've been thinking for it to actually be a thing.

Only a door separates me and the woman I can't stop thinking about. I breathe out and knock. I hear Ivy move around before coming to the door. It takes everything in me to keep my feet planted and not bolt.

She opens the door and smiles when she sees it's me.

I'm a fucking goner.

"Holland. What are you doing here?" The sound of excitement in her voice relaxes me. Or makes it to where I'm not concerned about my heart rate.

What am I doing here? I didn't think this through. Her eyes lock on mine.

"I… ugh… have to tell you something." I sound so unconvincing.

"Okay." She waits patiently. "What is it?"

Fuck. There is so much I want to say. Where do I start? Do I tell her how often she's on my mind? Or how she's the first person who makes me question what my future looks like? Or the way she makes me feel like I'm part of something?

"Holland," Ivy says, her voice low, as she reaches for my hand. She squeezes my fingers with her own.

I don't know if I can tell her. I could try to *show* her.

I step forward, put my hands in her hair, and my lips on hers.

The second I feel her kissing me back, those perfect lips and tongue on mine, I nudge her into her room. My hands find the wall, on each side of Ivy's face. She tilts her chin up and I dip down to be level with her.

Fuck. I dreamt of those green eyes.

When the door shuts, I pull away for a second.

"I can't get enough of you." I barely get the words out before I kiss her again.

She smiles under my lips and it's like I can fly.

"You're all I can think about," I confess.

CHAPTER THIRTY-EIGHT

THIS FEELS MORE like a movie scene than real life. Holland's kiss is eager and demanding—in the best way. With each second his mouth is on mine, the rest of the world falls away, piece by piece.

"I don't want you to leave," he says and my heart sings and sinks at the same time.

He doesn't want me to leave. Part of me doesn't want to leave either. No matter how much I could've planned, Jack put me on the trajectory to meet Holland. And I never saw him coming.

"I know the feeling," is all I can say before I get too emotional. The tears in my eyes are happy ones. I wrap my arms around his neck and try to explain myself with my lips. Feverish kisses.

"Have you been drinking?"

"Drinks were had. I wanted to come here and then I was fucking scared. I needed to sort my brain out." He looks around the room while he's explaining.

I grab his chin and lean in slowly to kiss him and bring my body to his.

Holland takes one of his hands and curls it around my neck. His fingers and grip are strong as he slowly brings my face closer to his. It's not overwhelming or uncomfortable but hot. *So hot.*

"I've been thinking of all the things I want to say to you, but between the bourbon and being up most of the night, I don't know if now's the time." Holland's voice is quick and I can hear the exhaustion in his voice.

"Shh. Don't worry about it. We can talk tomorrow." I do my best to reassure him. I lean in close and put my finger on his lips.

Our noses touch, and Holland locks his eyes on mine. From here, I can see flecks of gold in those rich eyes. Bright spots. Just like him.

And he kisses me.

Time slows and something changes at this moment. There's a shift. It's something that I feel down to my bones. Holland is someone. This is *something*.

I'm terrified because I didn't see it coming.

With my thoughts running wild and Holland kissing me like he is, I do the only thing I know to do. I nervously laugh.

"I have a rule about drunk men in my hotel room." I smirk at my own joke.

Holland is unbothered. He throws his head back and scoffs. "Honestly, just being near you is enough for me. Can I stay here tonight?"

My heart cracks. I know how difficult it is for him to ask me that.

"Of course." I put my hands on the side of his face, like he did when I was drunk in his shower. He closes his eyes.

I knew something. Before Holland was outside my door. Before he was kissing me like I was the air he needed. I knew I was in trouble.

Deep trouble.

When we're in bed—me in my matching pajamas and Holland in his briefs—he throws an arm over my stomach. He's on his side and his hand rests on my hip. It's like we're puzzle pieces. Almost like my hip was meant for his hand. We fit together perfectly.

Out of habit, I reach for my phone and open a social app. I scroll for a few minutes. A few notifications come in, vibrating the phone in my hand.

"What are you doing?" Holland asks, his voice groggy with sleep.

"Scrolling." It sounds dumb as soon as it comes out of my mouth.

"The light. The buzzing." He doesn't finish his thought but I know what he means. "Can it be just you and I tonight?" His voice is syrupy sweet and I'm going to melt into a puddle.

"Of course it can."

I put my phone in the nightstand drawer and then kiss Holland's cheek. I snuggle into the side of him and get comfortable.

A few minutes later, the phone buzzes. It's more obnoxious than if I would've left it out.

"Ivy." Holland sighs in exhaustion.

"I know, I know. I'm sorry. I'll turn it off." This is something I never do. I've learned to sleep through the buzzing and screens. It's like Holland can sense this.

"You're not working right now. Everything can wait until the morning."

He's right. It sounds so plain and obvious, when he says it like that.

I turn it off and place it back in the drawer. My smart watch lightly taps on the table, reminding me that it's there. I take it off, and put in the drawer, for good measure. Out of sight, out of mind.

When I lay back down, Holland pulls me closer to him. He twirls a piece of my hair as he drifts to sleep. Is there anything more amazing than a man playing with your hair?

I feel so wrapped up in him.

And that's the last thing I think about before I fall asleep.

The sun wakes me up. I look over to see Holland still asleep next to me. His face looks peaceful. With his perfect lips and long eyelashes.

I give him a kiss on the cheek and he stirs.

When he opens his eyes, a grin pulls at his lips. Again, I'm a puddle. Tears come to my eyes over the smallest of reactions.

It's like he sincerely wants me. The real me. I was so frantic when we first met, I had no chance to put on my cool-girl-costume. The mask you wear for the first few weeks of dating, to make sure you're pretty but not like you're trying too hard, fashionable but making it effortless, and hiding enough of your neurosis to make sure they don't run in the other direction.

I hate that costume.

Our first interaction was the opposite of the cool-girl-costume. And yet, here he is. In my bed, smiling like I'm exactly what he needs.

Since I've been stuck here at the lodge, he's found ways to cross my path. Goes out of his way to see me. When we're together, it's easy. Isn't that how it should be?

This isn't lust or instant attraction. I'm falling for a man who doesn't fit in my plan or my time zone.

What am I going to do?

I try to get out of bed and Holland's hand lands on my hip to pull me back.

"Not yet," he groans.

I don't even protest. Instead, I fall back into bed. I feel my back on his bare chest. For the first time in a while, I feel like I'm needed. Not needed in the sense of a job and productivity but in the way of companionship.

We lay together for a few more minutes. While it's lovely and I wouldn't mind doing this every morning, I'm itching to check my phone. It's a habit—a bad one—but it still exists for the time being.

I take my phone from the drawer and power it on.

Within fifteen seconds, my mood goes from great to complete panic. Missed calls, and texts, start coming in from Royce, Jack, and Stella.

I shoot out of bed and stare at the phone in hand before looking at the clock next to my laptop. It's after 10 a.m. We slept through the whole morning.

I forgot about my alarm. My stupid alarm on the stupid piece of technology I can't seem to function without.

"No, no, no." I sit down and open my laptop.

"What's going on?" Holland asks through a stretch.

"I have a bunch of missed calls from work—my boss to be exact. This is bad. I'm on a work trip. They should be able to get a hold of me." The words fly out of my mouth and the anxiety starts creeping up my entire body.

"Ivy. Take a deep breath. What could they have needed last night?"

"Last night? It's after ten! Half of the workday is over at the office."

"I didn't know it was that late," he grumbles as he looks out the window.

"Of course, you didn't," I snap back.

"What's that supposed to mean?"

"It means you don't need a plan. Why would you care about sleeping away half the day? You just wing it, right?!" The words are shrill. Holland is now out of the bed and staring at me from across the room. When he doesn't respond, I keep going. "You may be able to float through your days, doing whatever needs to be done, but that isn't how I operate. People count on me. I need to be responsible."

"Just because I don't choose to over-plan and prepare for any situation that could possibly happen doesn't mean I'm not responsible." His voice sounds foreign to me. "Do you even know what they want yet? Or are you just freaking out to freak out?"

My jaw is clenched. If it wasn't, it'd be hanging open.

"What they need isn't the point, Holland!"

"Then what is the point?! Explain it to me."

"This is my job! I've worked hard to be in this position and being reliable is a key part of that." Tears pool in my eyes.

"So predictable." He runs one hand through his hair.

"What do you mean?"

"Isn't that what you want? The ability to plan everything down to the nittiest grittiest detail. And not experience anything surprising, ever?"

"When it comes to my job, yes. That would be nice," I say. My voice is smug.

"You are something else. I wish you'd wake up and see that work is only a single part of you. A measly part of your life."

"How can you stand there and lecture me about work? You live at your job. You come running whenever there's the smallest issue. You haven't told me about a single friend, vacation, upcoming event in your life that's not *here*. You seem awfully connected to this job."

I see my blow lands.

"You don't know what you're talking about."

"I think I do; you just don't want to hear it." I'm standing at this point. "I have to go back to this job once this is over. Whatever this is." I throw my hands up. "I'm only staying here a few more days." My heart hurts as I say it, but I don't want Holland to see.

"Right. Whatever this is." Holland picks up his clothes from the night before and puts them on. "Well, I'll let you get back to it."

He doesn't look my way as he walks past me and straight out of my room.

When the door shuts, my heart cracks right down the middle.

Voicemails first. Inbox second.

I cry as I check the voicemails from Royce, Jack, and Stella. Royce needed to push the meeting out one more day, Jack was calling because Royce couldn't get a hold of me, and Stella had a clarification on the contract that was easier to talk through versus email.

Everything at work is fine. Nothing is urgent. No one is upset. Jack seemed a little annoyed, but he doesn't really count, in the whole grand scheme of things. The only action is that I need to confirm the meeting reschedule with Royce.

That's it.

I sit on the bed and stare at my laptop. And then at the side of the crumpled bed, where Holland slept.

Our argument replays in my head and so, I do what I do best.

I cry.

CHAPTER THIRTY-NINE
HOLLAND

I CAN'T GET AWAY from the conversation fast enough. Away from Ivy. At least I know how to get out of here without having to walk through the lobby.

My blood is hot. I need to go for a run.

I get back to my house, feed Slate, and change so I can get out of here and on the trails.

My feet pound into the ground. I'm running much faster than I'm used to. It's not long before my side aches and my legs shake. I can smell last night's bourbon on my skin. Nausea takes over and if I don't stop, I know I'll throw up.

I don't want to think about Ivy. Or what I said last night. Or what I said this morning.

It doesn't work.

Her tear-stained face and her panic when she saw the missed calls play on repeat in my mind. I keep hearing how she called me out for not having anything besides this lodge.

But then it's her smile when she opened the door last night. And when she squeezed my hand. And our pinky promise from days before.

Chaos. My thoughts are complete and utter chaos. I can't keep anything straight. The loop of our argument replaying over and over is horrible.

In attempts to not make today worse, I stop before I push myself too hard on this run.

While walking, I realize she's right. Well, sort of. I have no vacations to miss. No friends to meet up with. It's by my own choice, but it still stings.

How did I go from needing to tell her how I feel to leaving her as fast as I did?

It hurts. More than my cramping muscles. More than the headache coming on from too many bourbons.

I'm better off alone. I've told myself that for years. And I've believed it for longer.

Fucking Ivy. Why did I think it'd be different with her? That I could be different. I can't. I'm going to end up a lonely bastard because that's what I deserve.

Clearly, I wasn't paying attention to my route because I'm much farther than originally planned. Damn it.

I'm home, making dinner, when I hear the lodge radio going off. Slate barks at the radio like he always does.

"Holland, just wanted to let you know the flowers you asked for were delivered. She was in her room. It's all set."

Fuck. The flowers. I ordered those days ago. Before everything happened. Of course, they'd get delivered today.

CHAPTER FORTY

I SPEND THE ENTIRE day in bed. Which is ironic, considering this is the catalyst for my argument with Holland.

First, I try to read one of the books I picked up when I was shopping with Viv. I get about ten pages in before realizing reading a romance book is not what I need right now. I hate the characters, their names, the title, the small town they are in.

I order room service twice and do anything I can to stay in here, under the covers, with the curtains closed.

The sun outside is too bright. I swear there are birds chirping outside my window. I want none of it. It's like mother-nature is teasing me. I wish it'd rain. Are thunderstorms a thing out here? I'd pay a ridiculous amount of money to have it be a stormy, dark day.

Viv tries to FaceTime. I decline. Now's not the time. My mind is all out of sorts and I'm not ready to talk about anything with anyone yet.

My phone taunts me. I can't even stomach looking at it.

When all else fails, make a list. My therapist encourages me to make a list of how I feel when I can't crawl out of a hole.

Here's what I feel:

- Lost
- Foolish
- Pissed off
- Embarrassed
- Overwhelmed
- Sad. So, so sad.

Everything Holland said during our fight hit all my sore spots. He called out what I've been insecure about for a while. If I didn't have this job, who would I be? Would I still be fulfilled? Proud of myself? I know the answers but they sting too much to verbalize.

There's a knock at the door. I cautiously approach the thing that broke me this morning and look through the peephole. It's not Holland. A wave of relief and disappointment hits me at the same time. I open the door.

"Good evening, Miss Lawson. These are for you." A lodge staff member hands over a bouquet of flowers.

"Thank you," I say as I shut the door and take them inside.

Vibrant, peachy-pink dahlias are wrapped in craft paper. The petals are soft like velvet.

I wonder if they're from Viv. This is something she'd do. I find the card and my breath hitches.

No. Not from Viv.

JUST SOMETHING SPONTANEOUS...

-HOLLAND

CHAPTER FORTY-ONE

NO MATTER HOW many white noise playlists I went through, I could hardly sleep last night. I feel like I got enough to function but not enough to *function well*.

I tossed and turned, jumping from topic to topic. Holland. Royce. Work. Bliss4ul contract. Holland. Kissing Holland. Yelling at Holland.

Ugh.

Whether I like it or not, I must meet with Royce today. My last piece of business at the lodge.

I miss my Peloton. If I was home, I'd do a difficult ride to help mentally prepare. Instead, I'm forced to settle for a treadmill in the gym. I am not a runner so it's mostly walking and jogging until I'm out of breath.

One of my favorite pre-meeting rituals is a little dancing and music while I get ready. Not for every meeting, but ones that could have substantial outcomes. I do my best to move my body around but between keeping my mind quiet and eyes open, it's a sorry end result.

Less wallowing and more positivity. Again, I'd like to give the version of myself who packed this small carry-on suitcase a round of applause. The fact I have my lucky blazer and heels puts me in a better mood. Great things have happened in this blazer. My hair is pulled back in a low bun. Classic.

Professional.

Now the finishing touch to convince myself I'm unstoppable: dark red lipstick.

I'll take all the extra hype I can get because I'm kind of dreading this. Something has felt off with Royce this entire trip.

When there's nothing else to prepare or makeup to fix, it's time to go to the meeting. I wish we were meeting in the conference room back at Sparks. But unfortunately, we're in the inappropriately cozy room off the restaurant again. I cross my fingers, hoping we can get into contract details and talk less about Royce's personal life.

My heels click on the lobby floor and Bea—wearing another festive headband—waves. I haven't seen her in a few days since I was avoiding Holland. And really, everyone else.

Royce is at the same table. I let out a slow breath, holding on to as much composure as possible. He's clearly in work mode: earbuds in, taking a call, with papers spread out all around the table. My mood is on its way up. I instantly feel better.

He gives me a one-minute gesture when I approach the table. Quietly, I sit and pull up the notes on my laptop, careful not to disturb.

A few minutes later, when he ends the call, he sighs and leans back, cracking his fingers.

"Ivy, thanks for accommodating the schedule change." His demeanor feels genuine and like he's in a good mood, much different than the other night.

"Not a problem. I appreciate you fitting the meeting in." I'm being honest.

Things are already much better compared to our previous meeting. We start with my notes, some basic clarifications, and red lines. Royce laughs and reminds me of the guy I thought he was before this trip. Our focus is one hundred percent on the pages and contracts in front of us. To say I'm relieved would be an understatement.

Gone is the anxiety about coming to this meeting and now I'm getting excited. When Jack pulled the dickbag move of the year for this meeting, I thought it would be some bullshit check-in that could've been done via Zoom. But I can't wait to bring this back to the team. In my mind, I'm already crafting the overview email to Stella, hitting all the highlights. This extension will be awesome for Sparks.

"And that's the end of my notes. Do you have anything else we need to cover?" I ask, my eyes meeting his. I close my laptop.

One side of his mouth goes up in a smirk. "I just have a few things I'd like to propose."

This is expected. Royce has always been one for the dramatics. I never thought this would be completely straightforward; it'd need a Royce twist, which I think is coming.

We go through some changes, minor to my team but important to Royce, and there isn't anything I'm not comfortable saying *yes* to. So far, so good.

"Lastly, I'd like to request at least six, but no more than twelve visits to our headquarters each year." He stares down at a page, not looking at me.

Bliss4ul is located about three hours from this lodge. It's by no means a quick trip from the east coast.

"That's quite a bit more than currently. Is—"

Before I can get the rest out, he interrupts.

"I wasn't finished." His voice isn't what I'd call playful. "Back to it... six to twelve visits a year, for you specifically. Other team members can join you, but you must be present for each, unless you have other client responsibilities."

This must be a joke. So I laugh.

"What's funny?" He finally looks at me. His eyes are cold and has my laugh dead in my throat.

"Umm… why is it specific to me? That doesn't make sense." When he doesn't seem like he grasps what I'm saying, I continue. "I may not be at this company in five years. And you're asking me to travel once a month?" Maybe I misheard him.

"Are you looking for a new job?"

I'm caught off guard and answer him, even if it's not appropriate. "No, I'm not looking for a new job." I'm barely treading water at this point.

"Well, if you were…" His voice trails off and he stares at me. "I could create a position for you."

He isn't joking. I heard him correctly. My brain struggles to make sense of what's going on and my stomach flips. My blazer shrinks and my shoulders could rip it. It's tight around my wrists.

"Thank you for the offer but I'm happy where I am." I try to sound confident and level.

"Why do you look so confused?" He raises his voice and my heartbeat matches.

"Umm… I'm not sure what to do with your off-the-cuff job offer. I don't know how we got so focused on me in this conversation."

Royce drops his pen, reaches his hand across the table, and grabs mine. I should've put my hands in my lap. Or something. Anything.

He rubs the palm of my hand with his fingers. My nerves tingle and prick. His touch is slimy and disgusting.

I'm frozen. A statue. I'm unable to move or form a thought.

"You know I could give you whatever you want," he murmurs, his smile too wide. "Wherever you want it." He winks at me. "Take you anywhere."

Everything is moving too slowly and like it's sped up, at the same time. He lets go of my hand and instead, touches my face. His palm is sweaty and too warm. My breath catches in my throat. Sirens are going off in my head.

I keep waiting for him to stop and throw his head back in a cackle, that this is all this a joke. That he's just messing with me.

We're in a public place—well sort of. I wish there were other people here. My heart lurches when I think of the mostly empty restaurant I walked through.

"Royce," I say as I stand up, flustered, trying to get away from him. Even a little space would help. I'm clumsy and some pages fall to the floor. On instinct, I reach down to pick them up. If I focus on this task, maybe he'll get the hint.

"Don't worry about that right now."

He's crouched down to my level. He takes his hands and puts them around my arms, lifting me up as he stands. The papers I picked up leave my hands and float to the floor.

I'm afraid to breathe or say anything. Meanwhile, Royce is wearing a grin and is still way too close to me.

"I've wanted to do this for so long." He tips his head back in anticipation. He steps into me, touching his chest to mine. He takes his hands and lightly touches the top of my forehead before he brushes them down the side of my face.

Wrong.

This is wrong.

Alarm bells scream.

Red flags are flying.

I take my free hand and push against his chest. Instead of creating any space, he grabs my wrist and walks me backwards until my back hits the wall. He's being rough. He's holding my wrist—gripping tight and unrelenting—above my head. It smacks the wall when it makes contact.

"Come on. I know I'm what you want." He takes my head and leans in, whispering into my ear. Smelling my skin before kissing my neck and then my collarbone.

My body shakes. My teeth chatter. I'm lightheaded, unable to take a real breath. My vision is blurry. The tears are silent but flowing.

"Royce, stop. Please stop." My voice is barely a whisper. I'm surprised at the sound of it.

"You don't want me to stop." He's still smiling.

The hand not pinning my arm up grazes my collarbone and then right at the top of my bra.

Royce forcefully puts his mouth to mine. His mouth is rough and stale. He's pinning me in place. I'm stuck between him and the wall.

I know I can do better than this.

I squirm, shaking my head from one side to another. Royce's mouth follows me. I get a little space but then he slams me into the wall, still holding my wrist and my elbow banging into the surface.

I must do something.

Otherwise…

Otherwise…

I can't think of what will happen otherwise.

I bang my elbow into the wall again. I yell at him to stop, but his mouth covers mine. It's nothing but weird sounds. I try to knee him in the groin, but he catches my knee before I make contact.

He laughs. He actually laughs. Like he's enjoying this.

The only thing I can think to do is make more noise.

CHAPTER FORTY-TWO

HOLLAND

I'M IN THE RESTAURANT wrapping up the weekly bar order. No one's happy when we're out of beer or wine. I'm thankful for the distraction because I'm still replaying the fight with Ivy.

She was so pissed. She didn't even know what the missed calls were for but immediately found a way for it to be my fault.

She hasn't texted me. And I haven't texted her. This can't be the last time we speak before she leaves… right? I didn't think she'd say thank you for the flowers, but I thought she'd at least acknowledge them.

My breath hitches when I realize I don't know what day she's leaving. It could be today. This can't be it.

When I check the last item off on my list, I go to leave for my office, but before I can get out of the restaurant, I hear something.

It sounds like someone is knocking. Maybe on the wall? The music in the restaurant drowns out some of it. But it doesn't sound like your typical kid kicking the table or booth when they're eating. This place is also dead.

I'm immediately curious. What is that? It's not sporadic and I can hear it getting louder as I walk towards the room off the restaurant. Is it coming from the meeting room?

I turn the corner and immediately know something isn't right. There are two people, it looks like a man and a woman. The man's back is to me and he's pressing her into the wall. It almost looks like they're hooking up, but I can't tell.

This is awkward. I don't want to break up anyone's make-out session but this is a public place. The woman whimpers and turns her face to the side.

Ivy.

His hand pins one of hers above her head. She's struggling. Her elbow is repeatedly banging into the wall. That's what I heard.

My brain can't string together a set of words but it has no problem moving my body. I grab the man's shoulders, and pull him off her, my hands clasping the front of his shirt. Adrenaline runs through my body.

It's Royce. Fucking loser. He must not have heard me come in.

"What the hell are you doing?" His voice is gruff, and his hands come to mine on his shirt.

The balls on this guy.

"You first. What the fuck are *you* doing?" I shake him with my hands.

He has this dumbfounded look on his face.

"Talking. Ivy and I were talking," he pants. He looks disheveled.

I look for Ivy and see she's backed up all the way into the corner of the room. She's visibly shaken. Tears stain her face.

"You had your hands on her. You definitely weren't talking and you know that. Don't fucking lie to me."

"It was a business meeting that doesn't concern you," he says while leaning in, getting closer to me. "In a room that I paid for. I'm a guest."

I walk him a few steps backward.

"No, you're not. Pack your shit and leave the premises."

I let him go and he stumbles backwards.

"You can't throw me out—"

"Yes, I can. I should've thrown you out when you were drunk off your ass at your corporate event the other night. Fucking out of control."

"Ivy, tell him it's fine." He says it like the bully he is. He looks around me to try to get her attention. She's practically cowering.

I step forward. "Don't talk to her." My voice comes out like a growl. My jaw is clenched as I put a finger in his chest. "Get your shit and get out of here. As soon as fucking possible. No more meetings. You're no longer welcome here."

I turn and walk toward Ivy.

"She knew exactly what she was getting herself into." Royce pleads his case. He doesn't know when to stop. I know he's walking behind me. I hate that he's trying to convince me that his behavior was okay. Fucking pathetic. "She's the one who is about to land a massive contract for her company. I spent a lot of money at your little establishment and if you want that to continue—"

Without a second thought, I turn to face him and throw a punch. It lands perfectly in the center of his face. The crack fills the room, followed by Ivy's gasp, and then he's on his back. I walk and stand over him, picking him up by his shirt. He doesn't squirm or try to move, except to cover his nose.

"Don't say another word." Blood pours from his nose, and his lip is split open. "Get. The. Fuck. Out."

I drop him back to the floor. And he finally listens to me.

I nod to the staff from the restaurant, watching from the doorway. They walk in and escort Royce out. It's not often we have unruly guests, but they know exactly what to do. They'll take him to his room, watch him pack, call the local police, and file a report. Once the police are done with him, they'll escort him off the property.

I rush to Ivy in the corner and stand in front of her. It's just the two of us left. I don't want to touch her without permission. She picks her eyes up from the floor, red and panicked, and silently cries. When her gaze reaches mine, she falls into my chest.

And I catch her.

Ivy hangs onto me, her arms wrapped around my neck. It sounds like she's calming down, doing her best to gulp deep breaths. We sway, kind of like at a middle school dance, and I rub small circles on her back.

It doesn't matter how long we stay here. The room is empty except for Ivy's things strewn on the table. I want to ask her what happened but I know better.

Fucking Royce. I had a feeling he was a piece of garbage but didn't expect this. My face heats when I think of how he tried to pay for his behavior. He will not set another foot here. That's for damn sure. I can't wait to fill out *that* paperwork.

Ivy pulls her hands away and takes a step back, wiping her eyes. She stares at the floor.

"Are you hurt?" I quickly look her over and don't see much of anything.

She rubs her wrist, flexing her fingers and then shakes her head no.

"Are you okay?" I know her pain could be somewhere else.

"I mean, no. But. Nothing really happened. He tried to…and he kissed me… and…" She's nervously wiping her hands on the front of her blazer. Her face has a look of disgust on it.

I use my fingers to lightly tip her chin up towards mine. "What I saw was not okay. Not even fucking close." I'm trying to keep my anger in check because that isn't what she needs.

"I know. I know that." Her voice is flat. Her hands are now nervously touching the top of her head and sweeping her hair back.

"What do you need?" She doesn't say anything. "Do you want to call someone? Vivian?" I'm trying to be helpful.

"No, not really. I can call her later." She finally looks at me and the adrenaline starts all over again. I can't believe Royce made her feel this way. Put her in this position. "I want to change."

"Okay, let's go to your room." I take her things from the table and put them in her bag, swinging it over my shoulder.

I put my hand on her lower back, gently, careful not to startle her. I take her to the service elevator.

"Would you mind waiting outside my room?" she asks when we're inside the elevator.

"I already planned on it. We can go wherever you want after. Unless you want to stay here?" I want her to feel like she's in control. Whatever works for her, works for me.

"I don't want to be by myself. If that's alright?" The bright, vibrant Ivy I know has diminished. Seeing her small and shrunken makes me wish I got another good punch in.

"Whatever you want." I lean up against the door as she walks in.

"I need to take a shower," she says, seemingly conflicted.

"I'll wait here."

She's in her room for a few minutes, long enough for me to call down to the front desk and see if Royce is still on the property. The last thing I want is for us to inadvertently run into him. Apparently, he's taking his sweet time getting his belongings together. I ask the staff to keep him in his room for at least the next fifteen minutes.

I look at her door and it's overwhelming. The same door I practically slammed the other day after our fight. The same one I stood in front of, building up the courage to knock on.

When Ivy comes back into the hallway, her face is red but freshly washed. She's wearing leggings and one of the tops she bought on our shopping trip.

Her hair is out of its tight bun and the waves kiss her shoulders. I let her speak first.

"I know what I want," she says but her voice is quieter than I'm used to, and she sounds tired. She doesn't touch me but stands close. "A peanut butter bacon cheeseburger."

CHAPTER FORTY-THREE

WHY DOES IT FEEL like Royce stole a piece of me? Even if he offered it back, I'd never take it. I picture it dripping in black and frayed at the edges where he ripped it from me. My mind has always been too good at visualizing trauma.

It feels like hundreds of bugs are crawling over my skin. I wore a long sleeve shirt because I knew I'd want to scratch. That's how disgusting I feel.

Tears prick at my eyes when I think about Holland coming in when he did. There aren't words to express my gratitude. And I don't even attempt.

I'm in Holland's truck and we're driving in silence. He asked if I wanted to listen to any music. I don't. His voice is soft and kind. Much different than the last time we were together.

The whole nightmare with Royce spanned a minute or two and it's on replay in my head. His disgusting touch. His mouth, hurtful, on mine. Holland's face, full of rage. My body shaking.

I'm humiliated. And ashamed. Why didn't I scream? Or yell for help? Or get away quicker?

When we walked through the lobby, Holland stopped at the front desk. The concerned looks and hushed tones were hard to miss. I'm sure it was about Royce. There weren't many people who saw what happened between the two men, but I know some of them did.

Holland doesn't ask me anything about Royce or what happened and I'm grateful. He still looks rattled. I look at his hand, now on the steering wheel, and notice his knuckles are split open.

We get twenty minutes into the drive before I panic about the aftermath of this whole situation.

"Stella. I need to call Stella. I have to tell her. She's going to ask about the contract. What the hell do I say to her?" My words stomp over one another. I fumble my phone.

"Ivy. Breathe," Holland says while taking my phone from my hand, his other on the steering wheel. "You don't need to worry about this right now." He's trying to reassure me.

"I know... but she's expecting my call. She's going to think something happened."

"Something *did* happen." His eyes are soft when he glances at me, just for a second, before he's back staring at the road. "If you're comfortable, I can call Stella once we're at the restaurant. I can let her know what happened. That way, you can call her when you're ready," Holland offers. "We're not going to call her from the car, ok?"

"You'd do that? Call her?"

I know he can hear the tears in my voice. There are no jokes about crying. And he doesn't tell me to stop.

He doesn't hesitate to answer. "Yes."

Slumping back against the seat, I close my eyes. Holland rolls down both windows and the wind is loud in my ears. Like the best kind of white noise. Loud and distracting. I spend the rest of the drive doing my deep breathing.

Holland doesn't ask any questions.

Even though my brain and body are exhausted, I feel safe.

My mouth starts watering when we walk into The Bun Room. It smells like fried food and burgers. My stomach reminds me I haven't eaten since breakfast. When Holland asks if I want to stay here to eat or get it to go, I choose to stay.

I need some space from the lodge. Even if it's just for a meal.

It's a little busy but we get a table tucked away in the back. It seems like everyone knows Holland and is surprised to see him out. He doesn't let anyone pull him into a conversation; his focus is solely on me.

The server tells us the specials, which are mostly drinks, and leaves us to browse.

"How bad would it be to use alcohol as a coping mechanism right now?" I say as I scan the long list of local cider, beer, and wine. "Would you judge me?"

Holland smirks. "No judgment at all. You have a designated driver." He points at his chest. "If you want to have some drinks, I'll be sure to remind you about drinking water." He looks content and confident as he browses the drink menu.

"I'll keep you safe," Holland adds and it sounds like a throwaway statement. My heart picks up and I feel a little lighter.

When I can't decide on a cider, the server reminds me about a flight option. So I choose the flight but have the server pick them out—I don't want to make any other decisions.

I've finished my first cider flight when Holland brings up Stella.

"Do you want me to call Stella? I can step outside for a few minutes. Or if you want to listen, we can call her on speakerphone. Your choice." He's gentle, caring, and to the point. My face combs his, looking for a sign of annoyance, but I can't find one.

"What are you going to tell her?"

"I'm going to tell her what I saw. I'll be vague. And I'll let her know that we filed a police report on behalf of the lodge. And that he was escorted him off the premises." My eyes go wide when he mentions the police. "Lastly, I'll tell her you're safe and you'll get a hold of her when you're ready. Also, she can call the front desk if she'd like another statement from one of our managers." He's so calm and together. His words are intentional and he doesn't waver.

"Did you really file a police report?" Embarrassment floods my cheeks.

"It's our protocol whenever we have a violent guest. It's unconventional but I like to be cautious." It's like he's reading my mind.

A violent guest. Violent. That word makes me feel nauseous. The lump in my throat is hard to swallow.

"That doesn't mean *you* have to file a police report. That's up to you. You can think about it and decide… when you're ready."

I didn't consider this aspect. I think about Stella and what this could potentially mean for his company and mine. I worry about Holland's hand and if he'll be in trouble or feel financial repercussions. How am I in another situation like this? What Holland is saying sounds just like Vivian when I told her about Jack.

Ultimately, I decided not to go to HR. I still don't know if that was the right decision.

Before I can get sucked into a black hole of what-ifs, a basket of crispy, golden, cheese curds are set on the table.

"You can call Stella," I say as I hand him my phone with her contact open. "I'll feel better once that's done. I'm all set here." My jaw falls open in pure happiness at the mound of fried cheese. I mostly want to see if he's going to make the call.

Holland lets out a breath and stands up. He puts his hand on my shoulder. "Are you sure you're okay by yourself for a few?"

"I'm not by myself. I'm with all these people." I dramatically look around the room. "And fried cheese."

"Okay, okay. I'll be quick."

I can't help but watch him rush out of the restaurant. He looks back at me, before opening the door.

The back corner of the restaurant is getting a lot of attention. A microphone cuts across the music, announcing that it's karaoke night. People clap and holler.

Our server drops off my second cider flight. "You're in for some laughs," he says as he gestures to the stage.

I could use some laughs. Distractions.

The only thing I can think of right now is Holland. Him finding me. Punching Royce. Bringing me here. Talking to Stella. His knuckles cut on the steering wheel. How he held me up. His arms. The man with the tough exterior cracking to be the soft spot I need is such a surprise—and the best part of this whole thing.

At this moment, it feels like he isn't real. There must be a catch.

My body buzzes from the cider but the panic and anxiety are still within reach. I don't want to be drunk but want to feel something different.

Here's what clicks: I'm tired of worrying. Thinking about the big picture. I don't have it in me to wonder what I did that made Royce do what he did. Or wonder how this whole disaster is going to blow up. I don't want to worry about tomorrow, or work, or whatever heavy thing happens next.

There's nothing I can do to change today or this week. It's happened and that's it. The restaurant atmosphere is full of happy people. Friends laughing, partners holding hands, and people scouring karaoke lists to pick a song. I want to feel what they're feeling.

My brain needs a break. Hell, my body and soul need a break.

All I want to do is disassociate with today; I'll deal with it later.

I keep glancing at the door, waiting for Holland to come back.

Holland opens the door. We make eye contact right away. He nods and walks toward the table. His sleeves are rolled up to show his forearms. I'm not the only person who notices him.

But he's only looking at me.

CHAPTER FORTY-FOUR

HOLLAND

IVY'S SHOULDERS MOVE down and away from her ears the second she sees me. It doesn't matter that we fought the other day. Because this reaction? It's everything.

I'm not naive to think we won't have to talk about it. I know we will; just not tonight.

After I share how the call with Stella went, I can see the tension melt from her face. She was for sure waiting for me to say she was in some sort of trouble. Ivy seems to always expect bad news.

Stella was surprised to hear about Royce's behavior and was only concerned about Ivy and her well-being. She asked me to share updates with her until Ivy's ready to talk. She also promised to keep it between us—at this time.

Royce is an asshole and Ivy is entertaining the possibility she did something wrong. She's always wanting to take the blame. Her need for control is clear. I get it.

The rage I felt when I saw Royce handling her like a thing and not a person. The look on her face hits me all over again. Ivy—typically bright and brave, shaking and her eyes wide.

My face is hot and my heart beats in my ears.

At the bar, we sit through hours of karaoke. It's kind of a nightmare but it makes Ivy belly laugh. At one point, she stands up at our table and sings along with the person on stage. The crowd loves it and cheers her on. I make sure to get a picture of her, with her "fans," clapping for her in the background.

I hope it isn't insensitive. I'm sure there's a ton she wishes she'd never be able to recall about today. But seeing her dancing like she's the only person in the room convinced me that taking the photo was the right move.

After the day she had, I'm in awe. She's radiant. It could very well be fueled by rage and peanut butter, but who fucking cares.

I admire her and her resilience.

I nudge the glass of ice water her way. She takes a long drink. I move my chair close to hers and lean in.

"How are you feeling?" She's only had the two cider flights and is sober.

"Fine," she replies.

"Really?" I ask, my mouth close to her ear. The karaoke is loud.

"As fine as I can be," she confirms.

"I know you love a plan, so let's make one. Where do you want to stay tonight? I can take you back to the lodge, or you can stay at my place." My voice is level. Honestly, I'd be fine with whatever she picks.

She sits and contemplates for a few seconds. "Your place. You have Slate."

"Sounds good. He'll love it."

He's not the only one.

We're back at my place and Slate clearly missed Ivy. I haven't seen him greet someone like this, maybe ever.

Without the distraction of bad karaoke, Ivy looks tired. I can't imagine how she feels after today. Hell, the last couple of days.

Ivy is sitting on the living room floor, petting Slate—he can't get enough. I'm sitting on the couch and watching them.

When I think she's about to fall asleep, she says, "Today was not my favorite."

"Mine either," I reply.

Her facial expression goes from listening to confusion. She furrows her dark brows, creating these cute wrinkles in her forehead.

"What happened to you?" She sits up, sincerely concerned.

"I saw Royce with his hands on you. That's what happened."

She stands up and is in front of me.

"You punched him." She reaches for my hand. My knuckles are still pink with small cuts. I've had worse. She brushes those sore spots with the tips of her fingers, gently and deliberately. My heart races. "Does it hurt?"

"It's nothing. I'll be okay. It's fine."

"Hey… that's my line." Ivy dips her head down and plants a soft kiss on each of my marked knuckles.

I can't believe she's kissing me.

Her expression shifts and she takes her own hand, running it down her neck, her delicate collarbone. Her breathing picks up.

"He touched me here." I realize she's tracing the spots Royce helped himself to. "I hate that he touched me. With his disgusting sweaty palms. His skin was too slick. He tasted stale. Disgusting."

She's talking but it's more for herself than anything. She's working herself up, her chest rapidly rising and falling.

"Hey, how about a shower? Or a bath?" I propose.

"Do you have bubbles?"

"Believe it or not, I do." I answer.

I fill the bathtub with hot water and dig through my selection of bath accessories. Locals are always leaving products for me to try, in hopes that we put them in the gift shop or the rooms. There are quite a few I'm not really interested in, but I don't have the heart to tell them. That's how I've acquired various bath salts, oils, and bubble bath.

Next, I place a bottle of water and a piece of butterscotch cake on the ledge of the tub. Seems a bit like a hazard but I feel like if anyone would want to eat cake in a bath, it'd be Ivy.

Ivy's face is priceless when she sees the bath set up. She lets herself be happy, even if it's for a few seconds but it doesn't go unnoticed.

"You did this?"

"Filled the tub with water? Yeah." I shrug her off.

"You know what I mean."

I choose to bypass the compliment. "There's a whole box of salts, oils, whatever you want to use. Towels on the counter. Some things you can sleep in."

She smiles and nods.

"Are you going to stay here?"

"Like, in the house? Yes. Where would I go?"

"I don't know. I just want to make sure." She rolls her shoulders back and shakes her hands out. "I don't want you to leave."

"I'm not going anywhere." I make eye contact with her before I shut the bathroom door.

She stayed in the tub so long she needed to add more hot water. Her skin was pruned and flushed. I was already in bed when she stepped out of the bathroom.

Ivy crawls into her side of the bed.

My stomach flips. *Her* side. It feels like she has a side. We're both lying flat on our backs, hands over the covers, and looking at the ceiling.

"Holland. I owe you an apology—"

"Not tonight, you don't." I try to be gentle, but it sounds much bossier than I meant it. "You've been through enough today. I don't want to be another worry you add to your list." We both turn on our sides and face each other. "We can get into all that later."

Ivy takes a breath, holds it, and slowly lets it out. "Okay. Can I…?" She looks at the empty space between us, wanting to come closer.

"Of course." I lay on my back and put an arm out for her. She scoots in, puts her head on my chest, and her arm up and around my neck and shoulder.

Her heartbeat races against my skin until it finally slows down as she drifts to sleep.

CHAPTER FORTY-FIVE

AFTER BREAKFAST—courtesy of Holland—and a morning walk with Slate, I can already go for a nap. Holland had to run to the lodge but wanted to make sure I'd be okay here. He's been sweet and exactly what I need.

Holland didn't ask me a bunch of questions or try to get me to talk about anything. I'm thankful for that.

I'm also thankful for his couch, which holds me like a hug. It's way better than the one in my apartment. A headache pounds behind my eyes. Oh, the aftereffects of emotional turmoil. I know I need to call Stella. And Vivian.

The nap I desperately needed is cut short by my ringing phone. Slate barks at the interruption. It's Jack. Against my better judgment, I answer.

"Ivy, what the hell happened?!" He sounds frantic.

Even though we're not together anymore, we were for years. I want to give him the chance to talk to me if Stella told him what happened.

"I'm okay, Jack. It's okay."

"It is fucking NOT okay! Royce said you sabotaged the meeting."

My mouth hangs open. Did he call to scold me? Before my brain can catch up, he's raising his voice again.

"You blew it. How'd you manage to do that? I handed this to you on a silver platter." I can almost hear him angrily pacing through the phone.

"You're joking, right?"

"No, this isn't a joke. You screwed my promotion, your promotion, all of it."

"Royce is garbage. He's the one who forced himself on me, and in a public place. I begged him to stop!" Now I'm yelling.

"Quit with the dramatics. You're not a child," he says, more condescending than usual. "There's no way Royce did that. You're acting like he assaulted you."

Why did I assume he was calling to check on me as a compassionate person of the human race? Jack isn't capable of caring about anyone besides himself. I keep setting him up for redemption and it's never coming.

"He did assault me," I say. It hurts me to say these words aloud. They don't feel real on my lips. I'm angry I have to say them. My heart hurts at the same time.

Holland walks in and sees me screaming into my cell phone. His face is one of concern and confusion. He sits next to me and mouths, "Are you okay?"

I shake my head no.

"You're telling me Royce had sex with you against your will?" Jack's voice is sarcastic and shrill. It even pulls into a cruel laugh at the end.

"I didn't say that. He put his hand down my shirt and pushed me against a wall. Who knows what he would've done if someone wouldn't have walked in on us?"

"Whatever. That contract extension was going to fund my new position, your new position, and finally make it to where we don't have to work together anymore. When Royce called—"

"Wait… Royce called you?" This means Stella hasn't talked to him about it. Weird how Royce is immediately keeping Jack in the know.

"Yes! To tell me how dramatic you are. He was trying to help you. Can't you see that?" He's loud enough I need to pull the phone from my ear. Holland can obviously hear him. "And since you're literally a killer when it comes to business ventures, you can get back to the office ASAP. We can work it out here."

I hate that I'm crying right now. I don't want to waste another ounce of energy on Jack or Royce. They've taken enough.

My mouth is still open. For once, I'm at a loss of words. I have no idea what to say to someone who is so misguided.

Holland lightly places two fingers under my chin, which is almost touching my chest. He looks at me in this way that makes me want to sit up tall. He doesn't say anything, just nods.

I realize how Jack was making me shrink into myself, yet again. This time, for a despicable act that was nowhere near my fault. Jack has received too many chances, especially from me.

I make my voice as calm as possible and simply respond, "No."

"No?"

"You heard me, Jack. No. Or, fuck no. Whichever one resonates."

"You don't get to talk to me like that—when you get back here—"

"Actually, *you* don't get to speak to *me* like that. I'm not coming back to the office just because you're throwing a tantrum. You're horrible. A terrible human. The way you treat people like things and discard them as soon as you're finished, you should be ashamed of yourself." And then the words continue to fall out of my mouth. "You may be one step ahead of me at Sparks but you're not my boss. Stella is who I report to. Now that I think about it, does Stella know you canceled my vacation? Or did you manipulate that to fit your narrative as well?"

I glance at Holland and he's beaming. He's proud of me. Hell, I'm proud of myself.

"You think I'd do that? I'd stoop that low?" Jack scoffs into the phone but his voice is an octave too high. That's it. I've caught him in a lie.

"Yes. One hundred percent yes."

"Listen, just come back to the office—"

"You don't get it. I'm done listening to you. There's nothing you could say to make up for not only the things you've done to me, but the way you spoke to me after I went through what I did with Royce. I'm blocking your number and on every app. Do not try to speak to me again."

I hang up the phone. Holland claps. And then he picks me up and swings me around the living room. I put my head in the crook of his neck. He smells like sunshine and trees.

"That was awesome," he says as he sets me down.

"That was something!" The adrenaline is still rushing through my body. "I have to call Stella before Jack has a chance to spin his own story."

"Go for it. I'll give you some space," Holland says as he grabs Slate and takes him to the outdoor patio, closing the door.

I dial Stella's number with shaking fingers.

"Ivy. It's good to hear from you," she says, concern clear in her voice.

"Hi, Stella. Ugh, let me just say, I'm so sorry about all of this."

She interrupts before I can continue. "I know you're not about to apologize for Royce. This isn't your fault. From what I understand, Royce was criminally out of line." Her voice is stern.

"Have you heard from the company or anything?" While this would be a mess for us, it'd be much worse for them.

"Nothing from their camp yet. I'm betting they don't know about it. I'll let you know as soon as I hear."

"What about the contract?"

"Ivy, I don't care about that. We'll figure it out, but for now, I just want to make sure you're doing okay. Sounds like you've made some good connections at the lodge. I talked to the owner yesterday and he reiterated that you were doing well under these circumstances, which is all I care about."

"Have you told anyone else yet?" My stomach hurts from the idea of people whispering about me in the office, again.

"Not yet. There's no need to. Once we have more information, I'll share it with those who need to know."

"Thank you," I say and I mean it.

"I'd like to offer you additional days off to tack onto your vacation. Whether you choose to stay at the lodge or come back home, it's up to you. I want to make sure you have time to relax after this whole thing. You let me know when you're ready to come back to work and that will be fine with me."

Fucking Jack. I knew it. Maybe I knew the whole time and just didn't want to rock the boat at Sparks.

"Stella, about that..." And then I launch into the entire story.

Stella says nothing. She listens all the way until the end which makes telling it much easier.

"We've got quite the mess on our hands, don't we?!" Her voice is professional but also sounds villainous. "Well, this is my mess for now. I'm going straight to HR after this meeting."

"Okay. Let me know if you need anything from me—"

"You've given enough. What I want you to do is take some time away from the office. Not for anyone else but for you. Get through all of this. You can make your statement about Royce and Jack whenever you're ready."

"Are you sure?" I'm baffled.

"Consider this a sabbatical. A paid sabbatical. The only thing I want to hear from you is how you're doing. I'll handle everything at the office."

"Wow. Okay. Thank you, Stella."

"Ivy, I know I told you not to apologize for things that aren't your fault but I'm about to do that myself. I'm sorry this happened to you. I'm sorry you were at a work event—alone with someone like Royce, who ultimately couldn't be trusted. I'm sorry I believed Jack when he told me you volunteered to shift your time off and take the meeting. I'm sorry for all of it."

"I appreciate it, Stella. I really do."

We say our goodbyes and end the call.

Stella isn't an emotional person. She's clear and to the point, easily able to determine the best decision for whatever's on the table. Conversations like the one we just had are not the norm.

I'm a bit dazed when I walk out to the patio.

"Everything good?" Holland asks, Slate panting at his feet.

"Ugh, yeah. I think so." I sit down across from Holland. "I asked Stella if she knew Jack canceled my vacation and she didn't. She's going to HR and I'm on a paid sabbatical until I'm ready to go back to the office. It's clear I have stuff to sort out. Therapy is calling my name."

"Jack keeps outdoing himself, huh?"

"I guess you could say that."

"So, are you going to try and find an earlier flight home?"

The question feels loaded. Much bigger than travel plans. Holland and I haven't had the chance to talk about our fight. Or what we said. Or anything really. He's been careful and patient with me in a crisis and I owe us that conversation.

"I could. Or I can stay here for a few more days…?" My words come out like a question. My breath is caught in my chest. It's scary putting yourself out there.

Holland sits back and says, "You could stay here a few more days." It's a statement and a confirmation. "Think of all the time you'd have with Slate." He gestures to the dog sleeping next to me.

"Now, let's not make this next part weird. I'll call the front desk and put a note on your room file. Basically, you can stay as long as you want. But if you want to get some of your stuff so you can hang here at my place, that's an option too."

He rubs his hands over his cut knuckles. I can tell he's nervous.

"Whatever you're comfortable with."

My mouth is dry.

"I'm not expecting anything from you—" He's stumbling over his words.

"Holland. Take a breath. I'd much rather be here than an empty hotel room." I lightly touch his arm. "I know my room is still an option. I'll want to grab some stuff from there so I can stop sleeping in your clothes." I look down at the massive T-shirt and gym shorts I'm wearing.

"Whatever you need, Ivy."

Again, this doesn't feel real.

CHAPTER FORTY-SIX

HOLLAND

I'M OUT FOR A run while Ivy's on the phone with Vivian. I was around for the first five minutes of their video chat and that was enough. I needed to get out of there. Vivian was pissed that Ivy didn't call her about Royce right away.

Ivy mentioned a previous meeting with Royce, before the disastrous one, which surprised me. She didn't mention it. That's what sold me on a run. I don't want to overhear anything. If Ivy wants to tell me, she will.

I leave her in my house like it's something we've done a hundred times before. The ease of this whole thing nibbles on the edge of my mind.

My feet pound the trail as I fall into the rhythm of my run and feel the cool air on my warm skin. Moving my body like this is refreshing.

Before long, conversations with Bea and Vivian come back up. It's like a running agenda. I remember Bea saying Hazel would've liked Ivy. I don't doubt it. My heart is heavy thinking of how much I wish Hazel was here now, on this run, berating me for details.

Vivian told me Ivy was worth it like I didn't know. Since the first time I saw her, kicking her own ass, she pulled me in.

She's smart. She's brave. She tries to go out of her comfort zone and fights anxiety and self-doubt at every turn.

I'm in love with her.

My questions don't concern Ivy. They're about me. Can I risk this with wounds that are still healing? Hell, they'll probably always be healing and ripping open, for the rest of my life. Like the inside of your cheek you can't stop biting.

Am I willing to rewrite what I thought my future was?

If I can't have Hazel here, I wish I had some guy friends who'd punch my shoulder and make fun of me for being a pussy. Harass me over beers for repeatedly bringing up a woman. I don't miss much of anything from the city, but I had more connections there. It's not even those specific people, my old friend group; it's just the idea of having friendships.

There's a known stopping point on my right where I decide to pause.

While I'm staring at mountains, the open cloudless sky, and water in the distance, I ask myself a question looking for a gut-check reaction: *What do you want?*

The answer is simple.

Ivy.

For as long as she'll have me.

Loud music is coming from my place. I don't know if I've ever heard it this loud since I've lived here. I cautiously open the door, unsure of what I'm going to see on the other side.

"No Diggity" plays throughout the house. I take a few steps in and see Ivy in the kitchen. She's holding Slate to her. Ivy's dancing in my kitchen, to a nineties rap song, with my dog. Not only is she dancing, but she's singing and rapping. And it's fucking adorable.

She doesn't know I'm back yet. I let her dance around until she's facing me. My fingers itch to pull her to me, hold her, dance with her.

When she sees me, her eyes go wide, but she doesn't stop. She grins. Slate pants like he's having the time of his life.

"What's going on?" I ask over the music.

"A dance party!" She's still spinning around the kitchen.

When the song ends and goes to the next, she turns the volume down, and puts Slate on the floor. He slowly walks to me, smelling for treats. Spoiled bastard.

"Sorry. Everything has been so heavy. I needed to dance it out." She's out of breath with her hands on her hips.

"Why are you apologizing? I think Slate's going to end up loving you more than me, if you keep it up." I joke with her.

"Ha! How was the run?" She reaches down and scratches Slate's belly.

"Just what I needed. My version of dancing it out." I wipe sweat from my face and open the fridge. I bring out fresh fruit and put it on the table.

I want to invite Ivy to go with me to a lodge event tonight. I hate how nervous I am. Overthinking is making it worse. So, I go for it.

"Tonight. There's this thing. The lodge does this event every month. It's kind of like a build-your-own s'mores thing—"

"I'm in. I love s'mores. Say less," she cuts me off while clapping her hands together.

"I should've known. You sugar fiend." I point at Ivy.

CHAPTER FORTY-SEVEN

DID I EXPECT HOLLAND to invite me to stay at his place? No. Was it hard to pretend I didn't feel like a burden? Sort of.

These are the thoughts I have while I pack a few of my things.

Normally, I wouldn't agree to something like this. But after my call with Viv, where she both scolded and supported me, this feels like a solid decision. She's always telling me to take more chances. Plus, I'm hoping Holland and I might have time to talk.

I wait for him in the lobby and Bea approaches me.

"Ivy. I heard about yesterday." She spins me around and pulls me into a tight embrace. "I'm sorry. I never liked Royce and am happy he's not allowed back." She rocks us back and forth.

"Thanks, Bea. I'm alright. It's fine." I try to reassure her.

"No, it's not fine. Don't give behavior like that a pass. Ever." She's stern but still full of compassion. She's wearing a velvet headband adorned with small faux flowers. It looks like her very own garden.

"You're right," I say as I look at her. She looks at my bag but doesn't bring it up. I'm not sure if she knows I'm going to be at Holland's.

"We got new chocolate today," she says as she points to the gift shop. "Go see if anything catches your eye. I'll keep an eye out for Holland."

Well, she knows enough. Or she's assuming.

I browse the chocolate selection and my mouth waters. I walk out with a pineapple hazelnut milk chocolate. Maybe I'll use it for s'mores later.

Bea says she'll charge it to the room but we both know that's a lie.

Holland is waiting in the lobby when I get back.

"You good?"

"Yes. Let's go."

And I mean it.

The air is crisp enough to turn the tip of your nose and cheeks red. It's ideal s'mores weather. And I can't remember the last time I made a s'more.

The thought of being around a fire when the air is as cool as it is, seems like a wonderful way to spend an evening. I borrowed a scarf from Holland as the only one I had was from Royce's company and there was no way I was wearing it. Petty or not, I couldn't do it.

The three of us walk out to the outdoor seating area.

"Oh, Ivy. You're going to love this!" Bea exclaims. She stands behind a table where staff is working, leaving Holland and I on the other side.

"Here's a tray for your s'mores goodies. You can pick out whatever you'd like and come back if you need more. There's also mulled wine and hot chocolate." She points to a table in the corner with labeled drinks.

I've been to a ton of fancy hotels and never once did they offer up something like this. I hate to admit it, but I've been missing out.

The spread is over-the-top and it's what dreams are made of. There's different types of graham crackers and cookies, plus different flavors of marshmallows. The best part is the chocolate selection. There are probably twenty different types of chocolate bars and brownies… all in the name of s'mores.

"Oh wow!" It's all I can muster. "I don't know how to choose." I'm almost in a daze.

"I'm not picky. Grab some options and we'll share," Holland says, like the saint he is. "Do you want hot chocolate or mulled wine?"

"I'll try the wine," I reply as Holland leaves me to deliberate our s'mores supplies.

"What a guy," Bea says as soon as Holland is out of earshot.

What a guy is right. I watch as he gets our drinks. He's wearing a gray quarter zip, a black puffy vest that calls me to fall into it, and these sort of athleisure black pants. Usually, I find men in suits the most attractive. Not tonight.

I've decided to try to go with whatever happens tonight. I know Holland and I will need to address our argument eventually, but not now.

While I grab chocolate bars and see Holland filling cups with mulled wine, I'm hit with a wave of gratitude. It's not the first time this has happened, even just today. I think about the space Holland has given up and made for me in the last few days. My heart squeezes.

I realize I'm staring at him when he turns and looks for me. When he makes eye contact, he flashes a knowing look. One that says, "Caught you."

The lodge has outdone itself. I shouldn't be surprised since all the events have hit the mark. Tonight, fire pits and tables are arranged with different types of sitting areas, all equipped with blankets and throw pillows. Lanterns guide guests to different areas around the grounds.

Not one spot looks the same with a variety of chairs, love seats, and netted swings. Some are meant for large groups while others have seating just for two. It smells like roasted marshmallows and melted chocolate.

I'd never pick this place for a vacation. I think about timing and coincidence. No matter how convoluted the path, I'm thankful to be here with Holland.

"You want to pick a spot?" Holland asks as he carries our drinks.

"No, you pick. I bet you know the best one," I say.

Holland nods and we continue to walk. He takes us to the outskirts, kind of tucked away from everyone. I knew he'd find the best place for us.

There's a cluster of pine trees, a string of twinkly lights running through the branches, with a loveseat in front. Blankets are draped over the back. A smile spreads on my face. Holland sets our wine on tables placed on each side of the loveseat. I put our s'mores tray on the holder near the fire.

"This is amazing," I say in awe.

"Why do you sound so surprised?"

"I'm not. Just glad to be here. If you don't recall, this isn't my typical vacation destination."

Holland responds by opening chocolate bars and putting marshmallows on our roasting sticks. I take a sip of the mulled wine. It's warm and spicy in all the right ways. I claim my spot on the loveseat and Holland hands me a marshmallow to roast. My mouth waters.

"The real question is, are you a go-for-it or low-and-slow kind of guy?" I raise my eyebrows and cast a side glance at Holland as he sits down next to me.

He lets out a small chuckle. "Definitely low-and-slow. Gotta get it just right." His look is intense and fun. "For marshmallows, at least."

My lips tingle. The parts of my body I wish he was touching follow.

"Oh good," I say as I let out a fake but exasperated sigh. "I'd have to find a different s'mores buddy if you were one of the people who set it on fire as soon as it gets put on the stick."

I'm all talk. And he looks at me like he knows it.

"I'd never dream of it."

We roast marshmallows to the sound of cracks from the fire. I giggle when we go to put the s'mores together because it's a disaster. Holland shakes his head and makes fun of me with a look. I'll take the blame. I know I'm using more chocolate than what's needed, but how many times do you get to have a s'more with blueberry muffin chocolate? I have to cash in on this opportunity.

Biting into the s'more, I do my best not to make sex noises. It's unique and balanced. You can tell the ingredients are local.

"This might be the best dessert I've ever had," I say with my mouth full of sticky marshmallow.

With his brows knitted, he asks, "Even better than the butterscotch cake?"

I freeze. He's put me into a dessert corner.

"Gah. These aren't in the same category," I mumble a response. "Don't make me pick. I love that cake—"

"Fine, fine. Whatever you say," he replies before biting into his own s'more. "Good call on the weird blueberry chocolate." He smirks in approval.

When we take a break in the s'mores assembly line, we lean back into the loveseat, our shoulders touching the cushions. I rest my head on Holland's shoulder. The air smells like fire and sugar. We're far enough away from the main area that we can still hear chatters and bits of conversation but just glimpses. The fire in front of us cracks and pops.

I shiver. It's cooler than any other night I've been here. Without hesitation, Holland takes one of the blankets and wraps it around both of our shoulders. He puts the others across our laps. Before leaning back, he puts his arm around my shoulders and I melt into his side.

It's a small act; some might say minuscule. But not to me. The weight of it lurches my heart. My whole being. Where did this man come from? He's thoughtful and warm. It feels good to have him on my side. This realization hits me hard. There aren't many people I'd think or say that about.

Then, because I can't have anything nice according to my anxiety, a wave of panic rolls through me. There's no way it's *this* easy. It's like I'm at the right place at the right time for the first time in my life.

"I know I keep asking. But how are you feeling?" he asks, quiet and confident.

"Weird. I feel weird. I'm surprised I feel as fine as I do… about Royce, and just the whole thing. I know I have a lot of work to do in therapy. But that's okay," I reply as I look at Holland to reiterate my point. He's patient and I can tell he's ready to listen. "Right here, right now… I'm okay. I feel sort of… lucky," I continue. "I know how you are with thank-yous, but I'm thankful for what you did yesterday. You took care of me without a second thought"—I tip my chin up so I can see him—"Even when we weren't on the best of terms…"

"Stop it. It wasn't even a question," he says. "I take it you're not used to people being in your corner much…" His voice wavers at the end. Like he's unsure how I'll respond.

"That obvious, huh? It's something I've been working on. I spend a large amount of time taking care of everything and everyone else that I often forget about myself. It's not new."

He nods like he understands.

"When's the last time you did something for yourself?" he prompts me.

"Umm… Well, after the breakup with Jack, I got a massage. That was a few months ago." I'm trying to recall something more recent. "Oh! I bought this expensive pillow spray. It makes my bed feel like a sleepy paradise. I'm embarrassed by how much it costs but I love it and now I need it most nights to sleep." I nudge him playfully.

"Tell me it smells like lavender." He sounds like he cracked a code.

"Yes! How did you know?" I didn't expect him to say that.

"Because you've smelled like something familiar, but I couldn't figure it out." He sighs. "Not in a creepy way, but when we were in the truck with the windows down and the warm air, I kept smelling it." He's trying to gauge if I think it's weird or not.

I don't think it's weird at all.

"Your turn. When's the last time you did something for yourself?"

"I gave myself tonight off. So I could do this with you." He leans into me and bumps my shoulder.

"And just because we had that disagreement…"—he struggles to find the words—"it doesn't mean I don't care about you."

"I know. Honestly, you seem too good to be true." I say the phrase that's been on my mind the last day. I look up at him, his dark eyes reflecting orange flecks from the fire. "What's the deal? Why are you single?" I ask it in a joking manner but still want to know the answer. There must be a reason why Holland is currently spending time with Slate and not a partner.

Holland looks at me before shaking his head and looking around.

"Let me guess, bad breakup? I knew I could feel the tension between you and Bea." I fake dramatics and put hands on my chest.

He sighs and chuckles at the same time, like he knows he was meant to. It feels forced.

"Ummm, not really a bad breakup."

"Oh my god! You were engaged and she left you at the altar!?" I gasp.

"I was engaged, but no, not really that—" It feels like my body hits a wall. His voice is nonchalant and level.

He was engaged? Why is this information so jarring?

"Wait. You were engaged? To be married? What happened?!" I press like I'm looking for gossip. I sort of am because I want to know more about him. I told him how I caught my boyfriend having sex with his girlfriend at my place of employment.

He takes a deep breath, gazing at the sky for a second before looking back at me.

"Ivy. This is a sad story." His leg bounces a little, showing his nervousness. "It also will show you I'm not as good as you think I am."

This conversation is no longer good fun. It turned quickly. A brief memory flashes. The H tattoo on his arm. The sad story.

"I want to know your stories. Even if they're sad," I say as I push myself away from his side so I can make eye contact. "If you want to share, I'm here to listen." I sit back while he contemplates.

Holland takes another big breath. Rubbing his arms on his knees. His nervousness brings my anxiety to the surface. I hold the mulled wine, so I have something to do with my hands.

"The tattoo you saw the other night? The H? It stands for Hazel. My little sister." He steadies himself. I can see the color drain from his face. "She died."

CHAPTER FORTY-EIGHT
HOLLAND

I WONDER IF IVY can hear my heart slamming in my chest. I feel like it's echoing in the trees—like everyone could hear it if they listened.

Ivy puts her hand on her chest. I don't have it in me to tell her it gets worse.

On my run today, I knew I'd have to give her something. Open up. Give her more than what I've done. One, because she has this current idealistic view of me. Two, because if I want to give this a real chance, this is the first step.

"I used to live in the city. I moved there after college when I got a job in finance. I was your typical finance bro: ridiculous apartment, a job that owned me six days a week, the circle of friends from the firm, and the pretty fiancé."

Ivy's caught off guard. She's doing her best to mask it, but I can still see glimpses.

"You know that the lodge has always been in our family. My grandparents opened it, then my parents ran it. We knew Hazel would be next to take it over. She loved being outside." My voice and thoughts veer for a moment. "She moved out here after college and immediately started making it her own. It was her idea to have events like this for guests." I gesture to the s'mores tray.

I pause. Ivy nods. She's listening intently. We're on the edge of something.

"I thought I had it all." I roll my eyes sarcastically at the cliché. "I tricked myself into thinking it was everything I could ever want and then some. The money was great, but it was the kind of job where you never had a chance to spend it. My job became my focus. Everything else fell to the bottom of the list. Coming home was very close to the bottom."

"Hazel tried to get me to do short weekend trips, but I always said no. I never wanted to make it work so I didn't. I treated it like a chore. But one weekend, I finally made it work. It was a Thursday night departure and a Sunday night return. I remember the dread I had when booking that flight." I laugh because of how ridiculous I was. It sounds even worse coming out of my mouth now.

"I wanted to stay in the city with my current life and it felt like going home was a step back. My family was so excited. It was my birthday weekend and they were so glad I was going to be home for a few nights. The night we were supposed to fly out, my fiancé convinced me to go out for drinks—an early birthday celebration for the two of us. And I never could say no to Lauren."

I can't remember the last time I exchanged any kind of message with her. It's odd to think about. We almost tied our lives together and now I have no idea what she's up to.

"We had too many drinks and by the time I realized, I was drunk and had missed my flight home. I probably could've gotten on a later flight, but Lauren—the short-lived fiancé—convinced me it was no big deal. That I could just fly out the next day. So we stayed at the bar." My mouth goes dry. I can almost smell the bar now. Hear the sticky floors and too loud laughs. "We drank way too much and were complete idiots the rest of the night."

Ivy rubs my forearm.

"I rebooked my flight and texted the family group chat how something had come up and I'd be flying in the next afternoon. I had missed calls and voicemails, presumably from them, but I didn't even take the time to listen. I'd be with them the next day."

I take a few breaths. My chest aches. I'm hollow and my insides are nothing but black clouds. Ivy reaches over and squeezes my hand. It's warm and reassuring. I can't make eye contact with her. Not yet.

"I was hungover and miserable on that flight. I wished I was home on my thousand thread-count sheets, ordering takeout from a ridiculously expensive restaurant—the kind of place where people went for special occasions. But I thought I was above them—I'd get it and eat in bed." I let go of Ivy's hand. I stand up in between the loveseat and the fire.

I pace the short distance in front of Ivy. "When my flight landed, I grabbed a taxi to take me to my parents' house. My lifelong home. I didn't even tell them what time I was flying in so they could pick me up. I was so fucking selfish."

My heart could explode. It feels like it could break open in my chest.

"When I walked into my parents' house, I was annoyed that no one came to the door when I knocked. I rolled my eyes when I saw my parents sitting on the couch." My voice cracks. I know I'm going to lose it. Deciding to trade pacing for stability, I sit back down. My fingers grip the edge of the loveseat.

"And the moment I saw my mom; I knew something was horribly wrong. I just stood there. My dad was the one who got off the couch, once my mom finally let him go. And he just wrapped his arms around me. He was heavy." I wipe the corner of my eyes.

Ivy reaches over and places her hand on my back, barely moving it.

"My dad—a man I'd never seen cry my entire life—was sobbing into my chest. No one had said anything yet. I finally asked what was wrong. My dad picked his head up and grabbed me by my shoulders. His blue eyes were red where the white should be, and he took in a single breath. He told me Hazel had been in a car accident. He was in shambles. He couldn't finish his sentence. The strongest man I knew couldn't even say the words."

I put my head in my hands. They're cold from the chilled air and feel good on my face. I do my best to collect myself.

"My mom was still on the couch. She was the one who said it. She sighed and then it felt like she mustered all the strength she had left to say it. 'She didn't make it. Hazel. She died.'"

I think of the sound I made when my mom said those words. It was gut-wrenching. Couldn't believe it came from me. I don't share this detail with Ivy.

I let tears roll down my face. No use hiding it.

"My mom's voice sounded like gravel. I'd never heard her sound like that." My voice cracks and I cough. "She didn't stand up from the couch. Her body looked so frail. It was like she had used her last bit of energy to turn and look at me and say those life-changing words."

I wipe my face with the back of my hands.

"The worst part was when I was able to take in my surroundings. It was decorated for a party. *My* birthday party. And there was some squeaking in the laundry room off the kitchen."

My knees bounce and shake my whole body.

"My parents told me Hazel wanted to decorate for my birthday. She planned something small with my family. And then my mom jumped off the couch like she forgot something was on the stove. She opened the laundry room and out ran Slate. He was wearing a harness with a red bow on the back. My mom reached down, picked the dog up, and handed him to me."

"Oh no," Ivy says. Her voice sounds heavy and like she could cry too.

"He was a birthday gift from Hazel. We talked about how we were happiest with dogs. I acted like there was no room for one in my life, but it wasn't true. She researched and found a low-energy dog that would be happy in an apartment and on short walks. Hazel even had scheduled a few dog-walking services for me in the next few weeks. She wanted me to try them out and figure out which would work best. She was always one step ahead of me."

I take a pause to sniffle, wipe my eyes, and breathe.

"Oh, Holland." Ivy leans into my side, her arms wrapping around my far shoulder. She's pulling me into her.

"I don't know if things would've been different if I would've made it there when I was supposed to. But I would've been able to see her. Just one more time." I drop my head down. I hurt right down to my bones. This is the same hurt I've carried for years. I'm reminded why many people don't know this story… I can barely tell it.

We sit on the loveseat in silence. The fire crackles. Ivy doesn't ask any questions. She just lets me be. I do what I can to tell the rest of the story.

"After that, my life was immediately different. I asked Lauren and some of my finance friends to come to the funeral and they all told me they couldn't make it. Lauren could've made it, but told me funerals made her uncomfortable and she'd only met my sister once. *She didn't want to intrude.*" The last part comes out sounding sarcastic because of how bizarre it is. Doesn't seem like a real person would do this. But I have to remind myself that I wasn't that far off.

"And that was it. The life I thought I wanted, the person I wanted to be, crumbled down in front of me. I went back to my apartment to pack everything up and submitted my resignation. I moved into Hazel's place—now my place. She finished it a few months before the accident. She didn't even have a chance to show it to me in person. We did progress updates via FaceTime and photos."

"The first night I slept in the new place, Hazel's place, it felt like I was cracked open. She was everywhere and nowhere. I thought about how I couldn't remember what she was wearing the last time I saw her."

I look over and see Ivy wipe a tear from her face.

"A few days after the funeral, when I was ready to explode with every feeling, I needed to escape. I couldn't look at my parents for another minute. Couldn't handle the hugs and hands on my shoulders telling me how much Hazel loved me. It was fucking torture." I can hear the anger in my voice.

"I hid in my childhood bedroom and found a task I could accomplish. I listened to and deleted old voicemails from my phone." I'm rubbing my hands together hard enough for my knuckles to be white and my muscles to cramp. "There was a voicemail from Hazel. It was the night I missed my flight. It was my last piece of her. She was so fucking nice. I was a fucking selfish prick and she was still so nice to me. She didn't complain about me missing a flight or sound irritated. Instead, she told me how excited she was to see me the next day and that she had something special for me, and knew I'd love it. And she told me she loved me."

I take another break. Air is hard to find.

"I must have listened to that voicemail a hundred times. I couldn't move from that room." I wipe more tears away.

"This was Hazel's dream… the lodge. I came to do what she would've done if she'd had the chance. There was no other way. All the people who I thought were my friends in the city, all faded away. I got a few texts after the funeral but they stopped reaching out pretty quickly."

My eyes gaze at my arm.

"I got that tattoo so that it feels like she's close to me. When my arms are down, that H is close to my heart." I pull the arm into my side.

Ivy takes it in. My hurt. My pain. The saddest story I've ever told. The saddest story I've ever lived.

"Holland. I'm so sorry," she says as she wraps her arms around my neck, pulling me into a hug. "There are no words."

"I was such a dick. To be honest, I used to be more like Royce than I care to admit." I laugh it off like it doesn't make my stomach hurt. "He reminds me so much of my past life and people who I thought were my friends."

"Don't do that. Don't compare yourself to him. You're a kind and wonderful man. We all fall short sometimes but you are nothing like Royce." She's stern but makes her point clear.

I hug her back but don't say anything. There's more to say but I don't have any words left. Not tonight. Not about this.

"I think it's incredible you came back to the lodge. You could've stayed in the city, left this part of you and your family behind. But you didn't." Her words are full of empathy and her touch is full of care.

"When did this happen?" She's quiet when she asks.

"Three years ago."

She doesn't say anything in response but instead, she crawls into my lap. Ivy alternates between running her fingers through my hair and rubbing my back. Her forehead rests on the side of my face. The flames feel like they're hypnotizing me. The ache in my heart will never go away, but with each touch from Ivy, it shifts.

After my tears are gone and the hurt isn't roaring through my bones, Ivy takes my face in her hands.

"Holland. Listen to me. You're a good man."

She doesn't give me time to protest or respond. Instead, she presses her lips to mine. Her fingers trace my jawline, soft on my face. The kiss is slow and heavy. She tastes like wine and sugar.

I could live in this moment forever.

CHAPTER FORTY-NINE

I DON'T KNOW how late it is when we finally pull ourselves away from the fire. Everything is different. I know it was a substantial step for Holland to share Hazel's story. He was vulnerable and tried his best to be open. All I wanted to do was kiss him, over and over, like I could lessen the hurt.

And he let me kiss him. His cheeks. His forehead. And he didn't back away when I ran my hands through his hair.

When we open the door to Holland's, Slate picks his head up, barks and runs over. We both give him some attention while we take our shoes off.

When Slate is satisfied, he goes back to his bed. Holland stands at the foot of the stairs, reaching a hand out for me. I take it and we go up to the loft.

We move around each other, getting ready for bed like we've done this a hundred times. It helps that this bathroom is spacious. Hazel's bathroom. She designed this thinking she'd live here. Probably forever.

Holland's routine is shorter than mine, so he kisses my cheek on his way out.

While washing my face, thoughts of Hazel consume me. About Holland's pain. How he had another life before this. While I put on my moisturizer, I wonder what kind of person Hazel was. Did she build this massive counter for all her skincare or makeup? Did she happen to just like the space? I put on my pajamas and go back to the bedroom.

"You wear matching pajamas?" Holland asks, the faintest of smirks on his lips.

"Correction. I *only* wear matching pajamas." I crawl into bed, pulling the blankets up to my chest. Slate immediately readjusts on the bed, lying so he's touching one of my legs. My heart melts.

This bed is glorious. You sink into it, just enough, and the sheets are soft. I wiggle my body down. I must've been so wrapped up before that my brain didn't quite register the luxury of this bed.

I turn to the side, putting my head on Holland's chest, an arm draped up and over, touching the skin between his neck and shoulder.

"Is this okay?"

He pulls me close enough to place a soft kiss on my hair. "More than okay."

Holland turns the light off. I do a smaller version of my box breathing but find I don't need it. The feel of his muscles and the rhythm of his heartbeat are enough to pull me into sleep.

---△△△△---

When I wake up, Holland is looking at me. Light comes through the windows and hits his eyes, showing flecks of gold.

My apartment has blackout curtains; I'm not sure the last time I've woken up to beams of sunlight.

"Good morning," I say as I stretch and move my body under the covers.

"Morning." His voice is gravelly. He doesn't break eye contact and it makes me a little self-conscious. Before I can help it, a nervous grin spreads over my lips.

"What? Why are you looking at me like that?" I cover my eyes with my hands, peeking through my fingers.

Holland sits up, his lips turned up at the corners to match my own, and his eyes roam over me. "I can't believe I'm waking up next to you. You're stunning," he says.

I laugh, feeling ridiculous with my bedhead, and this gorgeous man giving me compliments in bed. "I doubt that, but thank you."

Holland leans over and says, "I want to kiss you. I need you to tell me you're okay with it though."

He wants to *kiss me*. I take a second to let me body feel and brain think. I feel safe and special when I'm with Holland. I want him to kiss me.

"You can kiss me."

His mouth is on mine. Slow and soft. Our smiles meet first and then I deepen our connection, wanting more. He nudges at my hip and helps me roll on top of him. My breath hitches. I'm straddling him, feeling him through his boxers.

He runs his hands from the top of my shoulders down to my ass, where they stay. I lean further into him, my breasts touching his chest.

Every inch of my skin feels hot, it's tingling and begging for his touch. I plant kisses from his jawline to his neck. I feel his heartbeat under my mouth and lightly bite. He grips my ass harder and lets out a low moan.

That sound. That sound makes me move my hips and curse the fabric between us.

Holland moves his fingers to the hem of my shorts. He moves his hands underneath the fabric and slowly makes it to the top of my thighs, delicate and teasing. I feel like he's getting me back for the kisses and nips on his neck. To be honest, he can get me back as much as he wants.

When his hands make their way back to my ass, no longer separated by clothing, I kiss him harder. My fingers are in his hair, pulling, anything to get him closer to me.

I sit back and reach for the bottom of my top. Showing him I want to take it off. Understanding, Holland nods at me. My body hums with anticipation. As I'm about to pull the top over my breasts, there's a noise downstairs.

Slate. He's howling. It sounds more like a scream.

Holland lets his head fall back on the pillow. "This has to be a joke." I can hear the exasperation in his voice.

"What's wrong?"

"He's going to do that until he gets fed. It will only get worse." His voice is flat. "I created a monster."

I wonder if we can tune it out. I reach down to kiss Holland. As our lips touch, Slate lets out this pathetic sounding howl. If I didn't know better, I'd think something was seriously wrong. But, no…he's just hangry. I can relate to that.

We pull apart, both of us breathing heavily.

Holland sighs in defeat.

"I guess it's time for breakfast," I say as I put a quick kiss on Holland's lips and get off the bed.

"I'll meet you down there. I need a minute."

CHAPTER FIFTY
HOLLAND

SLATE HAS BETRAYED ME. After I was in an appropriate state to come downstairs, I filled his food bowl. He has the audacity to stay in Ivy's lap. She's petting him while they are on the couch.

I hate to admit it, but he's a damn cute cockblock.

"Pancakes?"

"Yes! Pancakes." Ivy agrees as fast as I thought she would.

While I make breakfast, I can hear Ivy talking to Slate. She's using that voice, the one that fits both babies and dogs. I'm a gooey mess. Not from the pancake batter—which isn't helping—but from how much I love hearing her in the background.

Fuck. This will hurt when she leaves. Whenever that is.

When we sit down to eat, Slate also decides it's time for his breakfast. Not like the dog was howling thirty minutes ago, interrupting Ivy and me.

"This smells good," she says as she holds her knife and fork in her hands and hits them playfully on the table.

I set the French press coffee on the table between us. Grazing her shoulder with my hand.

We've been like this all morning. Finding ways to touch each other.

"Coffee?"

She nods enthusiastically. "You never have to ask me if I want coffee. The answer is always yes."

I pour her a cup and set it next to her plate. She reaches for my hand and squeezes it. "Since you're weird about thank-yous…" She jokes, winking as she says it.

In between bites, she asks, "What's the plan for today?" I swear it's her favorite question.

"We could hike? Something like the one we did earlier this week."

"I'm interested. I need to move my body. Didn't do much of that the last few days." She tips her head, side to side, stretching her neck.

"Should we do the same trail we did? Is this one much harder?"

I expected questions.

"I think it'll be fun to change it up. It's not much harder at all." I reassure her. "The key difference is that this one is a little longer."

She doesn't look convinced. Instead, she pulls her phone out and is paying attention to something on the screen. "It looks like it's going to rain," she says. "Is that still fine?"

"Light rain is okay. Your new jacket is waterproof. But we shouldn't bring Slate. He doesn't do well in the rain, even though he loves streams and ponds." I shake my head in disbelief. Ivy also looks perplexed. "I don't get it. We'd have to leave him back in this cozy house. What a travesty."

Ivy shakes her head in understanding. "Okay, okay. We can try something new. And as long as you're confident on the weather." She exhales.

"From what I can tell, the weather should be fine." I reassure her after looking at my own weather app.

She smiles in agreement. "What's the trail called?"

I tell her and she immediately grabs her phone again to start looking into it.

After breakfast is cleaned up, Ivy is researching and I'm taking care of a few things around the house. I glance at the calendar. My blood runs cold.

I forget to breathe. Fuck. How did I miss this?

It seems like the last week has all run together. I've been wrapped up in everything Ivy.

My birthday. The annual reminder of the worst thing I've ever been through. The day where loss could swallow me whole.

My birthday is in two days.

This is not light rain. It may have been light when we started but it's been steady ever since then. Ivy and I are much slower than we were even when we had Slate with us.

"Nothing like breaking in a new jacket. Making sure it's waterproof." Ivy claps her hands at her chest and then throws her arm in the air. Rain droplets fly off her sleeves. Her voice is upbeat.

"There's a good chance it will let up soon. Or if you want, we can turn back and cut it short." I want to give her the choice. Rain during this time of year isn't common.

"A little rain never hurt anyone." Since she's wearing her hood, she has to awkwardly move her head in order to see me.

She doesn't seem nervous or anxious. Either she's hiding it well or she's feeling good. I know how she likes to follow a plan and know what's coming next.

Me on the other hand, I'm a wreck. My mouth is dry. A cold sweat breaks out over my forehead. I feel like I'm on the verge of a panic attack. Wouldn't be the first one.

We walk in silence. Ivy tries to start conversations but I don't have it in me. I know I'm being an asshole. But all my other energy is going towards keeping my shit together. It's not going well.

She resorts to asking random questions.

"Favorite food?"

This one's easy.

"Chicken pot pie." My answer is always the same. "We have a family recipe. My grandma made it for my mom, and now my mom makes it for me. Only for holidays and special occasions. Sometimes, we put it on holiday menus at the lodge."

She's satisfied with that answer.

"Your favorite food?"

"I can't pick. There are too many!" She squeals.

"I'm not going to make you tattoo it on your body or anything. At this moment, what's your favorite food?" I try to sound easygoing, but it comes out all wrong. If Ivy notices, she doesn't let on.

"Fine. I'd say… noodles. Any type of pasta."

We walk for another minute before she's back with another question. I'm trying not to be irritated. My horrible fucking mood has nothing to do with Ivy, but I wish we were being silent.

"What's something popular that you don't like? It could be a person, song, food, restaurant, anything."

Another softball question. Thank god. "Cell phones. I obviously have one and use it. But there are so many times I'm at the lodge and see families on vacation, but they're just scrolling their phones somewhere other than their house."

"That's a good one," she says. "Being present is intentional." I look at her quickly. "That's what my therapist tells me. I can't take the credit."

"Being present is intentional," I say it back. I sound like a robot. "You?"

"Hmm." She contemplates. "Oh, I know! Plants. Everyone is in their plant phase and it's not for me. I killed succulents a few years back."

"Plants? You are literally named after a plant."

"I know, I know. It goes in line with me not really liking the outdoors. I don't know why my mom named me Ivy. I've never seen her garden in my whole life," she explains.

I nod and don't press for any more information. Ivy tries to catch my gaze with a sideways glance. I see her but pretend I don't. She lets the questions go and we simply hike in silence.

The rain lets up for a while as we stop for a snack and a stretch. There's thunder in the distance. It's not super common this time of year but it's still possible to have a thunderstorm or two. Ivy tries to check the weather but neither of us have service. I can tell she's on edge and I'm doing everything in my power to hold myself together. I can't do it for both of us today. I wish I could.

"Holland, is everything okay?"

"The weather shouldn't stick around long," I answer. Monotone. Without looking at her.

"No, not with the weather. Is everything okay with you?" she insists.

"Sure."

"Sure?"

"Yes. Everything is okay." I couldn't be less convincing.

"You're not even trying to sound believable. What's the matter?" Her big green eyes look up at me from under her raincoat hood.

What's the matter? There's a hole in my chest that I can't fill. It's like I'm trying to fix it with masking tape. It works for a while until something rips it open. All I have is this stupid fucking tape. It's not enough. I'll never be able to fix this hole.

I can think it. But I can't say it.

"Nothing. Let's keep going." We're both standing, awkwardly, as it starts to rain again.

"I don't want to keep going until you tell me what's going on. You've been stand-offish the entire hike. Which was your idea."

"Well, you don't always get your way." It stings me to say. It hurts Ivy when she hears it.

"You think I don't know that? Believe me, if this week taught me anything, it's how I don't always get my way." Her voice is sharp and she's getting pissed.

The whole argument plays out in my mind. The rock is rolling down the hill. I don't know how to stop it.

Instead, I don't say anything. I let out a breath and put my hands on my hips. Ivy lets that fly for about thirty seconds before she takes a breath and jumps back in.

"Holland. Why won't you let me in? Just a little." She sounds like she's trying to be patient but her voice still has an edge to it. It's like she's pleading but also agitated. "What are you afraid of?"

This question sets me off. I take a few steps back before I scream.

"EVERYTHING! I'M AFRAID OF EVERYTHING." My hands go to the side of my head and then out in front of me. "Where do you want me to start? How about that sometimes I hurt so fucking bad. My body physically hurts like I'm burning from the inside out. Or how about how I'm scared to answer the phone anytime my parents call? I think they're going to tell me someone else is gone."

"Holland—" Ivy takes a step toward me. I take another step back. I don't want to scare her.

"No. You wanted to know! I'm afraid to go home. The place full of childhood memories rips me to pieces. The smallest pieces that I spend months putting back together. Except they never quite fit right like they did. They never fucking fit. The only place—besides this lodge—that has any of Hazel left and I'm a fucking coward. It's so hard for me to be there. My parents always come here because they know I can't go home." My voice cracks. This is something that hurts me worst of all. I miss the feeling of home. It will never be the same.

"I'm terrified I'll be in that small town and someone I went to school with will forget my sister is dead and ask me how she is. Because that happens. THAT HAPPENS. And I can't stand it."

"Holland. How could anyone stand it?!" She speaks but I'm already onto the next rant.

"I'm afraid I'll go back to hating myself. The way I did when it all first happened. I didn't look in a mirror for months. It's exhausting feeling it all the time."

Ivy slowly takes a few steps towards me. The rain comes down harder.

"How about how the lodge will fail? The dream my sister had. Poof. Gone. I have to make sure that doesn't happen." I'm pacing back and forth, the only thing I see is the dirt and my boots. Fat raindrops turn the dirt to mud.

"And then there's you! Ivy. YOU." I look up from the ground and see her face staring back at mine. Tears silently stream down her face, mixing with the rain.

"Why are you afraid of me?" Her voice is calm and small.

"You fucking terrify me! You make me want you. And I haven't wanted anyone in years. I came to terms with what my life looked like and then you showed up for this stupid fucking event with those god damn boxes. I thought I could be alone forever." I stop and take a breath and wipe at my own tears. Fueled by pure fear.

"Now I can't picture it! And you live across the country. But I can't leave. And you made me love you and now you're going to be gone. You're going to make another hole in my chest that I'll have to pretend isn't going to swallow me from the inside out!"

Ivy grabs my hands with hers and pulls them to the front of her chest.

"Holland. Take a breath. Breathe." She stares at me, eyes matching the trees, and breathes so I can try to copy her. It works. It's shaky but I do it.

The rain falls heavy. All I think about is breathing. In and out. Over and over.

Her fingers are cold and squeeze my fingers tight.

"Is this coming up because you told me about Hazel last night?" She's tender and understanding.

I find another deep breath and close my eyes. I have to tell her. If I have any chance to keep her, I can't keep this to myself.

"It's my birthday. My birthday is in two days." My voice is a whisper, barely audible over the rain.

She doesn't say anything. Instead, she slowly wraps her arms around my neck and hugs me. Tight. Like she's trying to keep me together. I don't resist. I let myself fall into her. Both of our hoods fall and we're getting pelted with cold rain.

"Holland. I've got you," she whispers in my ear, before pressing a kiss on my cheek.

And I believe her.

CHAPTER FIFTY-ONE

I ASKED.

And Holland finally answered.

Ironic how he and I aren't all that different when it comes to focusing on others and sort of forgetting about yourself.

His birthday. A day typically meant for light, celebrations, and fun. But not for Holland.

Now, we're standing in the pouring rain. I'm hugging him as tight as I can. I'm holding him for all the times he's needed it and never asked. Or maybe never even realized he needed it.

Something he said crawls back. *"You're going to make me love you."* He screamed it. I heard it cut through the rain, the thunder.

Love.

He's afraid because he loves me.

I pull back to see his face, flushed crimson from the mix of cool rain and letting things off his chest. His jaw, set like concrete. And his eyes which make me forget to breathe if I stare too long.

I see him. And now I need to let something off my chest.

"You're scaring me." And before I can get a full thought out, he's already responding.

"I didn't mean to lose it, it's just—"

I lightly press a finger to his lips. "No, not that." I take my finger away. "You're scaring me because you're making me love you too."

"What?" His voice is muffled, dripping with defeat and dismay.

"I love you."

"You love me?" He sounds confused.

"Yes."

Without speaking, he walks us backward a few steps until I can feel a tree behind me. Holland picks me up, I wrap my legs around his waist.

If he wasn't holding me up, I'd be a puddle on the ground. The way he's looking at me right now—I can hardly stand it.

And then he kisses me. Like I'm air and he's drowning. It's the sort of kiss which makes you lose your footing. Good thing Holland is holding me up. Enjoyably frantic and the kind of touch that stitches you back together. Gone is the hesitation and curiosity. It's pure need. Understanding. Compassion.

Everything we try to say is in this kiss.

Holland slowly sets me down, my legs like jelly when they touch the mud.

"Ivy. I love you," Holland says with the smallest of smiles on his face and kisses my forehead.

In this forest, on an actual hike, I feel a wave of change. I don't know all the details but I know it's here. I can feel it in my bones. Touching on the corner of my soul.

"I know a shortcut. Let's go home."

It's funny, the way he says *home*. When I hear it, I don't want to argue. My brain doesn't panic and try to justify.

Holland feels like home.

I feel lighter when we're back inside, out of the rain. I sit down to take my boots off but Holland beats me to it. He's gentle with untying and taking them off. It feels good to be rid of the muddy boots and damp socks. We take off the first layer of rain-sodden clothes.

Holland walks to the kitchen and I follow. He washes his hands and pours me a glass of water. He sits down across from me. Our argument comes roaring back. I'm not sure which one of us will speak first.

Because I'm an anxious millennial and it's the way I am, I make a joke. "I definitely preferred the weather of our first hike."

"Agreed," he replies, tinged with exhaustion.

The silence engulfs us like a cloud of smoke. We sip our water and take a minute.

"I'm not trying to keep you out. I just don't know how to let anyone in anymore," Holland says, eyes fierce on mine. "I tried showing you with the shopping, and putting together the list of things for you and Vivian to do, her comped room, getting her a rental car—"

"Wait, you did that?" I didn't even know about the car or the room, and I thought Bea gave me the ideas.

"Yes, I did that."

"Why didn't you say anything?"

"I don't know. I can't explain it. I wish I could but I can't."

I know, all too well, what this is like. The random things my anxiety-riddled brain chooses to hold on to, are usually negative and never productive.

"You're one of very few people who knows the story of Hazel. From my side. Not from Bea or from someone else talking about it or on social media. I've only told that story a handful of times. And I wanted to tell you." He reaches his arm across the table. I put my own on top of it.

I look at him. It's heartbreaking and sad to think of all he's held onto this for so long. His gaze is intense and I know the words are hard for him.

When we make eye contact, I want to stay here, forever. I believe him. I know he's trying.

I stand in front of him. He turns the chair toward me. We're both jagged in our own ways. All I know is I feel better when I'm with him.

"There's a reason I'm here and not on a plane back to my apartment. I like it here. I like it here with you… and Slate," I share. "And you're right. I'm used to taking care of myself, to a fault." I look down at my feet.

Holland leans back in the chair, runs hands through his damp hair, before letting his arms hang to his side.

"I like it here with you too." His voice is quiet. His look is intense.

"And you need to take some of your own advice. Let me take care of you."

I place one leg over each of his, straddling him in the kitchen. My hands run through his damp hair, down his neck, and rest on his shoulders. He wraps his arms around my waist. There's a different type of anticipation in the air.

He tips his chin up and we take each other in. I kiss him like it's possible to kiss someone's pain away. All the things we both want to say, but haven't yet, are in this kiss. It's soft but powerful.

I dance my fingers along his jaw, the nape of his neck. His hands move down my back. Our breaths pick up and he pulls me into him so our bodies are pressed together.

"I want you for as long as you'll let me have you," Holland says, almost in a whisper. I can tell he's nervous.

Using my fingers, I tip his chin up. We're nose to nose.

I smile wide and tell him, "You've got me."

CHAPTER FIFTY-TWO

OUR KISSING IS FEVERISH. It's lips and bites and his tongue on mine.

"I like the taste of your lips on mine," Holland growls.

He stands up with me still wrapped around his waist. My breath hitches at how strong he is. He carries me up the stairs like it's nothing.

He sets me down at the top of the stairs and takes his shirt off. I lift my arms above my head and smirk. Holland grabs my shirt and pulls it up and off. Before I put my arms down, he kisses the skin surrounding my bruised elbow.

When I'm in just my panties and Holland is in his boxers, we pause. His smirk is mischievous. He closes the space between us and kisses me on the mouth, before lingering down my neck, and to the top of my breasts. My nipples are hard as he takes my breasts in his hands, his mouth.

I reach down into his briefs and wrap my hand around his dick. He lets out a low and tense growl when my hands make contact.

"How about a shower?"

I don't answer. Instead, I remove my panties, turn on my heels, and walk towards the bathroom. Holland follows and I can feel his eyes on me.

He turns the water on and comes back to me. He kisses me with urgency and excitement. My heart falls in line and races. I already feel euphoric. I can't get enough of how he touches me. Looks at me.

When the water is hot enough, he opens the curtain and gives me his hand. He guides me in before getting in himself.

There's nothing but the two of us. Waves of happiness and want hit me all at once. I throw my arms around him, put my fingers through his hair. His hands are on my waist. A place I usually hate to be touched. Definitely a different story when Holland is the one doing the touching.

Nothing about him makes me want to hide.

His muscles ripple and tense as we move in the shower. I go to take him in my hands but he moves back.

"Not yet," he says as he glides his hands down the front of my body.

He teases me, his fingers at the top of my thighs, a hand on my ass. After a few passes, I gasp. He's so close to where I want him to touch me but he's not there yet and he knows it.

"Is this okay?" he asks with his fingers right in front of my clit. So close I swear I can feel him.

"Yes," I reply in a breathy voice.

He strokes me with his fingers. My head tips back when he hits the right spot. I gasp and moan with each of his movements. He places his mouth on mine, mid sound, catching it for himself, and kisses me. His tongue lightly touches mine and I can't get close enough. It's just his mouth and his hand and the steam of the shower.

Surprisingly, he pulls his hands away. He comes back with soapy hands, the smell of his body wash filling the shower. He rubs my back, my legs, and my arms. He's careful around my bruised elbow and makes this the most sensual shower I've ever taken.

There's no rushing. We have nothing but time. He touches so much of my body but it feels like I'll never be sated.

When he's done with me, it's my turn. I spend most of my time on his neck and shoulders where he holds the tension, thick, wrapped around the muscles. I knead and dig in my fingers, while facing him. He closes his eyes, relishing in my touch, and it makes me feel powerful.

Turns out I'm awfully bold when I'm with Holland. I go from my hands on his back to reaching for his length.

I make my way to his cock and wrap it with my slippery, soapy hands. The sound that comes from his mouth is part sigh and part growl. I'm getting hotter by simply touching him.

I can't get enough. But what else is new?

His length is heavy in my hands. I stroke, up and down, and he puts one hand around my waist and the other to the shower wall. His head tilts back as my hand continues to move. I give him just enough, like he did me.

The way he reacts and presses into me, my touch.

I feel like a goddess.

We rinse off the soap, still kissing and touching. Our hands explore each other's bodies and the warm water eases some of the tension, physical and emotional, from the hike. Once we're both ready for what's next, Holland turns off the water, grabs a towel and quickly dries us off.

He helps me out of the shower, careful not to slip, and then carries me to his bed. Again, with the carrying. Why the fuck is this so hot?

Slowly, he lays me down on the bed, never breaking our kiss. Holland stands up and takes me in, from head to toe.

"What?" I ask, teetering on the edge of self-consciousness. I prop myself on my elbows.

"You're fucking amazing," he says while climbing over the top of me. His dick is hard against me and it's maddening. I want him. All of him.

"You don't need to use a condom; I have an IUD. Unless you want to," I say, clearly ready for him. I'm surprised by the confidence.

"Are you sure?"

"Yes." I'm confident and already reaching up for him.

Instead, he kisses me from my breasts down to my belly button. A trail from top to bottom. My breath is quick and his pace is slow. It's torture and bliss, all at once. I think I know where he's going next.

"You don't have to do that if you don't want to…" The confident woman is gone. Slight insecurity takes over.

Holland's face is confused for a few seconds until a look of understanding hits him. I'm grateful neither of us say what we know aloud. This isn't something I'm used to or have a ton of experience with.

"Are you kidding? Of course, I want to." He's genuine. Hopeful. And with that, he moves further down my body. My heart flutters with anticipation.

He swipes a finger against me, testing my wetness. "Ivy, you're so wet." His voice is low and tantalizing. "Even out of the shower, you're wet for me."

He teases me with his fingers. I want more but he refuses to give it up. Holland knows *exactly* what he's doing. His touch is delicate and soft. I think he senses my impatience and his lips turn up at one corner. He's loving this.

"What do you want?" Holland croons.

He looks up. When I see his head between my legs, eyes making contact, I feel wild. Like the only thing that would save me is his touch. His mouth. Him.

"Tell me."

"You." My voice is breathy as my hands are pulling at the sheets. "I want you." I arch a little off the bed.

"You have me." He teases me with his fingertips lightly touching the inside of my thighs.

"I want you to kiss me," I mutter. I'm for sure out of my comfort zone here.

He goes to kiss me on my lips. I put my hands on his shoulders. He stops.

"Not here," I say, with a finger to my lip. "Here." I trail a finger down and touch myself.

"Good girl," he says and licks his lips. Those perfect lips. I feel like I could pass out. No one has ever said that to me in bed before.

Before I have long to think about the whole "good girl" comment, he puts his mouth so close to my center. Teasing me as he did with his fingers, my hips move with and against him.

When he's done making me wait, he delicately licks my clit, with the tip of his tongue. I gasp and say his name.

"I love when you say my name." I can hear the satisfaction dripping from his voice. He goes from barely touching to pulling my bundle of nerves in with his mouth.

I want nothing more than to speed up the pace. I shift against him, chasing his tongue.

And then he's using his fingers and his mouth. Filling me with a finger, and then two, before lapping at me. The pressure is just what I need. One of his hands hooks around my legs and his fingers dig at my thighs. I whimper, loving it.

"Don't stop," I manage to say. My hands go to Holland's hair, itching to be in control. I move his head just right, putting his mouth, full lips, and tongue, right where I need it.

With that, Holland moans against me and I catch the wave I've been chasing. I come on his tongue. My body trembles and my muscles tense in that delicious way I've missed. My entire body feels too sensitive like the sheets are pricking at my skin.

I ride the waves with Holland still focusing on my clit, moaning in ecstasy.

I take a deep breath. Before I can get myself together, Holland grabs my hips and flips me to my stomach. His muscles make me feel like I'm weightless. He lays over me and kisses and nips at my neck.

"Holland." I try to say but it comes out sounding more like a moan.

He bites at my collarbone. I'm looking back at him and so badly want him inside me. I push my hips back and feel his erection. It's so close.

He taunts me with his dick near my entrance. It's clear what I want. I can feel him relishing in the anticipation.

"You're so eager and you already came once," he says and lightly pulls my head back by my hair. It's forceful but it doesn't hurt. I like it and can't help the smile on my lips. "Are you sure this is okay?" he asks without a bit of annoyance in his voice.

"Yes!" I practically yell. No hesitation. No second-guessing. I can feel him inch closer like my outburst is spurring him on. When he presses into me, I grip handfuls of the sheets. Holland is slow at first. I feel all of him, bit by bit. His hands wrap around the front of my hips and he pulls me towards him as he thrusts.

I push against him and he hits me deeper. My breath comes out in sharp pants. Short.

Each second brings me closer. Another orgasm on the edge, waiting to be pushed over. Another wave. I know he can feel it. He grips my hips and scratches my back while he speeds up.

"I'm close," Holland says. His voice is strained and sexy.

My legs quiver and shake with us both on the edge. Holland lets out a deep moan and I can feel him release. It's all my body needs to reach its own climax and tumble over the edge. My muscles tighten around his cock as he continues to thrust into me. He's trying to find his breath.

I collapse onto the bed when I can no longer hold myself up. My entire body is satisfied and exhausted. I roll to my back and try to slow my breathing. Holland lays down next to me, draping an arm over my stomach. My heart swells thinking how I can't get enough of this man. I want him right next to me. We look at each other. I can feel the flush in my cheeks and my swollen lips.

He hovers his lips in front of mine, brushing them, before he kisses me.

His hand plays with my hair and ends up on my chin, keeping his lips on mine.

"Thank you," I say. Part of me waits for Holland to scold me but instead he rolls his eyes with a smirk.

He kisses my shoulder before falling back on the bed. Holland doesn't say anything but instead, reaches for my hand. He brings it to his mouth before kissing it softly.

Holland reaches down for the blanket and pulls it up over us. He lays on his back and lets me drape myself over his bare chest.

Home.

CHAPTER FIFTY-THREE
HOLLAND

HEFTY RAINDROPS SPLATTER the windows. The roof. This is what wakes me up.

First, I have to make sure I'm not dreaming. Because Ivy's in my bed—sleeping on me, naked.

I rub my eyes.

Nope. Definitely not dreaming.

"I can't believe it's still raining," Ivy says, her voice covered in sleep. She rolls over and opens her weather app. "There's a flood watch."

I don't make fun of her for immediately reaching for her phone. I know she thrives with information.

"That happens a few times a year. You shouldn't worry." I brush her hair with my hand. "I'll check in with Bea, but everything should be fine at the lodge. They have everything they need."

"Will we be able to leave?"

"Not if it's flooding. It could be a day or two." I move a piece of hair from her face. My fingers touch her perfect pink lips. I'm preparing for her to ask at least ten more questions. I know how she likes to know anything and everything.

Instead, she does something else. Something better. In response to my touch, she reaches her hand over and touches me over my briefs.

"What a shame…" she says in a wicked way and climbs over me.

This isn't the woman I met a week ago. I love both versions but this one's moving the needle a bit.

She pulls my briefs down and my dick is already responding to a naked Ivy being in my bed.

"My turn." Her voice. That voice. That touch. It's like a fucking drug. And I'm addicted.

First, her fingers lightly brush the sensitive skin. Each movement is more maddening than the previous. I moan and pick my head up from my pillow. Ivy's dark hair touches the inside of my thighs, tickling me, while her hands are on my shaft. Seeing her down there, like that. Fuck. I'll never get over it.

"Someone feels a little greedy," she says as I inch my hips closer to her mouth.

Ivy's mouth puts a line of soft, and too gentle, kisses down my length. It's torture. But I fucking love it. I've never been turned on by someone like this.

When she gets to the tip, she slowly licks at the dot of wetness. I'm weak. A fucking goner. I'm so gone for this woman. I can tell she's relishing in my reaction. Her eyes are bright as she takes control.

I love it as much as she does.

She gives the tip an open kiss, putting my dick barely inside her mouth. Before my brain can compute, her tongue licks down to my base. Her teeth graze, just enough, and I'm losing my mind.

"What do you want, Holland?"

Oh, the tables have turned. She's going to make me say it.

"I want you to put those pretty pink lips around my dick. And then I want you to take as much of it as you can. With your mouth." My response is gruff, broken up.

Ivy smiles up at me. She loves turning the tables.

And then she does exactly what I asked.

My dick is in her mouth. Her lips surround me and I'm already close. She adds her hand. And she's stroking, licking, sucking, and I'm going to go fucking crazy.

"I'm… I'm close." It's like I'm cheering her on. And then it's like she flips a switch. Everything is more. She takes my shaft out of her mouth, flips her hair, and grins up at me. Wicked, wicked woman.

Evil.

Nothing like a good girl gone bad. I wonder if Ivy knows what I'm thinking because she moans. With that wicked mouth. I feel the vibration from her mouth on my dick and I can't fucking take it.

And that's all I need to fall in. She keeps her mouth on me while I come. Ivy scratches her nails into my thighs. She is un-fucking-real.

My climax continues to climb when she finds my eyes. She's full of mischief and satisfaction. Ivy doesn't pull away until the last of my tremors.

We finally head downstairs to feed Slate and ourselves. I put a bunch of treats near his bed and give him lots of attention.

"What's that for?" Ivy asks.

"Slate was a good boy and didn't bother us while we were upstairs." I pet him using that high-pitched voice.

Ivy laughs to herself but loud enough for me to hear.

Today, I feel lighter. Even though it's a mess outside, I'm sorting myself out on the inside. I'm not where I want to be and I still have a lot to share with Ivy, but I think we made solid strides yesterday. Not perfect but it's a start.

I'm in the kitchen, making scrambled eggs and hash browns. Ivy is on her phone.

"Oh wow," she says.

"What's up?"

"Message from Stella. It says Jack is out. They're letting him go today."

"Wow. Well, that's good news, right?" I feel better knowing she won't have to work with that dickweed again.

"I mean, I think so. The only other thing she said was not to rush back. They have a lot to figure out."

"For real? Wow." I pretend that I don't immediately think about her having more time. It's too soon to ask her if she plans on staying here. Part of me so badly wants to ask.

I focus on the eggs in the pan. I know I won't be able to keep my cool if she looks at me. I'll blurt out something idiotic.

"Are you sick of me yet?" She grins at me and her face is bright.

"Not even close." My voice comes out too serious.

"Are you sure?" Her voice is almost teasing.

"Fucking positive." I grin this time.

"Mind if I stay for a few more days? Eventually, I will have to go back to the city—"

The move is probably to play it cool. But I can't do it.

I pick her up from the chair and spin her around my kitchen. Slate barks and comes in to see what all the commotion is about.

"Hell yes! You can stay as long as you want," I say into her neck. I set her down and lock my eyes on hers. "I told you… I want you for as many days as I can have you." I reassure her with a smile.

"Isn't this kind of crazy? This whole… thing?!" She puts her hands on her forehead, taking it all in. "The sequence of events. What it took for me to get here. I can't stop thinking about it," she says.

Slate barks, interrupting whatever Ivy was thinking about.

Ivy laughs and it's the most wonderful sound. I know I'll do anything to hear that sound for the rest of my life.

And then I put my arm around her waist and dip her like we're in a cheesy romantic comedy movie and kiss her. Really kiss her. She continues to giggle and I know it's the right move.

She's worth it.

CHAPTER FIFTY-FOUR
HOLLAND

"I TOLD YOU, you don't have to take me to the airport," Ivy says for the fifth time. She zips up a bag in her room at the lodge. She's almost completely packed and the inevitable gets closer and closer.

Ivy is leaving. Going back to her apartment in the city. I knew this would happen but it still hurts.

This hurt is different. Maybe because I know it won't hurt forever? At least I'm hoping.

Hope. Can't remember the last time I felt that.

"And I told you, I was going to do it anyway." I'm short and to the point. There's no way I'm calling a car to drop her off at the airport. No fucking way.

"You probably have a ton to do—"

I interrupt her with a kiss. The quickest way to get this woman to stop rambling. Well, other than feeding her sugar. I feel the argument leave her body as she leans into me. She deepens the kiss, her hands in my hair.

I pull back. "Nothing more important than this." I kiss her on each of her cheeks.

She scrunches her face up and laughs.

That laugh. I've heard so much of it during the last week.

The flooding kept us inside for two days, so we turned the living room into a blanket and pillow fort and enjoyed a marathon of our favorite Spider-Man movies.

I'm not sure if Slate has ever been happier.

Or me.

We played board games to pass the time. Turns out, Ivy is ridiculously competitive and is also the type of person to read through the rules—even of games we know—before we start to play.

My girl and her plans.

At one point, Ivy let her phone die and acted like it was nothing. Oh, how things have changed in such a short time.

For my birthday, Ivy called the lodge and had a butterscotch cake dropped off at the door, along with ingredients for peanut butter bacon cheeseburgers. Brad was able to make the trip easily using one of the lodge's off-road-vehicles. A full circle moment.

Ivy somehow turned a day I can barely get through into something tolerable. She did just enough. We cooked dinner together—mostly in silence, but touched each other every chance we got. The thought of cooking with her for years to come was the distraction I needed.

What I respected the most was how she never once asked if I was okay. She knew the answer. No words necessary.

Hazel used to do the same thing. My heart pinches and swells at the same time. It's always been torture to think of Hazel, and somehow, Ivy makes it easier. She makes all this easier.

A closing closet door snaps me back to now.

"Plus, Slate wants to come," I say, knowing it's damn near her kryptonite.

Ivy says nothing as she wraps me up in a hug. Her arms around my waist, her head on my chest. I can feel her smile against me.

"Let's go get Slate," Ivy says.

I pull up to the airport departures and put the truck in park. My heart jolts to match. Without looking at Ivy, I open my door.

We leisurely unload her bags from the back. Slate, still buckled in, props himself up with his front legs, his head hanging out the rolled down window. Ivy gives him a kiss between each bag she unloads.

Everyone around us seems to be racing, getting in the airport as fast as possible. Doors slam, bags roll, and horns honk. It sort of smells like chaos and exhaust. Meanwhile, I'm taking my time. Because I know what's next.

When there's nothing else to grab, I turn to see Ivy petting Slate and him sneaking licks of her face.

She looks at me and my heart is on the floor. Her lip quivers. That perfect lip. Tears pool in those ferociously green eyes. Heavy like the raindrops that flooded the roads and kept us at my place for two whole days.

The air is gone. I can't breathe. My whole body feels heavy. It's almost hard to stand.

This is it.

I pull her in for a hug, resting my chin at the top of her head. We sway back and forth.

"Holland. I don't want to go," she cries into my chest.

My hand brushes the side of her hair before twirling a piece between my fingers. It's something that will calm her down—a trick I've picked up during our last week together.

I tip my nose and breathe her in. The comfortable smell of lavender—of Ivy.

"I don't want you to go." My voice is quiet because I know it's about to get all crackly. I suck in a deep breath and push us apart a little. Our eyes catch; hers are red with tears flowing and I bet mine aren't much better. I swear, my heart aches.

But at this moment, there's a shift. It's subtle but enough for me to feel it. It's like I was driving a car on two wheels and the third has touched the pavement. Stability. Consistency.

"This is weird." The words fly out of my mouth before I can stop them. Ivy's eyebrows scrunch, a confused look takes over her face.

"Weird?" Her eyes are big as she leans back a bit.

"I mean… it's just…" Truly a terrible start. "Look. I've never been good at this." I alternate between looking around and at Ivy. "Sharing. Talking about what I feel or whatever…"

"Holland, it's okay—" Ivy is trying to spare me but I won't let her. She deserves this.

"No, I want to try." My voice almost sounds like I'm pleading. Hell, maybe I am. "I think it's weird how I can look at you and feel this way. It's overwhelming… I'm fucking sad I'll wake up in my bed tomorrow and you won't be in it. But on the other hand, I'm so grateful and excited. This isn't the end, Ivy. You and I both know it."

Ivy falls back into my chest and squeezes. She says nothing but I can feel her shake with tears.

"I feel more like myself than I have in years and it's because of you." My voice cracks and a tear falls. I'm not embarrassed to be crying.

"Holland, stop—" Ivy tries to jump in.

"And I know you're terrible with fucking compliments, but I need to say this. You are unlike anyone I've ever met. You're brave. Resilient. A fucking force of nature… even though you sort of *hate* nature." We both scoff. Ivy wipes at her eyes.

"I can't wait to read menus before we go to restaurants, spray our sheets with whatever helps you sleep, wander around bookstores, compulsively check the weather app before we do anything outdoors, and find as many treats as possible. Thank you for making me love you."

Instead of responding, Ivy looks at me. The woman of my dreams who

I didn't know existed. The person who cracked the dark shell that's been around me. She's brought me back. And I don't care that it's only been a couple of weeks, because I love her.

I didn't fit in her original plan, and I threw out my own play book years ago. But here we are.

She puts her lips on mine and I pick her up. Ivy wraps her legs around my waist and her hands are in my hair, on my face, everywhere. We kiss like no one is watching because that's how it feels.

And I fucking love it.

Slate howls like he hasn't been fed. He startles everyone, including us. The dog can't handle not being the center of attention. I set Ivy down and we stand on each side of the most spoiled dog on the planet. Both of us pet him.

A stranger approaches, I assume to comment on Slate.

"I don't mean to intrude, but would you like a picture of the three of you?" she offers.

Ivy looks at me with her red-rimmed eyes but with a smile on her face before giving the woman her phone.

We stand on each side of Slate. I take my pinky and reach for Ivy. We make a pinky swear as the woman takes a few pictures.

"I love you, Holland," Ivy says to me, with Slate's head in the way.

I pull our pinky swear up and leave a kiss on her hand. Color floods her cheeks and it makes me weak. People around us whistle and clap like the end of a romantic comedy.

And you know what?

Who cares?

Because I've got the girl.

CHAPTER FIFTY-FIVE

Ivy

ONE MONTH LATER

I fumble the keys to my apartment. My hands are full with my yoga mat, takeout, and gym bag.

I've been trying to get to a yoga class at least once a week, but it seems I can only convince myself if it ends with the spiciest Indian food from my favorite restaurant down the block.

It's called balance.

There's also nothing more humbling than a yoga class. I need positive reinforcement.

I've been back in my apartment for a month. Leaving Holland and Slate was difficult, even though I knew it was coming. I glance at my fridge to see the picture of the three of us. I think this is the first picture I've had printed in years but it captured such a sweet moment. I couldn't help it.

The day I decided to go back to Sparks, I filed charges against Royce. It was delayed but there was enough video evidence to make it quick. I made myself physically sick before but I knew it was the right thing to do. I owed it to myself—and to every person Royce encountered—to speak out about what happened to me.

I was welcomed back to Sparks with open arms and an appointment with **HR**. I made a statement on Jack, including everything from the public sex to our conversation when he found out that the deal with Royce's company fell through.

The office is one hundred times better since Jack has been gone. He's facing hefty legal action from Sparks. Turns out, Jack had hacked Stella's email and would "interfere with correspondence". Stella never discussed my request to work remote because she never read it—it was Jack.

Despicable.

Therapy is going well. As well as therapy can go at times. I'm still dealing with the physical incident with Royce. I'm not sure I'll ever not be dealing with it. There's something truly awful about someone taking something from you that you can't even see. Some days, it feels like I have cuts that bleed just below the surface. I'm working on being honest with how I feel. Trying to get rid of all the cool-girl costumes I've perfected over the years.

My therapist recommended I take a self-defense class. I'm signed up for a four-week course which starts next week. I'm excited to learn how to better protect myself, and kick a little ass, when it's needed.

We're also working on me being less connected to my cell phone. I try to set blocks of time where I leave my phone somewhere out of sight. I'm not trying to go all cave woman but working on being present and using technology intentionally.

Adjusting to my space back home has gone better than I thought. I thought I'd be anxious about being home alone, or walking to my favorite spots in the city, but that isn't the case. It's clear that the two people who disrespected me, my boundaries, and showed lack of human decency were people I knew.

It's hard to grow but here I am, trying to do just that. Growing and changing is hard. It's not for the faint of heart.

I put my yoga bag and mat on the floor, freeing my hands to open the food.

I'm damn near shoveling the rich Tikka Paneer and rice into my mouth. The perfect reward to a grueling yoga class. I'm still waiting to enjoy the calm benefits of practicing because, at this point, it's just ridiculously hard.

There's a bark down the hall. Not uncommon. Many people have dogs in this building. One of my neighbors has a tan French bulldog but it's nowhere near as cute as Slate. Thinking of Slate and Holland squeezes my chest. I miss them.

A knock on the door. I can't even ask "who is it" because my mouth is chock full of paneer. I reluctantly get up and look out the peephole.

I'd scream if I didn't have a mouth full of food.

I swing the door open to Holland and Slate. I'm not sure which one looks more excited to be here.

"Oh my god! What are you doing here?!"

I wrap my arms around Holland. He holds me tight. I melt. He's wearing the same flannel shirt he wore on the first day we met. It could bring me to my knees.

"We missed you," he says while he's still hugging me.

We missed you. Swoon.

I pull away and kiss him. All over his face, like I can't control myself. Because I can't. Everything about Holland makes me wild.

"I'm supposed to be flying out to visit you guys in a few weeks."

"I hope you'll still do that. We're just here for the weekend."

His golden eyes stare into mine and of course he's going to make me cry. Instead of telling me not to, he pulls me back in, and runs his hand through my hair while I get myself together. His mouth finds mine and there's nothing else. It's just the two of us.

Slate barks at us. Pulling me out of my Ivy and Holland fantasy.

I let them in, sit on my kitchen floor, and Slate runs for me. He's smiling. The dog is smiling. I'm crying again.

Holland sets their bags down and sits next to me. The man terrified of leaving the lodge and who despises the city is in *my* apartment. The effort it took him to make the trip is more than most people could ever guess. The warmth spreads throughout my whole body. My soul.

He did this for me.

There we are, the three of us, on my kitchen floor. Slate flopping around trying to get any kind of attention. I rest my head on Holland's shoulder.

"I can't believe you're here. In my apartment. On my kitchen floor." I shake my legs in excitement before leaning over and kissing Holland's cheek. He leans in, like he knew it was coming.

"Wait, how was flying with Slate?"

"Oh, it was something. He was schmoozing all the flight attendants. He got a ridiculous number of cookies and snacks on that flight. More than I've ever been offered."

He laughs and my chest aches. It aches with how much I care for him. How thoughtful he is.

"Thank you for coming. I know it couldn't have been easy…" My voice is soft. He doesn't joke about me saying "thank you." He reaches down and grabs my pinky with his before he catches my eye. The gold flecks take the breath out of my lungs.

This man.

"You're worth it," he says before pressing a soft, sweet kiss to our interlocked pinkies.

"Well, you'll never believe what's on the agenda for today," I say, raising my eyebrows. Holland looks at me a little unsure.

"I'm not even going to attempt to guess. I never know with you," he says in a fake exasperated tone, but his plastered smile gives him away.

"Want to try baking peanut butter scones?"

EPILOGUE

Ivy

SIX MONTHS LATER

My phone buzzes with a text: Stella. She's eager to hear how the call went. I'm wrapping up my first conference call with the new director at Bliss4ul. Liz is a senior employee who knows the company in and out. She was the clear choice to replace Royce, who is starting to learn the court system in and out.

I spent a few weeks in the office and every member of the board made it a point to come see me. They all told me they were sorry about Jack and Royce. I thanked them but also reminded them not to apologize for what they had no control over. Every time I said it, I smirked a little bigger. It reminded me of the endless therapy sessions I've dove into. And Holland.

On my last day at the Sparks office, Stella threw me a Going Remote party. She invited Vivian and I cried in front of my co-workers. It was one of the nicest things anyone ever did for me. Stella also shared that she'd host a self-defense class, annually, for any employee who is interested.

Leaving Stella and my supportive colleagues was tough. Sparks restructured and offered me a new position, giving me the option to work twenty to thirty flexible hours a week, instead of forty. I have the option to work as much as I needed or wanted, from anywhere I chose.

No matter how tough it was, it was necessary. I thrive on a plan but I'd seen the end of this phase. I needed out. Out of the old life that almost fused with Jack's. There was no way I could go stay at my apartment and move forward on the same path. My soul craved a new landscape. I needed a new adventure. My tarot cards told me about the same thing for weeks.

Luckily, I knew the perfect place for a change of scenery. I moved in with Holland two months ago. We made trips back and forth to help with long distance. No visit was ever long enough. He came to the city and helped me pack up my apartment. I knew it was difficult for him to be there, but he didn't hesitate.

He always shows up. And he does his best.

After I went public on what happened with Royce, other women stepped forward. Some thanked me. Many told me their own stories. Hearing their experiences broke my heart and filled me with pure rage. It validated my decision to share my experience. I want to be part of the solution.

Some days are better than others. I'm a firm believer that there's never enough therapy. Holland and I go regularly—together, and on our own. We're far from where we need to be, but we're on the right path.

Liz and I say our goodbyes. I'm still going to play a key part in the Bliss4ul account. We're about to sign a five-year contract extension, but without Royce and Jack. I'm excited to work with Liz. A definite upgrade. Things feel like they're trending in the right direction.

As soon as I end the video call, I hear howling downstairs. I roll my eyes like I don't love it and go to the culprit.

"Slate! I'm right here. What's the matter?"

He paws at his empty food bowl. I grab it and fill it with dog food. As I set it down, Holland walks in.

"There's my girl." His smile is bright, full voltage. He comes in and picks me up, spinning me around the kitchen, while kissing me ferociously. The type of kiss that makes my brain short circuit and it's like I have no idea what I was doing before it.

"Stop that. I have to call Stella before I can wrap up my workday." I look at him mischievously. His eyes are golden and make me feel like I'm the only person who exists. Slate jumps up and puts his paws on his leg, clearly wanting attention.

Holland sets me down and gives me another kiss. The kind where it feels like the Earth slows. He moves his hands up to my hair before reluctantly separating.

"Call Stella. Wrap it up. We've got things to do." He winks at me and slaps my ass as I run upstairs.

I give Stella a run-down on the meeting with Bliss4ul. There's nothing but positive news to report. I'm killing it in my new role and learning quite a bit about work-life balance. I have no meetings on my calendar for the rest of the day and I tell her I'm logging off.

I change and practically skip down the stairs, leaving our makeshift office behind. We turned a corner of the loft into a co-working space. I can see outside from my standing desk. My favorite days are the rainy ones, where the sky is different shades of gray. The rain makes everything smell fresh and new.

Holland is also trying out a shorter schedule at the lodge. He's hiring a general manager and stepping into a different role. He's working on delegating and finding other projects he's passionate about. So far, it's been organizing events to support local charities and businesses. Tonight, we're hosting an outdoor karaoke night for the local animal shelter. Slate even gets to come.

"My parents are already at The Bun Room. If you want a cheeseburger before karaoke, we need to leave soon," Holland yells, not knowing I'm downstairs. "Otherwise, we'll miss Bea. You know she likes to go first."

"I'm ready!" I meet him at the door and give him a kiss on the cheek.

I'm so excited to see his parents again. We've made a few trips to

Holland's family home and it's just like I imagined. The first time we visited, I got to see pictures of Hazel when she first picked up Slate. It meant a lot to be let in and share this piece of someone they love and miss so dearly. My heart hurts when I think about not ever being able to meet Hazel, but we do our best to remember her.

While I walk out to Holland's truck, I see something on the side of the house. It looks like a set of tall planter boxes. They're full of fresh dirt and new plants.

"What's this?"

"Go check it out." He encourages me.

I walk over to the new planters and when I'm just a few feet away, my eyes tear up. Holland has planted lavender. Like, a ton of it. I can already smell the little plants. I dip my face closer to get a better look. When I stand up and turn around, Holland is there.

It seems like he's always there.

I swing my arms around him and put my head on his chest. We sway from side to side for a minute. He knows I'm crying but he won't say anything.

"I put them in these boxes. That way, they won't get drenched. These are movable so we can shift them during sunny days to make sure they're getting enough." He plays with my hair as he says it.

"This is so sweet. But I have no idea how to keep these plants alive—"

Holland interrupts my self-deprecating rant with a kiss.

"We can figure it out," he says through a smile.

"I love you." My words are intentional, genuine, and clear. He gazes at me in a way that makes me melt. I feel like I can be a puddle at any moment.

We've been seeing a couple's therapist and working on how to best work through our individual issues, together. It's clear that Holland shows he cares with acts of kindness. We both think we're not enough but the other one does their best to prove otherwise, every day.

We're disgustingly smitten and it's the best.

"I love you too." He kisses me. "But it's not a gift, it's a trade." His lips turn up at the corners into the cutest fucking smirk. The one that proves I'm a goner.

"What are the terms?" I look at him with a side-eye.

"You have to say that Andrew Garfield is the best Spider-Man." His face is serious but I know he's holding back a laugh.

I immediately roll my eyes and create more space between us. I let out an exasperated but sarcastic sigh. "You know I can't do that."

"And why is that?"

"Because. Holland is the best one. Hands down."

And it's true. Out of everyone I've met and tried to share parts of myself with, Holland is my favorite.

THE END

ACKNOWLEDGMENTS

Rachel

IF YOU KNOW ME, you know I'm crying while I write this; I'm a lot like Ivy in that way. Writing a book is hard. Sharing pieces of yourself is even harder.

To everyone who cheered me on with endless support and excitement, you've made one of my dreams come true. I have some special call outs for those that worked closely with me throughout this process:

Bob, for entertaining the littlest inkling of an idea—that was this book—while on a work trip. I appreciate the early encouragement. P.S. Tom Holland is the best Spider-Man.

Darren (and Caitlin), for giving me a title I loved and was a little jealous I didn't think of first. I received so many kind words about the title AND IT WAS ALL YOU. Drinks on me when I make it out your way.

Kelsey, Caroline, Caitlin, and Megan, for being the best early readers. Thank you for your honesty, eye for detail, and kindness. You played such a key part in this and challenged me to stretch this story.

Grace, Luna, and Kelsey, for being some of the best author friends a girl could ask for. I'm so lucky to have fell in each of your laps. SO SO THANKFUL FOR YOU.

Kaitlyn, Allison, and Dani, for allowing me to take over our Glam Fam Murderino group chat with anything and everything book related. You treated this like a major accomplishment which gave me so much confidence.

Shelbie, for telling me to write a book when we met in college. I'll never forget the times you'd look at me, so plainly, and you'd say "You're pretty good at this… you should write a book." You always made me feel like I could do this.

Patrick, for always making time for me. Whether it was questions, clarifications, or just a check-in, you always made the space. Thank you for reading my book early, even when it wasn't your genre, and leaving those voice memos with your thoughts. You gave me a key memory for this first book and I'll never forget it.

Dani (again), for never shying away from a plot question, or acting like it was normal to bring up Ivy and Holland like they were people we knew, and always being interested in what the next step was. I'm thankful for your design eyeballs because if there is anyone in the world I'd trust with formatting this book, with no detail left unturned, it would be you.

Chels, Ryan, FJ, and Stella, for treating this like such an accomplishment. You always were interested and in awe. Plus, you let me lounge on your couch quite a bit when my brain was mush.

Liz, for everything. EVERYTHING. You challenged me to make this book the best it could be. Your constructive feedback made me a stronger writer. I can't thank you enough for that. You always made space for me and made me feel seen. You were always there… whether it was a check-in, a marketing idea, or answering any of my thousand questions. Thank you.

My first novel wouldn't be finished without a shoutout to my parents. Thank you for teaching me cursive as a reward for good behavior, for buying me countless books, and for defending me when it came to that time in third grade (I wrote a *paper* about polar bears, used the word *majestic*, and the teacher was convinced I plagiarized. Really, I was just a nerd with a thesaurus).

And lastly, my sweet husband, Robby. Thank you for listening to me ramble about deadlines and things I was trying to figure out (which was a lot... baby indie author problems). You helped make this dream come true with your support, encouragement, and tough-love when it came to said progress/deadlines. Thanks for being proud of me, from start to finish, and giving me my very own happily ever after.

About the Author

RACHEL LABERGE is the author of *A Lodge Affair*. When she's not reading or writing, she's probably thinking about donuts, sour candy, or looking for her next hyperfixation. She lives in Michigan with her husband (Roberto), her two Frenchies (Rafa and Ruby), and cat (Riley).

You can connect with her on Instagram, TikTok, and Threads **@rachellabergeauthor** (no 'R' name required).